BRETWALDA

By

H A Culley

Book three about the lives and times of
Oswald and Oswiu, brothers who were
Kings of Northumbria, warriors and saints

Published by Orchard House Publishing

First Kindle Edition 2017

Text copyright © 2017 H A Culley

Cover Image: © Copora | Dreamstime.com

TABLE OF CONTENTS

List of Principal Characters 4

Place Names 6

Glossary 8

SYNOPSIS OF THE FIRST TWO BOOKS – *WHITEBLADE* and *WARRIORS OF THE NORTH* 10

CHAPTER ONE – DIVISION OF THE KINGDOM 11

CHAPTER TWO – DEEP INTO ENEMY TERRITORY 25

CHAPTER THREE – SAINTLY REMAINS 33

CHAPTER FOUR – LOVE AND WAR 46

CHAPTER FIVE – THE FALL OF WESSEX 70

CHAPTER SIX – RETURN TO ARDEWR 93

CHAPTER SEVEN – THE LAND OF THE PICTS 106

CHAPTER EIGHT – OVERLORD OF THE NORTH 125

CHAPTER NINE – WAR CLOUDS GATHER 135

CHAPTER TEN – TWO INVASIONS 151

CHAPTER ELEVEN – REGICIDE 162

CHAPTER TWELVE – WAR AND PEACE 171

CHAPTER THIRTEEN – PRELUDE TO CONFLICT 181

CHAPTER FOURTEEN – THE BATTLE OF THE WINWAED 199

CHAPTER FIFTEEN – AFTERMATH 211

Author's Note 219

Other Novels by H A Culley 227

About the Author 228

List of Principal Characters

(In alphabetical order)

Historical characters are shown in bold type

Acha – Widow of Æthelfrith and sister of Edwin, both kings of Northumbria

Æbbe - Acha's only daughter. Abbess and founder of Coldingham Priory

Ælfflaed – Oswiu's second daughter by Eanflæd. Later Abbess of Whitby

Æthelred – Youngest of Penda's three sons.

Aidan – First Bishop of Lindisfarne. He is credited with converting Northumbria to Christianity

Alchflaed – Oswiu's daughter by Rhieinmelth. Married Peada of Mercia

Aldfrith – Oswiu's eldest son (illegitimate)

Alweo – Nephew of Penda of Mercia.

Arthius – Son of Rand, Eorl of Elmet

Cadafael – King of Gwynedd in North Wales

Catinus – Briton born in Mercia who becomes one of Oswiu's warriors

Ceadda – Captain of Oswiu's gesith, later his Hereræswa.

Cenwalh – Cynegils' eldest son, King of Wessex from 342

Conomultus – Catinus' younger brother, a monk and later chaplain to Oswiu

Cuthbert – Monk at Melrose, later a warrior before becoming Prior then Bishop of Lindisfarne

Domangart – King of Dalriada

Dudda – Eorl of Norhamshire and one of Oswiu's counsellors

Dunstan – Oswiu's horse marshal

Eanflæd – Oswiu's second wife. Daughter of his uncle, Edwin of Northumbria

Eata – Novice at Lindisfarne, later Abbot of Melrose, then of Lindisfarne

Ecgfrith – Oswiu's elder son by Eanflæd.

Elhfrith – Oswiu's son by Rhieinmelth. Sub-king of Deira 655-664

Finan – Bishop of Lindisfarne after St. Aidan

Fergus – King of Ardewr and Ròidh's younger brother

Genofeva – Former queen of Ardewr and the mother of Ròidh and Fergus

Guret - King of Strathclyde

Hild – Oswiu's cousin. Abbess of Hartlepool, later of Whitby

James the Deacon – A Roman Catholic missionary in Deira; later canonised

Kenric – Eorl of Dùn Barra in Goddodin, fictional father of Cuthbert.

Œthelwald – Oswald's son; later King of Deira

Offa – Oswiu's youngest brother, his chaplain and later Abbot of Melrose

Osthryth – Oswiu's elder daughter by Eanflæd. Later married King Æthelred of Mercia

Oswiu – King of Bernicia. Later King of Northumbria and Bretwalda of England

Penda – King of Mercia

Peada – Penda's eldest son, Sub-king of Middle Anglia as his father's vassal.

Rhieinmelth – Princess of Rheged and Oswiu's first wife.

Ròidh – A Pictish prince who became Aidan's acolyte, now a bishop

Talorc – High King of the Picts

Talorgan – Oswald's and Oswiu's half-brother. Later High King of the Picts

Wigmund – Alweo's cousin. A monk, later Prior of Whitby

Wulfhere – Penda's second son, later King of Mercia

Utta – Former warrior in Eaochaid's gesith, later chaplain to Oswiu and then Bishop of Prydenn.

Place Names

(In alphabetical order)

I find that always using the correct place name for the particular period in time may be authentic but it is annoying to have to continually search for the modern name if you want to know the whereabouts of the place in relation to other places in the story. However, using the ancient name adds to the authenticity of the tale. I have therefore compromised by using the modern name for places, geographical features and islands, except where the ancient name is relatively well known, at least to those interested in the period, or else is relatively similar to the modern name. The ancient names used are listed below:

Austrasia – A part of Frankia (see below) centred on the Meuse, Middle Rhine and the Moselle rivers, with a coastline opposite that of southern Kent.

Bebbanburg – Bamburgh, Northumberland, North East England.

Bernicia – The modern counties of Northumberland, Durham, Tyne & Wear and Cleveland in the North East of England. At times Goddodin was a subsidiary part of Bernicia.

Berwic – Berwick upon Tweed

Cair Lerion – Leicester in the Midlands of England

Caer Luel – Carlisle, Cumbria, England

Caledonia - Scotland

Cantwareburg – Canterbury, Kent, England

Dalriada – Much of Argyll and the Inner Hebrides

Deira – Most of North Yorkshire and northern Humberside

Dùn Add – Dunadd, near Kilmartin, Argyll, Scotland. Capital of Dal Riata.

Dùn Barra - Dunbar, Scotland

Dùn Breatainn - Literally Fortress of the Britons. Dumbarton, Scotland

Dùn Dè – Dundee, Tayside, Scotland

Dùn Èideann - Edinburgh

Dùn Phris - Dumfries, south-west Scotland

Eoforwīc - York

Elmet – West Yorkshire

Frankia – The territories inhabited and ruled by the Franks, a confederation of West Germanic tribes, approximating to present day France and a large part of Germany.

German Ocean – North Sea

Gleawecastre – Gloucester, England

Goddodin – The area between the River Tweed and the Firth of Forth; i.e. the modern regions of Lothian and Borders in Scotland.

Gwynedd – North Wales including Anglesey

Hammaburg – Hamburg, Germany

Hamwic – Southampton, Hampshire, England

Isurium Brigantum - Aldborough in Yorkshire

Ledes – Leeds, West Yorkshire

Legacæstir – Chester, England

Lundenwic – London

Mamucium – Roman name for Manchester

Maserfield – Oswestry in Shropshire, England

Mercia – Roughly the present day Midlands of England

Neustria - The region of Frankia between Aquitaine and the English Channel, i.e. the north of present-day France

Northumbria – Comprised Bernicia, Elmet and Deira. At times it also included Rheged and Goddodin

Orcades – The Orkney Islands, Scotland

Oxenforda – Oxford, England

Pictland – The confederation of kingdoms including Shetland, the Orkneys, the Outer Hebrides, Skye and the Scottish Highlands north of a line running roughly from Skye to the Firth of Forth

River Twaid – The river Tweed, which flows west from Berwick through northern Northumberland and the Scottish Borders.

Rheged - A kingdom of Ancient Britons speaking Cumbric, a Brythonic language similar to Old Welsh, which roughly encompassed modern Lancashire, Cumbria in England and, at times, part of Galloway in Scotland

Strathclyde – South east Scotland

Wintan-ceastre - Winchester, Hampshire, England

Weorgoran-ceastre – Worcester, England

Ynys Môn – The Isle of Anglesey, North Wales

Yr Wyddfa – Mount Snowdon, North Wales

Glossary

Ætheling – Literally 'throne-worthy. An Anglo-Saxon prince.

Birlinn – A wooden ship similar to the later Scottish galleys. Usually with a single mast and square rigged sail, they could also be propelled by oars with one man to each oar.

Brenin – The Brythonic term by which kings were addressed in Wales, Strathclyde and the Land of the Picts.

Bretwalda - In Anglo-Saxon England, an overlord or paramount king accepted by other kings as their leader

Ceorl - Freemen who worked the land or else provided a service or trade such as metal working, carpentry, weaving etc. They ranked between thegns and slaves and provided the fyrd in time of war

Currach - A boat, sometimes quite large, with a wooden frame over which animal skins or hides are stretched and greased to make them waterproof.

Custos – A guardian or custodian, the word was used in a variety of contexts including to mean one left in charge in the absence of the lord or king.

Cymru - Wales

Cyning – Old English for king and the term by which they were normally addressed.

Eorl – A noble ranking between thegn and members of the royal house. In the seventh century it meant the governor of a division of the kingdom. Later replaced by ealdorman, the chief magistrate and war leader of a county, and earl, the ruler of a province under the King of All England; for example, Wessex, Mercia and Northumbria.

Fyrd – A militia that was raised from freemen to defend their shire, or to join a royal expedition in times of exceptional need. Service in the fyrd was usually of short duration and members were expected to provide their own arms and provisions

Gesith – The companions of a king, usually acting as his bodyguard.

Hereræswa – Military commander or general. The man who commanded the army of a nation under the king.

Seax – A bladed weapon somewhere in size between a dagger and a sword. Mainly used for close-quarter fighting where a sword would be too long and unwieldy.

Thegn – The lowest rank of noble. A man who held a certain amount of land direct from the king or from a senior nobleman, ranking between an ordinary freeman and an eorl.

Ulaidh - A confederation of dynastic-groupings that inhabited a provincial kingdom in Ulster (north-eastern Ireland) and was ruled by the Rí Ulad or King of the Ulaidh. The two main tribes of the Ulaidh were the Dál nAraidi and the Dál Fiatach.

Uí Néill – An Irish clan who claimed descent from Niall Noigiallach (Niall of the Nine Hostages), a historical King of Tara who died about 405 AD.

Settlement – Any grouping of residential buildings, usually around the king's or lord's hall. In 7th century England the term city, town or village had not yet come into use.

Síþwíf - My lady in Old English.

Weregeld – In Anglo-Saxon England, if property was stolen, or someone was injured or killed, the guilty person would have to pay weregeld as restitution to the victim's family or to the owner of the property.

Witan – The council of an Anglo-Saxon kingdom. Its composition varied, depending on the matters to be debated. Usually it consisted of the Eorls and the chief priests (bishops and abbots in the case of a Christian kingdom), but for the selection of a king or other important matters, it would be expanded to include the more minor nobility, such as the thegns.

Villein - A peasant (tenant farmer) who was legally tied to his vill.

Vill - A thegn's holding or similar area of land in Anglo-Saxon England which might otherwise be described as a parish or manor.

SYNOPSIS OF THE FIRST TWO BOOKS – *WHITEBLADE* and *WARRIORS OF THE NORTH*

Woken in the middle of the night to flee the fortress of Bebbanburg on the Northumbrian coast, the twelve year old Prince Oswald escapes his father's killer, Edwin, to establish a new life for himself on the West Coast of Scotland. He becomes a staunch Christian on Iona and trains to be a warrior.

He makes a name for himself in the frequent wars in Ulster and in a divided Scotland, earning himself the nickname of 'Whiteblade' and establishing himself as the greatest war leader in his adopted homeland. However, he is beset by enemies on all sides and is betrayed by those he should be able to trust the most.

After playing a leading role in deposing the treacherous Connad, King of Dalriada, he helps his successor to extend Dalriada to include the Isles of Skye, Arran and Bute. When King Edwin is killed in battle and those who try to succeed him are also killed by Cadwallon and his invading Welsh army, Oswald decides that his moment of destiny has arrived; he sets out with his warriors to confront Cadwallon and win back the throne of Northumbria.

Once secure on his throne, he enlists the aid of his friend Saint Aidan to convert his pagan subjects to Christianity and establishes the monastery on the Holy Island of Lindisfarne that will become the focus for the spread of the faith throughout the north of England.

Oswald's brother, Oswiu, marries the heiress of Rheged and becomes its king. Gradually he overcomes the ancient enemies of Rheged and allies himself to them to become the dominant force in Caledonia (Scotland) as well as North West England.

Meanwhile Oswald uses a mixture of force, diplomacy and threat to become the most powerful ruler in the whole of England. However, his enemies lurk in the wings and he is betrayed by his allies and killed in battle by the pagan King of Mercia. Oswiu vows to continue the work Oswald started and to take Northumbria forward into its golden age.

CHAPTER ONE – DIVISION OF THE KINGDOM

642 AD

Oswiu and his gesith rode as if the devil was behind them as they headed for the King of Bernicia's summer residence at Yeavering in the Cheviot Hills. His body slave, a boy called Nerian, struggled to keep up with them, burdened as he was by riding an inferior horse and leading a packhorse. The boys who served the twenty warriors who made up Oswiu's gesith lagged even further behind, but that wasn't Nerian's problem.

It was one hundred and seventy miles from Maserfield, where Oswald, King of Northumbria had been killed, to Yeavering; a journey that would normally have taken the best part of a week, even on horseback, but Oswiu, Oswald's brother, was determined to cover it in three days. His plan was to convene the Witan as quickly as possible to elect him as king in place of Oswald and then head for Eoforwīc, the capital of Deira, and convene the Witan there.

Although Northumbria was theoretically one kingdom now, it had a nasty habit of splitting into two parts: Bernicia with its client kingdoms of Rheged to the west and Goddodin between the River Twaid and Firth of Forth, and Deira with its satellites of Elmet to the west of it and Lindsey between the River Humber and the Kingdom of East Anglia. Oswald had failed to get support for the combination of the two Witans and so, like Oswald before him, Oswiu would have to get the agreement of both to his enthronement.

It was not going to be a simple matter. In Anglo-Saxon England sons did not automatically follow fathers to the vacant throne. The Witan, composed of the eorls, thegns, abbots and bishops of the kingdom, chose from amongst the eligible members of the royal house, called æthelings.

There were a number of contenders including Oswald's nineteen year old son, Œthelwald, who was in Kent the last Oswiu had heard. But he had two fast ships with him and it was only a few days by sea up the east coast. The other main contender for Deira was Oswine, son of the last King of Deira before Oswald.

Apart from Oswiu's tent, armour, weapons and other equipment, the poor packhorse was carrying Oswald's remains – the limbless and headless torso that Oswiu had removed from the crude crucifix where Penda of Mercia had nailed it - sewn into a leather tent.

Penda was a pagan and no doubt he saw some humour in abusing his enemy's corpse in this way. No-one knew where Oswald's head and limbs were, but Oswiu had vowed to recover them. His brother was already being referred to as Saint Oswald the Martyr and no doubt his remains would be highly prized amongst the faithful. The recovery of all his various body parts was likely to be something of an impossible quest.

Before Maserfield Oswiu had intercepted King Peada of Middle Anglia, Penda's son, and had soundly defeated him. Now here he was on a mad dash all the way across England to secure his brother's crown.

'Take my brother's remains to the church and lay it in front of the altar for now,' Oswiu told Nerian once they'd reached Yeavering.

'Yes, Cyning. Shall I see the carpenter about a coffin?'

'I'm not king here yet, even though I am the ruler of Rheged, so addressing me as one won't help my case if the members of the Witan hear you.'

'I'm sorry, lord.'

'Not that I don't appreciate the sentiment. You've been a good servant over the years; when this is all over remind me to talk to you about your future. Yes, go and see the carpenter by all means. Oswald wouldn't have wanted anything elaborate. A plain wooden box will suffice.'

Nerian was elated. Did that mean that Oswiu might grant him his freedom? He'd freed his predecessor, Raulf, when he reached fifteen and now he was a member of his gesith. He was so cheerful that he didn't even mind carrying the heavy bundle, which was now beginning to stink, into the church.

Oswiu took Dudda, the senior eorl in Bernicia, aside when he went into the king's hall, ignoring the others who had already gathered.

'Who are the other contenders?' he asked quietly.

'Œthelwald of course, but he hasn't arrived yet, your younger brother, Offa, your nephew, Talorgan the Pict and, of course, your sons Aldfrith and Ehlfrith.'

'Hmmm, I doubt that Talorgan will want to challenge me and one of my sons is still a young boy – and a bastard at that – whilst the other is a babe in arms. Have you heard where Œthelwald is?'

Dudda looked embarrassed. 'He arrived at Bebbanburg yesterday and demanded that the custos turn the fortress over to him as Oswald's son and heir.'

'And?'

'The custos admitted him but his crews, led by the shipmasters, Dunston and Cormac, refused to support him. He tried to have them arrested but no-one would follow his orders. He drew a sword and wounded Cormac before he was overpowered. I believe that he's being brought here under escort tomorrow.'

'Ha, that will hardly help his case. Is Cormac alright?'

'Yes, just a flesh wound, so I'm told.'

'You do seem well informed.'

'The Thegn of Bebbanburg Vill arrived here earlier and he was full of the news.'

'I see. How many have already arrived?'

'Just those who live close by. Your messenger only arrived yesterday morning, having practically killed his horse under him to get here.'

'So it'll be at least three days before the Witan can gather?'

'Yes, probably.'

Oswiu left him feeling a little concerned. It would be at least a week before he could reach Eoforwīc and state his claim before the Witan there. He wished Oswald had been able to combine the two witans.

'Nerian, go and find Ceadda for me.'

The boy ran down to the warriors hall and re-appeared with the captain of his gesith in tow a few minutes later.

'Ceadda, I need to send someone to represent me before the Deiran Witan and state my claim to the throne. It'll probably be quickest if you travel by sea. There are two birlinns at Bebbanburg with crews, tell Dunston I want him to continue as my horse marshal but it's his skill as a shipmaster I need now. He is take you down to Eoforwīc with all speed.'

'I'll leave immediately.'

'No, it's getting dark. Leave at dawn.'

'Who will you appoint to lead the gesith whilst I'm away?'

Oswiu thought for a moment. 'Who would you suggest?'

'Either Aart or Mannix.'

'Mannix is the elder so let it be him. Send him to me.'

~~~

Acha was distraught when she heard of the death of her eldest son.

'You would think that Oswiu would have found the time to come and tell me himself,' she complained to her daughter, Æbbe, the Abbess of Coldingham Monastery.

She had retired to the monastery, which Aidan had founded with Æbbe for nuns to complement his own monastery for monks a few miles further down the east coast on the Island of Lindisfarne.

'I'm sure he has other things on his mind, mother,' she replied, thinking - and not for the first time - that her mother was being rather self-centred.

'Such as? What could be more important than telling your mother that her eldest son is dead?'

'You're not being reasonable. He needs to confirm his own position as king, both here in Bernicia and in Deira as well, and he'll need to prepare the kingdom for a possible invasion by that odious pagan, Penda. Come, we'll go to the church and pray for Oswald's soul.'

The little timber church stood on the headland looking out over the German Ocean. Æbbe loved the location of her monastery, though her mother sometimes found the bitterly cold easterly winds unbearable in the winter. She was now approaching sixty and looked her age. Her one desire now was to visit her two remaining sons one more time before she died. That was one reason that she was so disappointed that Oswiu hadn't come to see her in person.

Offa was rather a different matter. He was her youngest son but he'd lived as an anchorite, firstly on Iona and now on one of the tiny Farne Islands to the south of Lindisfarne. The last time she had seen him was when he left for Iona at the age of twelve some sixteen years ago.

Mother and daughter offered up their prayers for the dead Oswald and then Æbbe left her mother to continue her mediation. Acha thought back over her life and regretted all the times she had argued with Oswald, and to a much greater extent, with Oswiu. The problem was they were all strong willed people with incompatible opinions.

'I can't go to my grave without seeing Oswiu and making my peace with him,' she said to Æbbe later.

'What will you do? You're getting too frail to ride, even the short distance to Bebbanburg. Of course, Oswiu's at Yeavering at the moment and no doubt he'll head for Eoforwīc as soon as he can.'

'Yes, I'll wait until he returns to Bebbanburg, which he'll do in October to spend the winter there, if he keeps to the tradition. I'll have to travel by sea, I suppose. Can you send for a suitable ship to convey me there? I want to go via the Farne Islands to see Offa one last time on the way.'

'But women aren't allowed there. Bishop Aidan might let you land at Lindisfarne, after all there are villeins and their families there who farm the land, but the hermitages are sacrosanct. Even the other monks are only allowed to go out to take food and water to Offa.'

'Nevertheless, this is probably my only chance to see him before I die. From there I'll go onto Bebbanburg and wait for Oswiu there.'

As the birlinn sailed into the bay below the monastery on the Holy Island of Lindisfarne a fishing boat put out from the shore.

'Greetings in the name of God and His Son, Jesus Christ. Who has come to honour us with a visit?' the monk standing in the stern called across.

'Greetings Brother Ròidh, do you not recognise me?'

'Abrecan, is that you? What are you doing here, is ought amiss?'

The fishing boat came alongside and Ròidh clambered aboard.

'A lot since the death of King Oswald. At least Oswiu has been elected as King of Bernicia.'

'What about Œthelwald? Did he not have a better claim as Oswald's son?'

'He scuppered whatever chances he had by wounding Cormac in an argument. He's seen as too hot-headed to rule in these difficult times; and he was forced to pay weregeld to Cormac as compensation for shedding his blood.'

'No tidings as yet from Eoforwīc I suppose?'

'No, not as yet, though the rumours say that Oswine, the son of that fool Oswin of unlamented memory, will be their choice.'

'We can only hope that the rumours are wrong. A nation divided will fall.'

'My sentiments exactly,'

Ròidh gave a start and turned to see an old lady making her painful way towards him with the aid of a stick and two women; one a nun and the other her body slave. He saw the chair mounted on the aft deck and assumed that was how she had made the journey from Coldingham.

'Síþwíf, my apologies. I didn't know that you were aboard.'

Ròidh bowed towards Acha and wondered what on earth she was doing there.

'I have come to see my son, if he will allow it. It will be my last opportunity to do so, I fear. Is Bishop Aidan here? I suppose I should seek his permission.'

'No, he's in the Land of the Picts at the invitation of King Talorgan.'

'Talorgan? My husband's grandson? Is he now king? I thought that was the duplicitous Talorc?'

'He is still the high king, yes, but Talorgan recruited a large war band when in the far north and so Talorc was forced to come to an agreement with him. Prydenn on the east coast was without a king and so Talorc gave Talorgan his support to take the vacant throne provided he acknowledged Talorc as his superior. Now Talorgan wants to convert his new subjects to Christianity.'

Talorgan's grandmother had been Bebba, King Æthelfrith's first wife - a Pictish princess after whom Bebbanburg was named. Acha had been his second.

Ròidh nodded. 'I would have gone with him as usual, but I was recovering from an illness at the time. He's taken two other young monks to train them as missionaries.'

Suddenly he realised that Acha was still standing.

'I'm sorry Síþwíf. Abrecan, is there something the Lady Acha can sit on?'

'Don't fuss. I'll go back to my chair in a moment, but first I need to know whether whoever is in charge in Aidan's absence will allow me to see Offa.'

'That would be me. Aidan made me prior of the monastery before he left.'

Aidan was Abbot of Lindisfarne as well as being the bishop.

'Very well. Do you think Offa will see me? Which islet is he on?'

Acha turned with difficulty and scanned the islets to the south, two of which had the distinctive beehive shaped huts on them in which the anchorites lived.

'He isn't, Síþwíf. He's gradually become one of the community. I think he's satisfied that he has spent enough time communing with God and now feels that he needs to be of more use in a practical sense. He's the Master of the Novices, and a very good one he is too. I think the boys respect his piety and he has a way of dealing with them that allows them to be boys, but also be self-disciplined when they need to be. He certainly seems to get the best out of them.'

'So he's stopped being a recluse?'

'Not entirely. He still seeks solitude from time to time. However, he hasn't felt the need to retire to the islets for two months now. I think that the last time he was away for a week he missed his young charges, though he would never admit that.'

Four rowers lifted Acha over the side once the birlinn had been beached and Ròidh sent for a horse and cart to take her up to the monastery. The buildings were scattered over the site, which was enclosed by a hedge of hawthorn to keep animals out. Apart from the church, kitchens and the hall, there were small huts for the monks to live in and a building with several large windows with shutters. This was the scriptorium where important documents, like the Holy Bible and books of prayer, were copied. The unglazed windows let in the maximum amount of light but work continued by candlelight if the shutters had to be closed in inclement weather.

Ròidh and a monk helped Acha out of the cart; the nun and her slave had been forced to remain on the birlinn. It was one thing to allow the former queen into the sacred precincts but three women would have been unthinkable.

She hobbled, leaning on Ròidh's arm, into the scriptorium. Several monks were busy copying and didn't even look up when Acha entered but at the far end a monk in his late twenties was bending over a boy's shoulder as he practiced illumination alongside a dozen other boys similarly occupied.

As he straightened up to move to the next novice he noticed Ròidh standing in the doorway with an old woman. His first reaction was outrage that a female should be here in the monastery, let alone in the scriptorium, then he realised that there was something vaguely familiar about her face. When he had last seen Acha he'd been a boy of twelve and she'd just entered her forties. He didn't recognise her now, but the way she was looking at him stirred a distant memory.

'Mother?' he asked uncertainly and then smiled a welcome when she nodded her head. 'I never thought to see you again, least of all here.'

As he said this he glanced at Ròidh with an unspoken question in his expression.

'Shall we go outside, brother?'

Ròidh left them to talk and went into the church to pray for the Lady Acha's soul. He had a feeling that she didn't have long left in this world.

'What brings you here, mother? You know that long ago I gave up the outside world to devote my life to serving God. I had reconciled myself to never seeing you or my family again.'

'I know that I haven't long to live, Offa, and the death of Oswald made me realise that I needed to see you and Oswiu once more before I died. I brought six sons into this world and you two are the only ones left.'

'I was sad to hear of the death of Oswald and the others, but I didn't really know them that well. Of course, Osguid, Oslac and Oslaph were with me on Iona for a while but after I completed my noviciate I became

17

an anchorite and saw little of them before Osguid and Oslac left to serve as priests. I was with Oslaph when he died though. He succumbed to a wasting sickness and I spent time in the infirmary tending him for his last few weeks. His was not an easy death.'

Acha wept for Oslaph in a way that she hadn't for the others, even Oswald. His had been such a short life.

'I must get back to my charges, mother. They are good boys but they need watching or they'll be up to some mischief. I know that I was the same at their age.'

'Offa, I came to say goodbye but also to make a request. Oslac served Oswald well as his chaplain. I know he had his wife and mistress to confide in and Aidan and he were always close, but he depended on Oslac a great deal and, as his chaplain, I know he made Oswald a better Christian. I realise that I have no right to ask, but Oswiu needs someone like Oslac now. He is devout but he is hot tempered and proud. He needs a chaplain to constantly remind him he is but a humble mortal and a child of God as well as a king.'

'And you want me to be to Oswiu what Oslac was to Oswald?'

'Yes, I suppose that's exactly what I'm asking.'

'I'll need to reflect on that and seek guidance from Our Lord. My years of quiet meditation and prayer eventually led me down my present path, but it may be that He has something more useful for me to do. Where are you going now? Back to Coldingham?'

'No, to Bebbanburg to await Oswiu's arrival.'

He nodded. 'I will either send a messenger there or, if I decide that the right thing to do is as you ask, I'll see you there in a little while. Goodbye mother. I may see you again but, if not, God be with you.'

Acha was assisted into the cart once more and, as she sat down with some relief, she looked back towards the scriptorium, but Offa had already gone back inside.

In the event, she didn't see either Oswiu or Offa at Bebbanburg. She died peacefully in her sleep three days after arriving there.

~~~

Oswiu arrived at Eoforwīc to find that the Witan had met but had adjourned until he and Œthelwald could be present, much to Oswine's annoyance. Ceadda took him to one side as soon as the formal welcome was over.

'The Witan is divided. Several of the eorls favour you; they know that keeping Northumbria together as one kingdom makes it stronger and better able to stand up to Penda, but James the Deacon wants Deira to be independent. I'm sure his motivation is religious. He is a member of the Roman Church and he seeks to counter the influence of Bishop Aidan and the Celtic Church. I have heard a rumour that he has petitioned the Pope to make Deira a separate diocese. Many of the thegns also want to split Northumbria in two again. It seems illogical but I suspect that they fear James and want to appease him. They mainly support Oswine. I suppose that the only good news is that Œthelwald seems to have few adherents, though he has been canvassing support since he arrived two days ago.'

'Thank you Ceadda. I'll not stoop to my nephew's tactics though. If I can't convince the Witan when it assembles, then so be it. I won't go around hiding in dark corners trying to bribe, threaten or charm people into supporting me.'

Hrothga, Eorl of Eoforwīc, presided, just as he'd done eight years previously when Oswald had been elected as King of Deira and Elmet. The hall was packed with the candidates and the earls seated on benches in front, and the thegns standing crammed in behind them.

'I'll call upon each candidate to state their claim for the crown in order of age and then invite the eorls and thegns to question them in turn. Oswiu, would you start please?'

'I'm the brother of King Oswald and son of the Lady Acha, daughter of King Ælle. I am King of Bernicia and Rheged and combining these territories with that of Deira and Elmet would establish Northumbria as a great power in England, powerful enough to resist the pagan Penda. I don't wish to boast of my military prowess, but suffice to say I am a warrior and successful commander whereas my rivals are as yet untried on the battlefield.'

When he sat down both Oswine and Œthelwald leapt to their feet. They glared at each other before Hrothga reminded them that Œthelwald was nineteen whereas Oswine was only seventeen.

'Thank you Hrothga. I am the only son of your last king, Oswald of blessed memory. I may not be as experienced a warrior as my uncle, Oswiu, but you would have my undivided loyalty. Deira is in danger of being swallowed up as part of a greater Northumbria. My uncle has always been more concerned with the north than with us here on the border of Mercia. He is allied to Dalriada, Strathclyde and many petty kings in the Land of the Picts and that is where his interest lies. Elect me and you will get a king who puts your welfare first.'

Oswiu glared at Œthelwald as he sat down. He would have liked to repudiate what his nephew had said but he'd missed the opportunity to address his criticism. He realised that he who spoke last had a distinct advantage.

'These two other æthelings are Bernicians, not Deirans,' Oswine began. 'Their father was the man who murdered my grandfather's brother, Æthelric, and took our throne by force. Do you wish to perpetuate this injustice? It's true that they can trace their ancestry back to King Ælle but I am the grandson of his youngest brother Æfric and I am descended through the male line back to Yffi, the founder of the royal house of Deira. Furthermore, my father, Osric, was king. I say I have the greater claim, and I will serve you and you alone. Finally, Oswiu says that he will save you from Mercia because a united Northumbria is powerful enough to resist him. That lie was exposed at Maserfield.'

Oswiu got to his feet at that.

'As you well know, the only reason he was defeated and killed was because he was betrayed by Eowa's men. He and his gesith gave their lives to allow the men of Deira to escape. It was the act of a hero and a martyr and Deira is in his debt.'

'Oswiu, sit down at once! I'll not allow this Witan to degenerate into a slanging match,' Hrotha thundered.

He had remained seated and he waved his hands at the other eorls who had sprung to their feet to indicate that they too should resume their seats.

'We are all aware of your brother's brave death and the sacrifice he made. Nevertheless it was the men of Deira who paid the price for his conflict with Penda; Bernicia wasn't present at the battle.'

'No, they were with me defeating Penda's son and the Middle Anglians. May I point out that, because of the losses they suffered that day, they won't be in a position to threaten Deira, Elmet or Lindsey for some time.'

Hrotha nodded to accept the truth of that and Oswiu sat down, still smouldering with anger.

'As I was saying,' Oswine continued smoothly, 'we should not interfere with Mercia. It would be better for us to agree a mutual policy of non-aggression with Penda. Then we can concentrate on making Deira a prosperous and peaceful kingdom once more.'

With that he sat down and Hrotha opened the meeting to questions from the eorls. The first to speak was Rand, the Eorl of Elmet, a previously independent kingdom before it was absorbed into Deira.

20

'We would, of course, welcome peace with Mercia as we border it on two sides; however, Penda's invasion with Cadwallon ten years ago was unprovoked. I don't think a policy of appeasement, as advocated by Oswine, would give us security. I prefer to be able to defend ourselves and, for me, that means electing Oswiu.'

'I disagree,' another eorl, this time from the north of the kingdom, bordering Bernicia, said. 'When one king ruled both Bernicia and Deira he didn't stop raids across the River Tees to steal our livestock. I say we want a king who can defend us against Bernicia. My choice is Oswine.'

The debate continued in like vein for a while then, when it became apparent that nothing new was being said, Hrotha opened the discussion to the rest of the Witan.

'Bernicia is a Christian kingdom, as is Deira,' James the Deacon said. 'However, Bishop Aidan is from Iona and the rest of England now follows the Roman Church. The Celts do not observe the correct date for Easter and much of what they teach is false. Furthermore, Aidan is now in the Land of the Picts and we are neglected. I believe that we need to re-establish Deira as an independent kingdom which acknowledges the Pope in Rome as our spiritual leader.'

Most of the thegns who spoke seemed to favour Oswine and Oswiu was already resigned to defeat when the vote was called. The majority of the eorls selected Oswiu but two thirds of the thegns voted for Oswine. Œthelwald secured five votes and he stomped out of the hall in disgust, not staying to swear fealty to Oswine. It wasn't until he'd cooled down outside that he wondered what he was now going to do. He had burned his boats with Oswine and he couldn't see his uncle giving him any responsibility. He was without a place in the world.

Oswiu approached Oswine and congratulated him.

'I hope we can work together as allies, cousin,' he told him.

Cousin was stretching it a bit. They were in reality second cousins.

'I hope so too, Oswiu, but I won't be entering into any alliances against the Mercians.'

'There may come a day when you'll bitterly regret that decision. Goodbye Oswine.'

Outside he found Œthelwald pacing up and down in indecision.

'What will you do now, nephew? I hope you're not expecting me to offer you a position. You and I have never been friends and, to put it bluntly, I don't trust you.'

'I wouldn't accept if you did offer me a post,' he replied fiercely. 'I'll take my father's birlinn and recruit a crew from amongst my friends and sail for Ulster. I always liked Eochaid. I'll learn to be a great warrior there, like my father did.'

'You'll never be like your father, boy. You couldn't be more different. I wish you well though, and I won't contest your right to take the Holy Saviour. I have enough birlinns without it. Give my regards to King Eochaid.'

~~~

Oswiu and his mother had often been at odds but her death saddened him. Having always been a member of a large family, he didn't like being almost alone. He was therefore glad to find his younger brother Offa waiting for him at Bebbanburg. Offa was two years younger and they had played together as boys; however, they were never close – not in the way that he and Oswald had been close.

He was devout but even he found Offa's piety a little too much. Nevertheless, he readily accepted his offer to become his chaplain. The two of them travelled to Coldingham for the funeral and, for this occasion, Æbbe had lifted the ban on men entering the monastery.

'It's good to see you both, it seems a very long time since were all together as children at Dùn Add.'

'It must be all of sixteen years; a long time as you say. You're looking well, sister.'

'Yes, I think the sea air and tranquillity of this place suit me,' she said with a smile.

'It's what I loved about Lindisfarne too,' Offa said.

'Do you miss it, now that you're our brother's chaplain I mean?'

'Yes, very much. But I know that I am doing God's bidding and so I am content.'

'I'm sorry that you didn't inherit all of Oswald's domain,' she said to Oswiu.

'So am I, but I will be King of all Northumbria in the end. However, my first priority, after we bury our mother, is to recover the rest of Oswald's body.'

'Do you know where they are?'

'His head is on a spike outside the gates of Tamworth and one arm is reportedly hanging from a tree near the battlefield. Until I have recovered these we shan't bury him. Meanwhile his torso is at Bebbanburg preserved in a cask of mead.'

'Where will he be interred?'

22

'On Lindisfarne. It's the centre of Christianity in the north and it's a fitting place for his shrine.'

The group fell silent for a moment thinking of Oswald's untimely death and what else he might have achieved had he lived. Then Æbbe broke their reverie.

'It's time we went in for the service. Mother will be buried beside the altar.'

So saying, she went into the church followed by her brothers. Ròidh was present with a small contingent from Lindisfarne, as were two eorls and several thegns. After the internment, Oswiu and Offa headed back to Bebbanburg. On the morrow the king would leave to recover what he could of Oswald.

When he got back to Bebbanburg he found two boys waiting for him. He'd almost forgotten that he'd sent Raulf with a few mounted members of his warband to collect them. Alweo was the son of Eowa, Penda's brother and Oswald's ally who'd been murdered by his own men at Maserfield, and Wigmund was his cousin. Both were Penda's nephews but he knew they'd be useless as hostages. To be truthful, he wasn't quite sure why he'd rescued them. Penda had little regard for anyone other than himself and he'd have killed the two boys out of hand because of Eowa's betrayal of him.

'Did you have any trouble?' he asked Raulf.

'No, Cyning. I just told the custos that Eowa had sent for them. Luckily word of the defeat at Maserfield and Eowa's death hadn't reached them yet.'

'Good. I wouldn't want to be in the custos' shoes when Penda finds out.'

'Er, what shall I do with them?'

'How old are you?' Oswiu asked, turning to the two boys, the younger of whom looked both miserable and fearful at the same time whilst the other glared at him defiantly.

'I'm nearly thirteen and Wigmund is twelve,' Alweo answered without a trace of deference in his voice.

'Confident little sod, aren't you,' Oswiu told him with a grin. 'I like that; you'll make a good warrior one day. I can't say the same about the shrinking violet beside you though.'

'Wigmund's alright, but you're correct, he's not warrior material.'

At this Wigmund glared at his cousin and kicked him hard in the shin, causing the other boy to grunt in pain.'

'Ah! He has got some spirit then. Good. Now what am I going to do with you?'

At that moment Offa appeared.

'Excellent timing. Do you think Aidan could do with some more novices?'

'Always, he can never have enough monks to help with his work. You mean these two?'

'What's a novice?' Alweo asked curiously.

'A monk in training; not that I'm suggesting you should become one, though the life might suit Wigmund. No, I'm sending you to Lindisfarne to be educated and turned from a little pagan into a civilised Christian. If you behave, I'll admit you into my warband for training as a warrior. Wigmund can decide what he wants to do after two years there.'

'Thank you, I suppose.'

'What for saving your miserable lives?'

'Oh yes, that too.'

'Offa, will you take them up the coast and hand them over to Brother Ròidh? Come straight back though, I want you to come with me when we leave tomorrow.'

CHAPTER TWO – DEEP INTO ENEMY TERRITORY

October 642 AD

Oswiu knew it was a stupid risk but he would not be dissuaded. He was determined to recover his brother's head, which was on a spike outside the gates of Tamworth and the one limb he knew about, which had reportedly been thrown up into a tree near the battlefield. The only reason he knew about the latter was because a peddler had told Fianna of a miracle he'd heard about at a nearby tavern when he was selling her some cloth for a new tunic.

The innkeeper's niece, so the story went, was paralysed from the waist down but, when she was laid down under the tree where some of the blood from the arm had drained into the soil, she was cured and walked back to the tavern.

'You don't believe it do you?' Sigbert asked him when Oswiu relayed the story to him.

'You don't?' Oswiu asked.

'Well, it seems a little implausible to me. I've heard of the relics of saints performing miracles in the name of Our Lord but King Oswald isn't a saint and this was supposedly performed by earth on which a drop or two of his blood may or may not have fallen.'

'Our brother may not be a saint yet,' Offa said quietly, 'but he most assuredly is a martyr. He was slain most foully by a pagan.'

'You think Oswald may become a saint?' Oswiu asked, surprised.

'I believe so, yes. He was a devout believer and spread Christianity throughout Northumbria, with Bishop Aidan's help of course, and now his remains are performing miracles.'

Oswiu thought that his brother was being a little naïve, but he could see the political advantage of proclaiming Oswald a saint. It would harden every Christian's heart against Penda.

'I must consult Aidan about this when he returns; in the meantime I'll travel to Lindisfarne tomorrow to discuss it with Brother Ròidh. Now, we were discussing my plans for recovering the head and this miraculous arm. Taking the warband, or even part of it, is not practical. I'm not seeking confrontation with Penda, or the blasted Welsh, at this stage. We need a small party who can ride fast and fight well, and that means my gesith. It's now thirty strong, which is large enough to protect me against anyone we are likely to meet accidentally, but not so big as to be impossible to hide.'

'Very well, will Father Offa be coming along?'

'Offa was about to say no when Oswiu surprised him.

'Yes, of course. I don't want to go anywhere without my chaplain. If I should be killed I don't want to die unshriven. I'll also take Nerian; and I suppose the gesith will want to take some servants too. Three should suffice. No tents or unnecessary baggage, only what can be carried on the horses. The servants can each lead a spare horse, just in case we lose any. Now, any questions?'

'Provisions?'

'Oh, yes. Thank you.'

Oswiu was annoyed with himself for overlooking something so basic but his mind was totally focused on recovering what he could of his beloved brother.

'Each man is to take a water skin and some cheese, bread and apples – enough to last two days' he continued. We'll have to find isolated farmsteads or shepherd's huts to raid and those who have bows better take them. Nerian's quite good at tickling trout too.'

'If we raid even isolated places won't word get around about us?'

'Not if we kill everyone and bury the bodies where they won't be found easily,' Sigbert replied with a grin.

'Oh, how barbaric!'

'No, you're wrong Offa. It would be barbaric if it was wanton killing. In this case it is necessary to save our own lives.'

'Perhaps, but it's still a sin. Warn me, please, so I don't have to be a witness to such brutality.'

It was at times like this that Oswiu was reminded what a sheltered life his brother had led up until now.

After the other two had left, Oswiu's mind turned back to Fianna, who had brought the peddler to him. She was a widow now but she was the mother of his eldest son, Aldfrith. The boy was back living with her and, in addition, she was looking after his two children by Rhieinmelth with the help of a wet nurse. She hadn't said so directly, but it was obvious she entertained hopes that they might resume their old relationship now that his wife was dead.

26

Oswiu had no intention of doing that. He needed to find a wife who would strengthen his position and that meant someone of royal blood, not a villein's daughter from Bute. He had no intention of following Oswald's example and to keep a wife and a mistress. In any case, no-one else would be as understanding as Cyneburga had been. That was another problem. She and Keeva were still living in the fortress. He had spoken to Cyneburga briefly and she had expressed a desire to become a nun. If her brother agreed, that might be the best solution. He thought that Keeva would probably want to go with her. He'd have to talk to his sister as soon as he got back, but he was certain that Æbbe would accept them at Coldingham.

He went to bed wondering who he might approach with a marriage proposal. He couldn't sleep and so he ran the possibilities over in his mind. When he'd thought about it at length he came to the conclusion that the obvious choice was Eanflæd of Kent. Aside from Wessex and East Anglia, Kent was the most important of the southern kingdoms. It was founded by the Jutes, who were jealous of the growing power of the West Saxons and therefore keen to make allies.

In addition to being the cousin of King Eorcenberht, she was the daughter of Oswiu's uncle, Edwin of Northumbria, who had usurped the throne when Oswiu's father had been killed. Marrying her would placate those who had been loyal to Edwin as well as reinforcing the friendly relations Northumbria had forged with Kent. Of course she might look like the back end of a cow, but her mother had been accounted a beauty in her day.

Satisfied with his decision he drifted off to sleep.

~~~

Raulf was talking to Nerian when Oswiu and Ceadda emerged and mounted their horses. Raulf and Nerian had become, if not comrades, then at least friends. Nerian admired Raulf and the older youth felt a bond with the boy as he too had been Oswiu's body slave in the past. The rest of the gesith were mounted already and Raulf hastened to do the same. Nerian mounted his pony and, leading the packhorse carrying his and the king's gear, he moved to join the other servants in the middle of the column.

The early morning dew clung to the grass as they swept out of the gates of Bebbanburg heading south towards Hexham. Oswine might be King of Deira instead of Oswiu, but he didn't anticipate any problems travelling down through Elmet to the Mercian border. He'd decided to head for Tamworth first to recover his brother's head before seeking the severed arm near Maserfield. From there it wasn't more than a two day ride north into Rheged.

The first part of the journey went without incident. Oswine might be their king but no-one in Elmet was going to challenge the mounted party of thirty experienced warriors. They paid for what provisions they needed instead of foraging and that earned them the co-operation of everyone they encountered. Oswiu's one worry was that word of their passing might reach Penda, but they were travelling so rapidly that it seemed unlikely.

The northern boundary of Mercian territory was marked by several rivers, from the Mersey and the Weaver in the west to part of the Aire in the east. Between them lay a large area of boggy upland called the High Peak where practically no-one lived. Oswiu decided that this was his best route into Mercia. From the southern edge of the peaty morass it was still fifty miles to Tamworth through more populated country but he hoped that, by avoiding settlements, he could cover this undetected.

The black peat hills looked impassable at first glance.

'Are you sure there's a way through this?' he asked Ceadda.

'So these two boys assure me.'

The scouts had found two brothers of fourteen and twelve looking after a flock of sheep in the valley through which a river called the Derwent ran. They seemed to find the prospect of leaving their boring task in exchange for a bit of an adventure attractive and went with the scouts willingly, once they'd been promised that no harm would come to them. The scouts weren't great proponents of personal hygiene but even they found that the stink given off by the two young shepherds was overpowering and they gave them a good wash in the Derwent before they continued. Now they nodded eagerly when asked whether they knew their way through the black hills facing them.

Oswiu still looked sceptical. 'Let the elder act as guide and keep the younger boy close. If the guide doesn't do what he's promised or gets us lost, cut his brother's throat.'

He repeated what he'd said in Brythonic as the boys didn't understand English. They apparently had no idea whether they lived in Mercia or not – indeed they claimed not to have heard of it. They were Britons, part of the original population before the coming of the Anglo-Saxons.

'I give you my word that I'll guide you true, Brenin,' the fourteen year old said, sounding highly offended that he wasn't trusted.

Oswiu was suprised to be address as *Brenin*, which meant *king* in most of the Brythonic languages. The boy wasn't entirely an ignoramus it seemed.

What's your name boy?'

'Catinus, my brother is called Conomultus.'

'Well, Catinus, I believe you. Lead on.'

Nevertheless he kept the younger boy by his side.

Their young guide led the way up beside a stream which trickled down the hillside. The going was soft, but not dangerously so. Once they reached the top Oswiu saw a large plateau stretching in front of them. It was covered with bare patches of black peat, clumps of heather and the occasional outcrop of rock. The boy jumped down into a deep trench that wound its way through the peat bog. The bottom was of gravel with a couple of inches of water running through it.

'We call these groughs,' his brother helpfully confided to Oswiu.

The grough twisted and turned and it took them two hours to traverse the boggy wasteland, but then they descended the hill to cross a small river before climbing up again. This happened once more and then they emerged at a point where the stream they were following flowed over the edge and down a rocky course to the valley below. Their horses picked their way down the escarpment carefully whilst the boy leading them on foot kept stopping impatiently and waiting for them to catch up.

Eventually they reached the valley floor through which a larger river ran.

'This is the River Ashop. It'll be dark soon so we can camp here tonight, Brenin,' the guide told them. 'Tomorrow we climb up there.' He pointed to the top of the steep escarpment facing them. 'Then it's no more than two or three miles through the last area of bog before we descend to the valley below. That's the start of the inhabited country but I've never been further than that.'

The next day dawned dank and chilly. Oswiu looked up at the escarpment but the top of it was lost in low cloud. This part of the country was bad enough in fine weather; it was going to be a miserable day.

'Can you find your way across in this murk?' he asked Catinus when he appeared chewing a piece of cheese.

The boy looked up, swallowed his mouthful and grinned.

'It's a plateau, Brinin. You can hear the waterfall that drops over the cliffs to the west and there's a river below us to the east so, as long as we can see a green valley below us with low hills beyond when get out of the cloud, we'll be fine.'

And so it proved. Oswiu was hoping that the cloud would lift but in fact the weather deteriorated as the day wore on and the valley they sought was barely discernible through the rain as they descended. The one good thing was the poor visibility hid them from the two settlements in the valley.

Raulf put an arrow through a solitary sheep that was lost and bleating piteously and so at least they would have fresh meat that night. Catinus and Conomultus proved their worth by skinning and expertly butchering the animal ready for the spit once they found a copse with a stream in which to camp. Oswiu thought that they were probably now no more than forty miles from Tamworth – a day and half's ride if they knew where they were going, but they didn't. All Oswiu knew was that they were due north of their destination.

His problem now was what to do about the two boys. To Ceadda the solution was simple.

'We cut their throats so they can't tell anyone we were here and bury them in this copse.'

'Yes, that is an option but they have done what they said they'd do and I don't like to reward good service with death.'

'Well, we can't take them with us. They'll slow us down. You could just cut out their tongues I suppose? I doubt if either of them can write, so they couldn't tell anyone about us.'

'I agree that's the sensible course, but they could be useful to us when we get to Maserfield. They could enquire amongst the local Welsh as to the whereabouts of my poor brother's limbs.'

'I suppose so but, now we are in open country again, we need to move fast.'

'They can double up with the servants leading the packhorses. If we change them round every couple of hours that shouldn't tire the horses too much. It isn't as if they weigh much. I suspect that they've eaten better since they joined us than they do normally.'

'If you say so, Oswiu, but I still say we should cut out their tongues.'

~~~

Aidan and his two monks disembarked at Dùn Dè from the currach that had brought them north from Lindisfarne to be greeted by Talorgan. The bishop had been surprised that the King of Prydenn found it necessary to be accompanied by fifteen warriors for the journey back up to his fortress, and said so.

'Bishop, you obviously don't know King Talorc. He gave me Prydenn to buy me off when I threatened to topple him from his throne, but he doesn't expect me to keep it. He's already made two attempts on my life, an ambush in the streets of my own capital and an assassin who managed to reach my bedchamber. On both occasions I was lucky. I don't intend to give him a third chance.'

'I see. Well, let's hope I can convert your people before he succeeds.'

He gave the startled king a smile to indicate that he was in jest, before they continued their journey in silence. Later, when they were alone, Aidan wasted no time in coming straight to the point.

'What is it exactly that you want of me?'

'Most of the other Pictish kingdoms have followed Christ, thanks to your missionary work amongst the Picts years ago, but Prydenn wasn't included. My mother was a Christian, as was my father - for a time. I am too, as is my wife, but my people aren't. I hope that you can convert the people here and give us a bishop to carry on the good work in the rest of the kingdom.'

'Well that's direct enough. I suggest that I start with the warriors in the fortress and we'll see how that is received.'

'Excellent. By the way I had expected to see Ròidh with you.'

'He was ill when I left but hopefully he'll recover soon.'

'I hope so too. I understand that he was a Pictish prince at one stage?'

'Yes, but that was when he was fourteen. A lot of water has passed down the river since then. I believe that his brother is now King of Ardewr?'

'Yes, they are my neighbours to the north-west. I know that I have no right to ask this, as Ròidh has been your companion for so long, but I can't help but think that he would make an excellent Bishop of Prydenn.'

'Ah! So it wasn't me you wanted, but my assistant.'

'I'm sorry, but yes. Ròidh is a Pict and moreover of royal blood. That will be a great help to him as a missionary here.'

'Very well. I'll return to Lindisfarne and send Brother Ròidh to you as soon as he is well enough.'

'No, please don't go. I can see that I've offended you and for that I apologise. I hope that you'll stay a few weeks so that you can see something of my kingdom. It is, of course, all new to me as well. I was born in Fortriu, where the high king now has his main fortress.'

'I can see why, as it borders both Strathclyde and Dalriada.'

Talorgan nodded. 'And Goddodin near Stirling, if I remember correctly.'

'Yes, it's wild country for the most part, except around Stirling. Its fortress is near on impregnable and its position dominates many of the routes into the rest of Pictland.'

'Much as I'd like to see something of your kingdom, I fear I should get back to Lindisfarne. I'm concerned about Ròidh, and about Lady Acha, who is increasingly frail. I'm also anxious about King Oswald's foray into Mercia. However, provided you'll allow me to make a start on converting the people here in your capital, I'd like to stay for a week or two before facing journey back by sea.'

It was two weeks later, just as Aidan was thinking about returning to Lindisfarne, that a small birlinn arrived from Bebbanburg. The news of the death of both Oswald and Acha shocked Aidan and even Talorgan was worried.

'I'm sorry about the death of Oswald, - and his mother, of course - but I'm now concerned about my own position. Power is a dangerous game and one of the reasons Talorc was wary of me was the fact that Oswald was my uncle. Perhaps I indicated to the high king that Oswald was friendlier towards me than he was in reality, but now he needn't fear any interference from Northumbria.'

'Why not? Oswiu is also your uncle and he has more influence up here as King of Rheged and conqueror of Goddodin than Oswald had?'

'Perhaps, but now his attention will be directed southwards, as Oswald's was. After Maserfield, Mercia is the most powerful of all the English kingdoms and there is no guarantee that Oswiu will be able to resist them. I'm sure that his northern border is the least of his concerns at the moment.'

'All the more reason for me to sail south today. Oswiu will need my support. Don't worry, I haven't forgotten my promise to ask Ròidh if he'd be willing to become your bishop.'

When he reached Lindisfarne he found Ròidh completely recovered but Oswiu, having failed to secure the throne of Deira, had disappeared with his gesith and no-one knew where he was.

CHAPTER THREE – SAINTLY REMAINS

Autumn 642 AD

'Now, you're quite clear what I want you to do?'

Oswiu looked the two boys in the eye. He was risking a lot in trusting the two young Britons. Ceadda clearly thought his king was mad.

Catinus and Conomultus both nodded earnestly. They were extremely nervous and, given the fact that the captain of Oswiu's gesith had promised to cut out their tongue and castrate them if they failed, that wasn't surprising. However, they had little option but to carry out the task that Oswiu had given them, dangerous as it was. They had effectively thrown in their lot with the Bernician king and their fate lay in his hands. They had nowhere else to go now.

'Right. God be with you then. Off you go.'

The two boys set out along the path that let out of the woods where Oswiu and his gesith were hiding and across the cultivated land that lay between them and the gates of Tamworth. Even at this distance they could see the rotting head of King Oswald sitting on top of a stake near the gates. Their task was made even more difficult by the fact that the stake wasn't more than ten yards from the four sentries who were stopping all those entering Penda's capital to levy a tax on all those who'd brought produce to sell at the weekly market.

The two boys joined the queue waiting to enter and a boy sitting on the back of the cart in front of them grinned at them and threw them an apple, which Catinus deftly caught. He took a couple of bites out of it and passed it on to his brother.

'Thanks,'

'You're welcome. Those arseholes on the gates will pinch a few anyway, in addition to charging us to enter. You on your own then?'

The two boys saw that a man and a youth sat on the seat at the front of the ox-drawn cart and assumed they were the boy's father and elder brother.

'Yes, we're orphans,' Conomultus volunteered.

He would have said more but at that moment the cart moved forward in the queue and a man leading a cow and a calf came up behind them followed by two more carts full of produce.

'We're not here to make friends. Don't tell anyone anything you don't have to,' his brother whispered quietly in his ear. 'Now get that sack ready.'

A few minutes later they moved forward again. The cart in front of them was being inspected by two of the sentries and, as the apple grower's son had predicted, they helped themselves to a couple of apples each. The grisly head was now only a few feet away and, when the two sentries moved back towards the gate, Catinus seized his chance.

The head was just out of reach and so he jumped up and pushed it upwards with his fist. For a moment he thought it wasn't going to budge, but then it toppled off the spike and Conomultus caught it deftly in the open sack. For an instant everyone was caught by surprise and the two boys were able to turn and start to run away before anyone reacted. A second later uproar broke out and the men manning the gate came running to see what the matter was.

Two of them started to run after the boys whilst the other two ran back to the gate. One remained at his post, telling everyone to clear the gateway, whilst the other ran towards the king's hall to raise the alarm. He desperately hoped that his fellow sentries caught the thieves; Penda had a nasty habit of killing those who let him down.

The boys were a hundred yards clear of their pursuers and, although the latter's longer legs meant that they were gaining on them, they were hampered by their spears and helmets and so they discarded them. One was wearing a leather jerkin but the other was wearing no more than a thick woollen over-tunic. Now they were gaining on the boys, who were no more than fifty yards in front of them.

Undoubtedly they would have caught them before they reached the trees but, just as they were about to overtake their quarry some sixty feet short of the woods, several arrows hit them in the chest and they fell, one dead and the other seriously wounded.

As the boys reached safety a few men ran forward, slit the throat of the surviving sentry, and carried the bodies into the trees. Oswiu hoped that there would be a delay before someone could organise further pursuit. The dead Mercians were bundled into a depression in the ground and covered with fallen leaves. Penda would certainly know by now that his grisly trophy had been stolen but he wouldn't know who'd taken it or why. The use of Britons to steal it might confuse things for a while, or so he hoped.

He led his horse forward to the edge of the woods and looked towards Tamworth. The carts waiting to enter had blocked further pursuit for a few precious minutes. Now he could see a group of horsemen starting towards him. They would reach him in a couple of minutes so, pausing only to congratulate the boys and take the sack from them, he mounted and led his men deep into the trees following an animal track. It had been made by large animals, perhaps deer, and was just wide enough to allow men on horseback to traverse it slowly, pushing overhanging branches out of the way as they went. The two boys ran on, leaving footprints in the muddy road until they turned and made their way, with some difficulty, through the dense undergrowth to join up with the animal track that Oswiu and his gesith had taken.

For a moment Catinus thought that Oswiu had abandoned them but half a mile along the track they found Raulf waiting for them with Nerian. Catinus grasped Raulf's hand and he pulled the boy up behind him whilst Nerian did the same for his brother, then they set off after the rest.

The Mercian horsemen pounded along the road until the man in command spotted where the boys had taken to the undergrowth. There was no way that they could follow on horseback, so they dismounted and used their swords and seaxes to cut their way into the mass of shrubs and brambles. They followed the boys' trail, which was all too evident because of broken twigs, trampled vegetation and the like, but they couldn't take their horses with them without cutting back the undergrowth.

They eventually emerged onto the trail that Oswiu and the others had taken but, by the time someone had gone back to bring the horses along the main trail, whoever they were chasing had a good head start. Nevertheless, the man in charge of the pursuit knew that he daren't go back without the head, so the Mercians set off in pursuit.

~~~

'You do know that they'll keep on after us, Oswiu?'

'Yes Ceadda, I'm not a fool. How many of them would you say there are?'

'Perhaps twenty?'

'We need to slow them down. Who would you say are our best archers?'

'Raulf and Edmund. They're not the fastest to get the second and third arrows away but they are the most accurate.'

'Good. I want them to kill the leader of our pursuers. That will cause confusion and, hopefully, the rest will be a lot more cautious.'

The two warriors climbed up into the lower branches of two oak trees, one either side of the trail. Catinus and his brother waited a hundred yards further along, around a bend and out of sight, holding the archers' two horses.

The undergrowth was dense and the trail narrow but the trees were bare of leaves, therefore the two men knew that they would be spotted as soon as the Mercians appeared. They would have barely a second or two to strike before they would have to jump down and run.

They waited nervously, their bows strung and the arrows nocked but they would have to wait until the first rider appeared before drawing the bow and letting fly. The arrows were tipped with iron and had no barb. At close range they would have enough power to force their way through the links of chain mail, tear through the clothing underneath and, with any luck, penetrate the torso underneath. Both prayed to God that the first man to appear would be the leader. If he'd sent a scout ahead the ploy would fail.

The trail wasn't wide enough for two men to ride abreast so the Mercians would be in single file; that would work to the archers' advantage. Suddenly they heard the sound of twigs snapping and a few seconds later the first Mercian appeared. He was about fifty yards away and well dressed – wearing a well-polished byrnie over a leather liner, red trousers tied with yellow ribbons up to the knee and leather shoes stained black. His saddle was made of leather with two horns at front, both decorated with silver, and his helmet dangled from the right hand front one. His shield hung on his back and he had a sword and seax hanging from the studded leather belt around his waist.

Raulf took all of this in during the second or so it took for him to draw his bow and loose an arrow. However, the Mercian captain had seen him as soon as he rounded the bend in the trail and he'd hauled back on the horse's reins so that it had started to rear up on its hind legs by the time that the arrow arrived. Instead of hitting the leader in his chest it hit his mount in the neck.

The horse neighed in agony and reared up before coming down on all fours and shaking its head violently, trying to rid itself of the pain. Edmund had been a fraction slower in drawing his bow and, luckily, had paused when he saw the horse rear up. As soon as he had a clear shot at its rider, who was desperately trying to stay in the saddle, he released the bow string. He watched as the arrow sped towards the rider and, although the horse was twisting and turning out of control as its lifeblood poured down its chest, he was lucky. The arrow didn't hit its intended target – his chest – but it hit his unprotected neck and the tip passed clean through it, only halting its passage when the point had emerged from the back of his neck by a good six inches.

It had smashed his windpipe and cut his spinal cord in the process. If he lived he would have lost all control of his limbs and bodily functions. The man fell out of the saddle and his horse collapsed beside him, effectively blocking the trail.

Well satisfied with their work, Raulf and Edmund quickly climbed down their respective trees and ran off to where the two brothers waited with their horses. A quarter of an hour later they re-joined the others and told Oswiu of their success. That night they camped in a clearing in the trees and Oswiu sent two scouts back to see if there was any sign of their pursuers. They went back for several miles along the trail but saw nothing.

'Now all we've got to do is find out where the bloody hell we are and how we get from here to Maserfield,' Ceadda grumbled to Oswiu as they ate a meal of cheese, dried meat and apples. The king was still thinking about Oswald's rotting head and didn't reply. The birds had pecked out the eyes and the flesh had started to decompose so some had fallen away from the skull. His hair was matted with blood his teeth had been smashed. Oswiu shuddered; it wasn't the brother he'd known and it wasn't the way he wanted to remember him. He thrust the head at Nerian.

'Sew it into a leather bag with some herbs to counter the stench.'

Tomorrow they'd go in search of the severed arm that supposedly performed miracles.

~~~

Penda looked at the warrior standing before him with anger contorting his scarred face.

'So you lost them? Or did you just give up through fear once Ingram was ambushed?' he asked contemptuously.

'We didn't know what to do for the best, Cyning. It was a very narrow trail, probably one made by animals, and Ingram and his dead horse were blocking it. The undergrown was dense and by the time we'd cleared enough space to move the bodies off the trail, the fugitives had long gone.'

'So why didn't you pursue them as soon as you could?'

'We didn't like to leave Ingram lying in the forest for animals to devour, so we buried him. We set off in pursuit the next morning but the trail ended when it emerged onto the main roadway from Tamworth to Shrewsbury.'

'Forgive me if I'm being dense, but tell me why you didn't set off towards Shrewsbury where the men who stole Oswald's head were presumably heading?'

The sarcasm stung Irwin and he bit back an angry retort.

'We didn't know which way they had turned once they reached the road, Cyning.'

'Oh, so you thought it likely that they would return to Tamworth did you?'

'No, I suppose not.'

'You suppose correctly. Right. I'm going to give you a chance to save your miserable life, and those of the men with you. Head back towards Shrewsbury and pick up their trail. Come back with their heads and that of Oswald or you'll find out what it means to fail me. Now get out of here.'

Irwin, who was Ingram's cousin and who had taken over leadership of the Mercian patrol after his death, stomped out of the king's hall in a furious temper. The king had treated him as if he was an imbecile. He was certain of one thing; he had no intention of returning to face Penda without the heads, but he knew that seeking men who he couldn't identify was futile. He didn't even know how many of them there were. From the tracks in the mud there could be anything from twenty to fifty of them. He had less than twenty.

'The king wants us to find these men and the two little thieves who stole Oswald's head. If we fail he'll kill us,' he told his men.

As he'd expected there was an outcry at the news. They had been tired and lethargic when they'd returned empty-handed to Tamworth. Now they were more animated than he'd ever seen them.

'What are we waiting for?' one asked. 'Let's get after them!'

'After who?' Irwin asked quietly.

'The people who stole the head, of course.'

'And how will you find them? Do you know what they look like? We know that there were two boys and two archers, but how many more are there? Their tracks indicate that there far more of them than there are of us.'

The men looked at each other and grew silent.

'Now let's talk some sense. None of us knows what to do to apprehend a group of people when all we know is that they have a head – and they could have buried that already for all we know.'

'What do we do Irwin?' one asked eventually.

'I don't know about you but, faced with the choice of either succeeding at an impossible task or suffering a painful death, I know what I'm going to do.'

The warriors looked at each other puzzled.

'Doesn't sound like much of a choice to me,' said the man who'd been all for setting out blindly a few minutes ago.

'It isn't, which is why I've decided to take the third option.'

'What's that?'

'Collect my wife and children and flee to Wessex.'

An hour later the group of horsemen set out once more, this time accompanied by two carts filled with supplies, tents and, most importantly, the families of the four married warriors hidden under a tarpaulin.

~~~

Like his brother before him three months previously, Oswiu skirted Shrewsbury to the north and headed for Maserfield. They camped that night by a small river, a tributary of the Severn that ran around Shrewsbury. The next day they headed north into an area of bog to confuse any Mercians who might still be following them, then crossed it where the water was only two feet deep. An hour later they joined a muddy track that led north eastwards. Occasionally they passed the remains of Northumbrian men who had been killed during the rout after the battle and the odd broken weapon that wasn't worth looting.

The mood amongst the men grew even more subdued as they neared the hill fort at Maserfield where the battle had been fought, but Oswiu sensed that he wasn't the only one feeling a growing sense of anger at the betrayal that had led to the death of King Oswald and their countrymen. Even Catinus and Conomultus attracted the odd angry look as they were Mercians, albeit Britons rather than Angles.

The gesith scoured the area but there was no sign of the supposedly miraculous arm.

39

'We're going to have to ask the locals about it,' Oswiu told his men. 'Catinus, I want you and your brother to go into Maserfield and see if there is a tavern. If there is come back and let us know; if not I'll have to think of something else.'

No-one paid the two boys any attention as they entered the settlement. It was a poor place of scruffy hovels and a decrepit hall for its lord that looked as if it would blow down in a strong wind. There was no palisade for defence, or even to keep animals out. Pigs and chickens searched through the stinking mud for anything worth eating. There was, however, a small tavern. It looked in better repair than the rest of the place and had a stables at the rear. Presumably its relative prosperity resulted from its location on the track that led into the interior of Powys.

'What do you boys want?' a voice suddenly interrupted their examination of the tavern.

The man had spoken in a language that wasn't the same as the Brythonic that they spoke but it wasn't so different as to be unintelligible. They realised that the man must be Welsh.

'We heard of a miraculous arm up a tree. My brother has never spoken since he was born, yet no-one can find anything wrong with him. We thought that perhaps it could cure him,' Catinus replied using the cover story that Oswiu had suggested.

'Aye, it might. It cured my daughter and she was paralysed from the waist down after being kicked in the back by a horse. She never walked again until we laid her under the tree and left her there overnight. The next morning she managed to stand unaided. Her leg muscles were wasted and it's taken time for her to fully recover, but she can now walk as well as ever she could, and run too.'

'What made you lie her under the tree with the arm?' asked Catinus.

'I had a dream. I wasn't a Christian but I'm sure it was an angel who came to me in the night and told me what to do. When a monk came to the village a month ago he baptised all of us, for my neighbours were as amazed at my daughter's cure as I was.'

'Thank you. It's the story we'd heard, though the man who told it to us said the girl had been carried there by Jesus Christ himself.'

'Well, that's bards for you, they do like to embellish the truth.'

'Where can we find this tree?'

'Go back the way you came and turn south off the road when you come to a small copse. It stands alone half a mile further on.'

'Thank you for your help.'

'Yes, thank you,' Conomultus said, forgetting that he was meant to be mute.

The man looked at them suspiciously and wondered what they were playing at. He was about to sound the alarm so that the headman could question them when they took off giggling and ran out of the settlement on the road back towards Shrewsbury. He shrugged, thinking they were both soft in the head, and went back into the tavern.

Oswiu sat on his horse and looked at the withered arm hanging from a branch of the apple tree. It was a solitary tree, not part of an orchard, and had presumably grown there from a seed blown by the wind or dropped by a bird. That in itself was unusual. Strangely the arm, although the flesh had shrivelled, hadn't been attacked by birds. Below it, where some blood had presumably dripped down, there was a hollow where people had taken away earth because of its reputed healing properties.

Conomultus climbed up the tree until he was above the arm, then he lifted it up carefully and handed it down to Oswiu. He put it in another leather bag and handed it to Nerian for him to sew it up later. Oswiu debated whether to take some of the earth from the base of the tree, but he decided to leave it. He had what he'd come for.

The journey from there north was uneventful until they reached the River Mersey, which formed the border between Rheged in the north and Mercia in the south. Oswiu turned right and followed the river towards the old Roman ruins of Mamucium, a military fort and civilian settlement on the road between the two major Roman centres at what was now called Caerlleon and Eoforwīc.

From Mamucium they crossed several small rivers and then started to climb into the hilly country that divided Rheged from Elmet. Oswiu and his gesith had started to relax as they were now well north of Mercia and, although the border was far from clearly defined, they felt that they were in friendly territory. It was a mistake.

They had just dropped down into a valley and were climbing up the far side when they became aware that the crest of the hill in front of them was lined with armed men. About a dozen of them were mounted and they were all well-armed and wore helmets and some sort of body protection. Those on foot were clearly from the fyrd; all wore their everyday clothing and few had helmets. Swords seemed few and far between and most were armed with a spear and a dagger. About half had a shield of some kind.

Oswiu rode forward accompanied by Ceadda and two of his gesith. One of the horsemen facing them did likewise, also accompanied by three mounted warriors.

'That's far enough. Who are you and what is an armed warband doing here in Elmet without my permission,' the man in the front of the four horsemen demanded.

'If I recognise you, Rand, you must surely recognise me,' Oswiu said cooly.

Rand was the Eorl of Elmet and had been present at the Witan in Eoforwīc when Oswine was chosen as king in preference to Oswiu.

'You have no business here, Oswiu. You are a long way from Bernicia and King Oswine believes that you are up to no good. You are to be disarmed and will accompany me to Eoforwīc.'

'I'm going nowhere at the behest of that simpering fool, Oswine, and you'll do me the courtesy of addressing me as Cyning.'

'You will do as I say – Oswiu – or my men will cut you down.'

'What, that load of farmers and tradesmen? Half of them have pissed themselves at the very thought of being attacked by my battle-hardened warriors. Now, get out of my way before I kill you for your impudence.'

'You will soon find out that three hundred of Elmet's fyrd are more than a match for two dozen Bernician oafs and a few boys.'

Oswiu gave him a cold look. 'Don't say I didn't warn you.'

He turned and rode as fast as he could for a nearby hilltop and his men did likewise. It was a good defensive position and they hastily dismounted and formed a shield wall facing the Elmet army about a hundred yards away. The ridge on which they stood was the same height as the circular hill which Oswiu's gesith had occupied, but there was a deep defile between the two positions.

Rand was still riding about on his horse, clearly undecided what to do. Oswine's instructions had been clear. As soon as Oswiu's presence near the border had been reported to him, he saw a chance to strengthen his position. He was scared of Oswiu and he thought that, if he could capture him, he could demand Oswiu's children as hostages in return for his release. That way he would have a hold over the King of Bernicia and he would feel safer on his throne. He clearly didn't know Oswiu though. He would never have submitted to Oswine, a man he despised.

As it was there was something of a stand-off. Rand didn't fancy attacking an experienced shield wall at the top of a steep slope with his untried, poorly armed and ill-disciplined rabble and Oswiu wasn't about to flee and allow Rand to claim this petty skirmish as a Deiran victory over Bernicia.

'Edmund, Raulf. Come here. Do you think you could hit that preening fool on a white horse over there?'

He nodded his head towards Rand.

'It's a bit of a tall order, Cyning. It must be at least a hundred yards away and there's a bit of a breeze blowing. I might be able to hit his horse though,' Edmund replied cautiously.

'What about you Raulf?'

'I agree with Edmund, Cyning.'

'Well, I'm not standing here all day. Give it a try, but release together, understand?'

The two men went and fetched their bows and prepared them out of sight behind the shield wall.

'Now,' Edmund shouted and the centre of the shield wall parted to allow them to step through it. Both men took aim and let fly together. They had both aimed two yards in front of Rand's horse to allow for the wind and had aimed up to allow for the fall of the arrow over that distance. Both had judged it perfectly, though there was a modicum of luck too.

One arrow struck the horse in its rump causing it to rear up just as the first arrow struck Rand's byrnie. At that range the arrow pierced the chainmail but it lodged in the leather shirt the eorl was wearing underneath. It didn't matter though as Rand toppled over the rear of his saddle and fell to the ground head first. His neck broke as he landed and his wounded horse bolted, scattering the fyrd out of its way as it went.

The men from Elmet were stunned by the death of their eorl and, when Oswiu sent his other archers forward to threaten them, they broke and ran. They had a few archers of their own who aimed a few arrows their way before leaving, but none carried as far as Oswiu's men. The dozen men of the eorl's gesith stood there uncertainly until one fell to another of Edmund's arrows, then they hastily put the two bodies across their horses and rode off over the crest of the ridge. Oswiu watched them go.

'I'm grateful to both of you,' he said as he handed them both a gold arm ring and went to mount his horse.

It wasn't unusual for him to reward his gesith, and other members of his war band, with a silver arm band, but a gold one was exceptional.

~~~

Oswine was visiting the east of Deira when he heard of Rand's death. Not only had Oswiu escaped but he had done so by killing one of his chief supporters; and he'd done so without alienating the people in the process. He felt far from secure on his throne and the death of his father at the hands of Cadwallon still haunted him. Now Oswiu's popularity would have increased because he had escaped the trap without harming a single Deiran - except for Rand and one of his men, of course - and he'd been made to look a fool. He knew that Oswiu wouldn't rest until he'd re-united Northumbria and he wasn't sure that he was the man to stop him.

Oswiu returned to Bebbanburg in triumph.

'What will you do with your brother's body,' Aidan asked.

'I'd like to bury his torso and his head on Lindisfarne but place the miraculous arm in a silver casket to be kept at Bebbanburg.'

'You believe in the stories about the miracle cures then?'

'Yes, I have no reason to doubt them, especially as we've heard directly from the tavern keeper whose daughter was cured.'

'You've only the word of Catinus and Conomultus for that.'

'Why would they lie? And the tavern keeper gave them directions to the tree. I certainly believe them.'

'What will you do with them? They're Mercians after all.'

'I don't think that the concept of being Mercian or Northumbrian has much relevance for them. They're Britons who happen to have been born inside Mercia. I am certain as I can be that their loyalty is now to me. As to what happens to them, I haven't made up my mind. They've served me well so I've decided to take a personal interest in their future.'

'I gather that their grasp of English is poor.'

'Yes, but they're quick learners and good mimics. They already understand the basics and can make themselves understood.'

'How old are they?'

'Fourteen and twelve.'

'Why don't you send them to me and I'll educate them as novices for a year or two? Then they can decide whether they want to train as warriors or to become monks.'

'That's kind of you. I'll arrange for them to be ready to accompany you when you leave. I'll be coming too – for Oswald's funeral.'

A hundred and twenty miles away Penda was raging against Oswiu – who else would have had the temerity to ride through Mercia unopposed gathering up the dismembered parts of his brother's body? He vowed that one day he'd do the same to him as he'd done to Oswald.

His first task was to find someone close to Oswiu who he could subvert and use against him. He considered all the possible contenders and finally decided on Œthelwald. He didn't need to be turned against his uncle: they detested each other already. Œthelwald would need to become powerful enough so that his eventual betrayal of Oswiu would bring about the latter's downfall. He grinned in anticipation, but he knew he'd need to be patient.

CHAPTER FOUR – LOVE AND WAR

643 AD

'This is my third son, Cuthbert, Cyning. I hope that he will be able to enter the monastery at Lindisfarne when he is older.'

Oswiu smiled at the nervous nine year old boy.

'Don't worry, Cuthbert, I don't bite, contrary to what you may have heard. Why do you want to be a monk and not a warrior like your father?'

He and Aidan were visiting the north east corner of his kingdom and were staying with Kenric, the Eorl of Dùn Barra in Goddodin.

'I would quite like to be a warrior, Cyning, but I really want to be like Bishop Aidan and convert the heathens to Christianity. It's still fighting, but in a different way. But I wouldn't mind being a warrior first.'

Oswiu laughed at the boy's precociousness and Aidan looked at him with interest.

'You see spreading the Word of God and his Holy Son, Jesus, as a fight do you, Cuthbert?'

'I do, as a struggle at any rate.'

'That's not a bad analogy, though I hadn't thought of myself as one of Christ's warriors before.'

'When would you be able to take him as a novice?' Kenric asked.

He was rewarded by a startled gasp from his wife.

'You sound as if you can't wait to get rid of him, husband. He's only nine,' she said.

'He'll soon be ten and I believe that the king went off to Iona to be educated when he was eleven?'

'That's correct, but I was big for my age and there were other reasons why I was sent away early,' Oswiu replied.

'Twelve is normally the youngest we take boys, though we have accepted some as young as eight if they are orphaned and it was the dead parents' wish.'

'What about Melrose instead of Lindisfarne? You must need novices there.' Oswiu said.

The settlement of Melrose was some forty miles due west of Lindisfarne. Aidan had recently proposed to Oswiu that a daughter house of Lindisfarne be established on land that the king owned near the settlement.

'Yes, work will start on constructing the essential buildings soon and I have already selected the man I would like as abbot as well as the first few monks. It's true that we'll need a large number of novices to build up the community quickly. We should be ready to admit the first cohort of boys in a year or so. Cuthbert could go there as a novice for a couple of years and then decide whether he wants to train as a warrior or not when he reaches fourteen. At least then he'd have a basic education behind him.'

'Who have you selected as abbot, you haven't mentioned it to me?'

'I apologise. I shouldn't have said anything. I did want to discuss it with you first, especially as it affects you personally.'

'Offa? You mean to suggest my brother as abbot?'

Oswiu looked around him as Offa had come north with him and Aidan. However, his brother wasn't in the hall. No doubt he was still praying in the nearby church. He often disappeared for hours at a time to meditate.

'Have you mentioned it to him?'

'Not yet.'

'What makes you think he'll accept?'

Aidan shifted uncomfortably in his chair.

'I'm his confessor so I can't say anymore, except that I have reason to believe he might find the idea attractive.'

'Ah! He finds his brother a trifle too warlike and he seeks a more tranquil community than my court?'

'Something like that.'

'I think it's an excellent idea. If Offa is happy with it, then I'm content.'

Aidan did his best to hide his surprise. Oswiu had been one of six brothers. Now, at barely thirty one, apart from his sister, only his youngest brother and he survived. He had thought that he'd want to keep Offa by his side and was pleased that Oswiu seemed to be putting his brother's feelings first.

Kenric's wife, relieved that she would have her youngest son for at least another year, left the men to talk of other matters, taking her son with her; though he'd have preferred to remain and listen to the men.

'I'm heading south soon - to Kent - and I need someone to act as regent. I'd like you and Aidan to look after things whilst I'm away. Things are quiet at the moment but both Oswine and Penda will be smarting after the events of last year and my absence might tempt them to get up to some mischief.'

'Wouldn't one of the other eorls…' Kenric began.

'No, they are good administrators but some are old now and the younger ones lack your military experience.'

'Have you thought about making Melrose a mixed house?' Oswiu asked Aidan a little later when they were on their own.

Aidan frowned. 'No, why do you suggest it? I know that there are other mixed houses of monks and nuns elsewhere but I always thought it better to keep men and women segregated.'

'I suggest we visit Æbbe at Coldingham on our way south and see what my sister thinks. I'd like to see her again in any case.'

Aidan grunted in a non-committal way before quickly changing the subject.

'You haven't told me why you are intent on visiting Kent. Œthelwald may have been more of a hindrance to you than a help but at least he seems to have cemented an alliance with Eorcenberht.'

'I'm thinking of asking for the hand of Eanflæd, not just because she's the king's cousin, but because she's Edwin's daughter and therefore of Deira's royal house.'

'So you hope that by marrying her it will strengthen your claim to Oswine's throne, I suppose? I see. Well, I support your aim to re-unite Northumbria, of course, but I hope you are not thinking of deposing Oswine by force. He is a Christian king who was duly elected by the Witan of Deira.'

Oswiu was beginning to realise that using Aidan as his counsellor had its drawbacks.

'No – at least not at the moment, but individually we aren't strong enough to stand up to Penda and his allies. Northumbria needs to be ruled by one man if it's to survive.'

The two said nothing for a while then Aidan broke the silence.

'I hear that Hengist is now King of Lindsey.'

'Yes, his predecessor was always a sickly boy. He was the last of the old royal line and it seemed natural for their Witan to elect the man who had been regent.'

Neither mentioned the rumour that the boy king had been killed by Hengist.

'Hengist was ever Oswald's man but Oswine will no doubt try and forge an alliance with him now.'

'And you think I should approach him first? Perhaps. I'll call in and see him on my way south. It may be sensible to visit Anna of East Anglia as well. If I can form an alliance with all three kingdoms I may be able to contain Penda's ambitions.'

~~~

Offa was only too happy to exchange the role of king's chaplain and return to a quieter monastic life, even if it did mean that he would have to take on the responsibility that being an abbot entailed.

'Who do you recommend as my brother's replacement?' Oswiu asked Aidan just before he was about to set out by sea for the south.

'Yes, I've been giving that some thought. I think that the vills around Bebbanburg need a priest separate from your chaplain. You are often on the road these days and that leaves them without a spiritual leader. I have a monk who would make a good priest and I have approached Utta to see if he would be your chaplain. I would have suggested Ròidh had he not already left to be Bishop of Dùn Dè. Utta is a strong character as well as a devout Christian and I think you'll find him useful.'

'Um. I don't think I've met Utta. I'll reserve judgement until I've done so. Can you arrange for him to visit me here tomorrow morning? We leave the day after.'

'He's waiting outside the hall, if you'd like to meet him now?'

'Yes, by all means.'

Utta was a tall bull of a man. Oswiu couldn't help but think that he'd be a formidable foe in a fight. Then he noticed the cut on his cheek and the fact that two of his fingers were missing from his right hand.

'I assume that you used to be a warrior before you became a monk, Utta?'

'Yes, Cyning; as did many who are now monks.'

'Whose warband were you in?'

'That of King Eochaid. I was in his gesith until I lost these fingers so I couldn't hold a sword properly anymore.'

'Eochaid? How come you ended up at Lindisfarne then?'

Eochaid had been his brother Oswald's closest friend until he'd become King of the Uliadh in Ulster.

'I became a novice on Iona after I was wounded and then I was sent here when the monastery was established.'

'I'm surprised that we haven't met before then.'

'I've seen you and King Oswald plenty of times at Lindisfarne but I'm nobody important so I kept in the background.'

'And do you want to be my chaplain?'

The man nodded and smiled for the first time, revealing a row of teeth sharpened to a point. It was something that some Irish warriors did; it turned a smile into a frightening grimace.

Oswiu laughed. 'Yes, I think we'll get along well.'

~~~

The visit to Hengist had been a success. The former captain of Oswald's gesith had been only too happy to conclude a treaty of mutual assistance whereby Oswiu would come to his assistance if he was attacked by either Penda's Mercians or Peada's Middle Angles. Oswiu also promised to send him a few of the more experienced warriors from his warband to help Hengist train his own men.

However, when he arrived at the court of King Anna of the East Angles he found a messenger waiting for him. Cadafael ap Cynfeddw, King of Gwynedd and successor to Cadwallon who Oswald and Oswiu had defeated at Heavenfield eleven years previously, had invaded Rheged from the south. This had to be at Penda's instigation, or at least his with his connivance.

He stayed only long enough to secure an alliance with Anna and then he returned in his birlinn to Bebbanburg whilst sending Utta on to Kent with an offer for Eanflæd's hand in marriage and to negotiate a new treaty of friendship.

Arriving back at Bebbanburg, he assembled his warband and sent out messengers: to Caer Luel to say that he was on his way and to the Eorls of Hexham and Hawick to call out the fyrd and muster at Hexham. He also sent them to every other eorl asking them to join him with their war bands and to King Guret of Strathclyde asking him to come with his war band to meet him at the ford over the River Esk six miles north of Caer Luel. He believed that he would have enough men to defeat Cadafael without the sixteen year old Guret, but it would be a useful test of the alliance they had agreed the previous year. He had no doubt that Guret would want to help him, but whether he was yet strong enough to impose his will upon his nobles was another matter.

He was pleased to see that his nephew had joined the army with his war band. To keep Œthelwald out of mischief Oswiu had made him Thegn of Yeavering. Apart from being custos of the royal palace, he had been given two vills as well, centred on the settlements at Akeld and Yetholm. It was a large area, but populated more by sheep than by men. It was a backwater except for the times that the king was there in the summer months and Oswiu thought that it would prevent him from building up a power base from which he could challenge him.

When he reached Hexham he found that he had two hundred and fifty experienced warriors in the various noble's gesiths and war bands and another six hundred members of the fyrd. His scouts came back to report that the Welshmen of Gwynedd were besieging Caer Luel with about a thousand men but half of those were absent during daylight raiding and foraging in the surrounding countryside.

Oswiu wasn't sure how many men the Eorl of Rheged would have inside the walls but at least three hundred was a reasonable assumption. He made his plans accordingly.

He was relieved to find Guret waiting for him on his side of the border at the crossing over the Esk. He was accompanied by about fifty men wearing some form of body protection - leather jerkins or byrnies - and helmets, and about three times that number who wore little or no armour. All carried a spear and a small shield and had a sword or a seax at their side.

'I've only brought two hundred men with me but they are all mounted and are experienced warriors.'

'Guret, I'm delighted to see you again. Have you brought Brandon, Cunobelinus and Nechtan with you?'

The three nobles had been Guret's council of regency the last time they had met.

'No, I'm sad to say that all three met with an untimely death. I now rule alone.'

'I see, and how did your other nobles react to that?'

'None of my other nobles seemed very keen on insisting on another regency. Oh, I didn't have them killed secretly or anything. I found out that they had been plotting with an agent of Penda's to kill me and invade Rheged from the north, whilst the Welsh did so from the south. I had them formally tried and executed and their families were exiled. They fled to Gwynedd or Powys I believe. So, when your request for help came I was in the right mood to do anything I could to thwart Penda's machinations.'

'I'm impressed. I always thought that you were a more astute man than your father.'

The youth was pleased at being called a man, especially by someone he admired. He was short of stature and looked a year or so younger than his actual age. Most Anglo-Saxon men had now eschewed the beard and grew a long moustache instead. A good growth on the upper lip was a sign of manhood. His lack of facial hair was therefore something he was embarrassed about.

'What is your plan? You don't seem to have that many men with you?'

Oswiu had only brought his own warband and that of Œthelwald with him – about a hundred men in all, all mounted.

'Oh, by the way, this is my nephew, Œthelwald, Oswald's son.'

The two nodded at one another, Guret with a smile and Œthelwald somewhat sulkily. Guret didn't take offence; he was well aware that the young man must have resented the fact that the throne had gone to his uncle instead of him.

Oswiu, Ceadda, Œthelwald, Guret and the captain of his warband dismounted and stood around a bare patch of earth in which Oswiu drew a crude map.

'Cadafael's men are camped to the south of Caer Luel between the Rivers Eden and Caldew. My main army, numbering about seven hundred, is here at Thursby. It's six miles from the enemy camp and it's on the old Roman road, so it shouldn't take them much longer than two hours to cover that distance. We'll cross the Eden here to the east of Caer Luel where there is a good ford, so I'm told, and then cross the Caldew, which isn't very deep, to the east of the Welsh Camp. The rest of my men will take up a position to the west of the camp and we'll trap them between our forces and the walls.'

'Excellent,' Guret grinned. 'We should be able to slaughter them easily, if it works. When do we attack?'

'Mid-morning tomorrow.'

'Why not attack at dawn?' Œthelwald asked.

'Because men can get lost during a night approach and there's more chance of some of the enemy escaping in the chaos of a mass attack on their camp. This way they'll form up when they see our main army approach. Only when they're committed do we appear and take them in the flank. Hopefully the garrison will sally forth as well so that Cadafael is surrounded.'

'But the forage parties will have gone forth to plunder by then?' Guret said.

'Precisely. So the enemy will have no more than half their strength on the field. We can deal with the foraging parties later.'

~~~

Aldin, the Mercian thegn that Penda had sent with Cadafael to make sure he did what he wanted him to, was sitting morosely on his horse wondering when Oswiu would appear. Penda was no fool. He knew that Oswiu would rush to relieve Caer Luel and had planned a trap for him. Instead of going off to forage and pillage the surrounding vills, half of Cadafael's army was waiting three miles to the west together with a hundred well-armed Mercians. Their intention was to sweep in and trap Oswiu's men between them and the Welsh besieging the old Roman city.

As soon as the Bernicians appeared and took up their position several hundred yards from the Welsh camp, Cadafael moved into formation to oppose them. It looked like a traditional struggle between two shield walls supported by the less experienced fyrd on one side and the ill-disciplined Welsh tribesmen on the other. The archers on both sides opened proceedings but then the gates swung open and three hundred men of Rheged tore into the rear of the Welsh formation, where the more cowardly men always gravitated to.

Chaos ensued and it began to develop into a slaughter of the Welsh when the Mercians and the other half of Cadafael's men appeared from the east and attacked the Bernician's flank. The battle turned and now it was Oswiu's men who were trapped. However, the efforts of the Rheged garrison kept one half of the Welsh from pressing home their attack.

Then Oswiu, Guret and their three hundred horsemen splashed across the Caldew. Although neither Britons nor Anglo-Saxons normally fought on horseback, Oswiu knew how effective the tactic had been in Ireland. The horsemen rode up to the rear of the Mercians and one half of the Welsh and threw their spears. Over a hundred men were killed or seriously wounded. More importantly the sudden attack by a mass of mounted warriors caused panic.

Oswiu withdrew his horsemen and they dismounted before advancing on foot. Now the two halves of the Mercian/Welsh army were trapped between two armies each three hundred strong on the outside and over six hundred in the centre. Although the latter had suffered about a hundred casualties, the invaders had already lost well over two hundred and more were dying all the time. They were surrounded and outnumbered; more importantly they were totally demoralised.

Suddenly about thirty horsemen appeared from the centre of the Welsh camp and cut their way through the mass of men, killing Welsh, Mercians, and Oswiu's men indiscriminately. Many of the horsemen were cut down but six managed to ride clear. Unfortunately for Oswiu, one of them was King Cadafael.

After the cowardly flight of their king, the heart went out of the Welsh and they started surrendering. The Mercians, however, fought on and so the battle continued, surrendering Welsh men being cut down along with the last of the Mercians. The last one to die was Aldin. He had fought on despite the loss of one hand and numerous wounds to his arms and legs. Oswiu chopped his head from his body himself.

By the time that the body count had been done the sun was sinking in the west. One hundred and fifty of those who had fought for Oswiu had died and another thirty were too badly wounded to ever fight again. All one hundred Mercians had perished and another three hundred and fifty Welsh had also died or been killed as being too badly wounded to be sold into slavery.

'I want you to collect up the heads of every Mercian who died here today, Œthelwald, and pile them in a cart.'

'What will you do with them?'

'Send them south to Legacæstir, the nearest Mercian centre, with a message pinned to them requesting that they be sent on to Penda. The carter can leave them outside the gates at night, otherwise he'd be killed in revenge, no doubt.'

'Well done, by the way, you fought well today.'

'Don't tell me my father would have been proud of me,' he sneered. 'He never was when he was alive.'

'Accept a compliment in the spirit in which it was given, Œthelwald. I have no ulterior motive, other than to give praise where it is due.'

Oswiu left two hundred of the slaves with the Eorl of Rheged as compensation for the pillaging of the country and gave another hundred to Guret as thanks for his help. The other three hundred were destined to be sold to pay his nobles and his men. It was how a successful king kept his people loyal.

~~~

Catinus was in two minds about becoming a novice on Lindisfarne. He wanted to train as a warrior but, at the same time, he didn't want to be parted from Conomultus – and he was too young for military training as yet. In the end he decided that they should both become novices, at least until they were a little older – and bigger.

Britons tended to be smaller than the Anglo-Saxons and the two boys were no exception. They both had black hair whereas the other novices had lighter hair, ranging from fair through to brown. They therefore stood out from their fellows. They entered the hut that they would be sharing with twelve other novices carrying their new habits when they were immediately accosted.

'We don't want dirty Britons sharing with us, you stink! You can sleep outside.'

The boy who spoke was fourteen, the same age as Catinus. He pulled the new habits from their arms and threw them out of the hut. It was a mistake.

Instead of going outside to retrieve the garments before they got soaked in the heavy rain that had just started, Catinus punched the bigger boy hard on the nose. The boy, whose name was Seward, staggered backwards and cannoned into one of the other novices. Blood streamed from his squashed nose and tears from his eyes; for a moment he couldn't see. Before he could recover Catinus hit him again with both hands in quick succession: once in the chest and once in the stomach. Seward doubled over gasping for breath and Catinus brought his knee up, smashing it into the other boy's chin.

Seward would have been in agony from a broken jaw but he was mercifully unconscious. Catinus went to kick the comatose boy but Conomultis pulled him back. Most of the other novices stood there in a state of shock but one came forward with a grin and shook Catinus' hand.

'Well done. He had it coming. I wish I had the courage to do that myself but he threatened to beat my cousin to a pulp if I opposed him. I'm Alweo, by the way, and this is Wigmund.'

The small boy by his side nodded his head and then gave Catinus a shy grin. Fighting was strictly forbidden in the monastery, though occasionally Seward hit other boys who didn't do what he told them. No-one had stood up to him before and, after a brief period of stunned silence, the others started to cheer.

The noise attracted the Master of Novices, a monk in his thirties called Wiglac, who arrived just as the boys had lifted Seward and dumped him onto his bed, which consisted of a pile of straw covered by a rough woollen blanket.

'What's happened here?' Wiglac asked. 'Is Seward alright? Why is his face covered in blood?'

His questions were greeted by silence but it didn't last long.

'He insulted me and my brother and tried to throw us back out into the rain. He said he wouldn't share his hut with a couple of stinking Britons,' Catinus said defiantly.

'Oh dear.'

Wiglac was quite out of his depth. Unlike some monks in charge of novices he believed in the power of reason, rather than using the rod. He had usually managed to resolve differences between his charges by calmly asking them to explain to him what the problem was and brokering a reconciliation. He was aware that Seward was a bully and he had spoken to him about it. The boy had promised to behave but he hadn't changed. Secretly Wiglac was delighted that someone had taken Seward down several pegs, but he couldn't condone violence, of course.

'I'm sorry, Catinus. I'll have to report this to Bishop Aidan. We don't tolerate that sort of behaviour here.'

'Good! I wasn't certain I wanted to come here in the first place.'

'Don't take that tone with me. I'm Master of the Novices and deserve your respect!'

'Why? Seward was obviously intimidating the rest of these boys, judging by their reaction when I knocked him out, and you've done nothing about it. I don't think that's the conduct of someone who deserves respect.'

'He's right,' Alweo said, coming to stand beside him. 'You must have known what a bully he was.'

Wiglac stared at the two of them open-mouthed. The newcomer, who was in danger of being expelled from Lindisfarne, had the cheek to berate him and now Alweo, who he had always liked, was taking the wretched Briton's side against him. He didn't like confrontation but he was very conscious of his own dignity. He grabbed Catinus by the ear and started to drag him from the hut, intending to take him to Aidan. He didn't get very far. Conomultus stood in the doorway, barring the exit and Alweo joined him.

'Let go of my brother now,' he demanded in his high boy's voice. It would have been comical if it wasn't for the look of sheer determination on his face.

'Get out of my way, you little bastard. You too Alweo.'

Wiglac was not a man given to swearing - or to losing his temper, but he was dangerously close to losing control.

'Good evening, Brother Wiglac. I came to see how my two new novices are settling in.'

Aidan had suddenly appeared behind Conomultus and Alweo. He gently put a hand on the boy's shoulder and whispered in his ear, 'I think you can both stand aside now. '

The boys did as they were bid and Wiglac now saw to his horror that the king was standing beside Aidan.

'What seems to have happened here? What's wrong with that boy?' he asked gesturing towards the unconscious Seward's bloody face.

'Nothing for you to worry about, Cyning; just a little disciplinary problem. I fear that this new novice and his brother are troublemakers. They seem to have corrupted Alweo too,' the master of novices whined.

Wiglac had immediately let go of Catinus' ear when Aidan had spoken. The boy rubbed it, looking at him resentfully, something that Oswiu noticed.

'Aidan, I'll leave you to sort this,' he said tactfully, but the expression on his face betrayed the fact that he was far from pleased.

'Brother, may I have a word?'

Wiglac nodded uncomfortably and followed Aidan out into the rain. Completely ignoring the downpour, Aidan turned when they were out of earshot and faced the unhappy monk.

'Am I correct in assuming that Seward tried to intimidate Catinus and Conomultus in some way and that they stood up to him?'

'I believe that something of the kind happened, yes, but Catinus seems to have attacked Seward and hurt him quite badly. Then Alweo joined them in opposing me when I tried to deal with the situation.'

'So I assume that you imposed discipline straightaway and have sent for the infirmarian to tend to Seward?'

'Yes, well, no. I'll send one of the novices to find him straight away.'

At that moment a loud wail reminiscent of a stuck pig could be heard from the hut.

'I think that would be sensible. It sounds as if Seward is recovering consciousness. Then come and see me in my hut, and bring Catinus and Alweo with you. I suggest you don't try and drag them by the ears though.'

'Well, I assume you got to the bottom of the altercation in the novices hut?' Oswiu asked Aidan quietly during the simple supper of cheese and bread that evening.

'It seems that Seward tried to intimidate your two fiery little Britons as soon as they entered the hut and, to put it bluntly, Catinus beat him up, breaking both his nose and his jaw in the process. The infirmarian has bound his head until the jaw mends which means that he will have to drink and consume thin soup through a reed for now. Alweo confirmed that Seward had been bullying the rest of the novices for ages so I have little sympathy for him.'

Oswiu sighed. 'I suppose you want to send the two Britons back to me? Though I'm not sure what I'm going to do with them. Perhaps Ceadda was right. I should have disposed of them when they'd stopped being of use.'

'You would never repay loyalty and valuable service with betrayal, and that's what it would be. No, I think Catinus and Alweo will make fine warriors when they're older. Perhaps Conomultus and Wigmund are too gentle for that; they are probably more suited to life as a monk. As to their immediate future, they can stay here until they can read and write.'

'Will you flog Catinus?'

'No, he and Alweo can look after Seward until his jaw mends. However, I'll have to replace Wiglac. He should have sorted out Seward's unacceptable behaviour long before this. Masters of Novices tend to be too strict or too lenient; Wiglac was the latter and he didn't have the moral courage to tackle Seward. I suspect that he might even have been frightened of him.'

'And Seward?'

'Oh, I think he's learned his lesson. If not, I'm sure that Catinus and Alweo will remind him. The two seem to have become friends but how long that will last I'm not sure. I've made Alweo senior novice and I do wonder how good a follower Catinus will prove to be. He strikes me as more of a leader. I just hope that Alweo doesn't turn out to be like Seward. He can be arrogant at times.'

'Perhaps but, if anyone, it's Conomultus I'd worry about if I were you. He lives in his brother's shadow too much and is too reliant on him. I suspect the same may be true of Wigmund and Alweo.'

~~~

The rain had stopped by the next morning and Oswald's funeral was conducted in the open in bright sunshine. The whole community was there for the internment, even Seward with his swollen nose and bound up face. He kept giving Catinus nasty looks but the other boy just smiled back at him. Of course, that just made the other boy even angrier. Oswiu believed that the struggle between them was far from over, but he had other more pressing concerns. Hopefully Alweo would manage to keep the peace.

Afterwards Oswiu stayed to pray by his brother's grave for a long time. The two had always been close, especially when they were younger, and Oswiu missed him. However, now he wore the crown of Bernicia and he needed to concentrate on what Penda was up to.

The next day he set off for the south of his domain.

~~~

'You're certain of this?'

Oswiu was talking quietly to one of Hengist's nobles in the hall of one of his thegns whose vill lay on the north bank of the River Tees - the border between Bernicia and Deira. The man had come to seek him out and had stayed quietly amongst the crowd in the hall until he managed to get close to Oswiu.

'My king is certain, yes. The information came from someone in the warband of King Peada who is in Hengist's pay.'

Oswiu was struck by the idea. He could understand the usefulness of a spy in the camp of the enemy, but he had no idea how one might go about recruiting or inserting someone like that. He would have to ask Hengist how he managed it the next time he saw him, although he didn't know when that might be as Hengist of Lindsay formally acknowledged Oswine of Deira as his overlord.

'If Oswine has agreed to this arrangement with Penda, do we know when he is due to launch this raid?'

'No, it appears that Penda may be waiting for more information about your strength and the disposition of your forces.'

'But that would mean that I have a traitor amongst my own men.'

'So it would seem. Who knows of your plans in advance?'

'Very few. Ceadda, of course, but I'd trust him with my life. Bishop Aidan, the eorls who I intend to visit, and my inner council.'

'Then I would look closely at the latter if I were you, Cyning.'

'Thank Hengist for his timely warning. However, there is little I can do until I know what Penda plans.'

'I'm sure that King Hengist will send a messenger as soon as he knows more, but my guess would be next spring.'

'Yes, mine also.'

After the man had left to return to Lindsey, Oswiu's thoughts turned to his inner council. Some men could be bought, as he knew from experience. Penda had managed to bribe the Custos of Bebbanburg for information years ago. The more he thought about it, the more he was convinced that it had to be Œthelwald. His nephew had little cause to love him and, when he'd returned from Ulster in a huff after an argument with Eochaid, he'd been persuaded to include him on his council as a way of keeping him under supervision. Well, it seemed that hadn't worked too well if he was managing to communicate with his enemies. He wondered whether he was in touch with Oswine as well.

He could understand Oswine being wary of him, and even wanting him dethroned as he saw him as a threat to his position as King of Deira, but plotting with Penda was something he would never have suspected. It just proved what a naïve fool he was.

Œthelwald was a different matter. He was still held in high regard by some, mainly those who didn't know him, because he was Oswald's only son. There were even those who had suggested that he should be made King of Rheged as Oswiu's vassal to compensate him for not being chosen as King of Bernicia. This unmerited popularity made it difficult for Oswiu to deal with him as he would wish.

He returned to Bebbanburg for the winter wondering what perils the year 644 would bring. However, when he got there he found a very pleasant surprise awaiting him. Not only had Utta managed to negotiate his betrothal to Eanflæd but he had brought the girl back with him, chaperoned by her uncle, Eormenred, the King of Kent's younger brother.

As soon as he saw the girl he fell in love. She was fifteen and extremely beautiful. He couldn't wait to wed and bed her. However, Utta tried to dampen his passion somewhat.

'She doesn't know you, Cyning, and she is wary of you. She is very young, half your age in fact, and has grown up hearing fearful tales of you and Oswald. Not surprising really as her father killed yours and took his crown. You have been portrayed as someone to be feared; a vengeful enemy to be precise. And then there is the complication in the eyes of the Church that you are first cousins. I think you need to take things slowly.'

Oswiu was a virile man who had been without a woman for too long. He could, of course, have had any number of willing bed mates since his last wife died, but he was also a devout Christian and he believed that fornication outside marriage was a sin. He had never really forgiven himself for taking Fianna as his lover when she was a year younger than Eanflæd was now.

He was therefore angry with Utta for pouring cold water over his lust. Later though, when he had had time to think, he could see that his chaplain was being prudent. Eanflæd wasn't just shy in his presence, she was like a trapped bird being stalked by a cat. He sighed. They needed to get to know each other and he would have to win her love the hard way, by courting her.

He started by taking her to visit Lindisfarne. He needed to get Aidan's dispensation to marry his cousin in any case. Naturally Eormenred came too and Oswiu discovered that the young prince and he had a lot in common. Of course, it helped that the prince, who was only eighteen, admired both the late Oswald and Oswiu and kept asking about their time in Dalriada and Ulster as young warriors.

Normally women weren't allowed inside the monastery but Aidan made an exception for Eanflæd, though she wasn't allowed to sleep there. They therefore stayed with the thegn on the mainland opposite the island. Oswiu saw the novices being taught by their new master and had to hide a smile when he saw that Seward still had a bandage around his head, though the bruising had disappeared from his face and his nose was back to normal, if a little bent.

The two Mercian brothers were bent diligently over their work, though Catinus did glance his way and gave him a tentative smile. Oswiu shouldn't have encouraged the boy's impudence but he couldn't resist smiling back. There was something about the boy that Oswiu liked. He found himself hoping that he would decide to become a warrior and not a monk. Alweo and his cousin sat opposite them and it was obvious that the four were a close knit group. It wouldn't be long before the two elder boys were old enough to train as warriors and he decided there and then to ask Ceadda to oversee their training.

The next day they travelled on to Coldingham and Oswiu introduced Eanflæd to his sister. She took Eanflæd off to meet Cyneburga and Keeva and they didn't reappear for over two hours. Oswiu was left kicking his heels with Eormenred, Ceadda and the rest of his gesith but he didn't mind. He knew that his prospective bride would be learning a lot about him, hopefully most of it good.

When they rode back to Bebbanburg the next day Eanflæd rode beside him and she was far less shy. They talked amicably, learning about each other, and there was even a little mild flirting.

Over the next week he took her to visit Yeavering and she marvelled that the first snow had fallen on the tops of the Cheviot Hills so early in the year. They had snow in Kent, of course, but never before January or February. The wild hill country was so very different from the cultivated rolling countryside of Kent and she was captivated by it.

They went hunting the next day and managed to bring a stag back. Of course, Eanflæd was only a spectator but the chase had excited her and, far from being reticent and shy, she was now full of chatter and laughter. Oswiu decided to set a date for their wedding the following week.

~~~

Eanflæd lay in the bed nervously watching as her husband disrobed and climbed under the blankets with her. Over the past two weeks she had come to know and to like Oswiu and he had always behaved towards her with consideration, but his reputation as a violent man and the lustful way he looked at her made her fearful.

To her surprise he started by kissing her gently and then used his hands and his tongue to excite her. This was not what her mother and the other women she knew had led her to expect. Gradually she found herself becoming more and more aroused. Her whole body was tingling and she moaned in excitement.

'I want you inside me, Oswiu,' she told him.

He smiled to himself. He had forced himself to control his lust so that he could awaken her libido first. He knew that he wanted to spend the rest of his life with Eanflæd and he didn't want her to just like him, he wanted her devotion. He'd fancied himself in love with Fianna and with Rhieinmelth but he had been attracted to the elfin qualities of the first and the pretty face of the second.   From the conversations he'd had with his new wife he knew that he was attracted, not just to her beauty, but also to her personality.

Once he'd overcome her shyness he found her witty and knowledgeable. He actually enjoyed her company and missed her when they were apart. He knew that this wasn't another infatuation but love, and a love that he was certain would grow deeper as time went on.

Finally he did what she wanted and she screamed, not in pain, but with pleasure when he inserted himself into her. Yes, it had hurt a little, but he had done it slowly and allowed her to get used to him inside her, then gradually increased the pace until she felt a euphoria she hadn't thought possible as her whole body shook with pleasure. They made love three times more that night and once again when they woke. By the time that they joined the household to break their fast in the hall she was utterly besotted with Oswiu.

That morning he introduced her to Fianna as his children's nurse and to Aldfrith, who was now ten, the four year old Ehlfrith, and his baby daughter, Alchflaed. She was enchanted by the younger two but Aldfrith just scowled at her. Oswiu sighed. He'd neglected the boy since Rhieinmelth's death when he'd returned to his mother's care. He'd be eleven in two months and he knew that the boy hated being expected to help look after his half-siblings. He didn't want him to turn into another Œthelwald but he wasn't sure what to do to improve their relationship.

Smitten as he was with his young wife, he soon forgot about his eldest son and, despite the imminent onset of winter he took her on a tour of his kingdom. They spent Christmas at Caer Luel and had reached Dùn Phris on the way back to Bebbanburg in March when the news reached him that Penda had crossed the River Wharfe inside Deira.

He was sitting eating the evening meal with Kenric and their respective wives when the messenger arrived. Cuthbert and his two elder brothers had also joined them and Oswiu was reminded that he needed to do something about Aldfrith, who was the same age as Cuthbert.

'Penda is ravaging Deira on his way north towards the River Tees, Cyning,' the messenger told him. 'It looks as if he is making for Bernicia.'

'So much for Oswine's treaty of friendship with Penda. He might have known that a pagan's word wasn't to be trusted. How old is this news?'

'The message came from the Eorl of Eoforwīc and arrived at Bebbanburg yesterday. It came by sea so I imagine it's three of four days old by now.'

'You did well to get here so quickly, I'll reward you later. For now go and wash and get some sleep.'

'Thank you, Cyning.'

'Well, if tidings of Penda's advance reached Eoforwīc three or four days ago, we can expect Penda to be well on his way to the Tees by now.'

He turned to Kenric.

'Can you send out messengers at dawn to the other eorls in Goddodin and meet me with their war host at Heavenfield in ten days' time? I shall make my stand on the Tyne.'

'I've a birlinn to take you back to Bebbanburg, if you need it.'

'Thank you, Kenric, I'll do that. There's no point in sending a messenger there as I can reach it by tomorrow night with a fair wind. However, can you summon the Eorl of Rheged to join us with as many men as he can muster in that time?'

'What about me, Oswiu?' Eanflæd asked timidly, a little scared by what was happening.

He looked at his wife and smiled. 'You'll be coming with me to Bebbanburg. You'll be safe there whatever happens on the Tyne.'

~~~

Oswiu had based himself at Wylam, some three miles from where he expected Penda to cross the Tyne. It seemed the sensible choice as there were only six possible places where you could wade across the river, and four of them were within three miles of Wylam. Beyond the easternmost ford there were a couple of ferries, but they couldn't take more than ten men at a time. His scouts were across the other side of the Tyne shadowing Penda's advance.

So far he had gathered some four hundred trained Bernician warriors on foot, a few dozen mounted men in addition to his gesith, and fifteen hundred men of the fyrd, including Britons from Rheged and some Deirans who had fled north. According to his scouts Penda's army consisted of sixty mounted warriors and another five hundred wearing armour of some sort. There were another two thousand members of the fyrd. Oswiu was therefore outnumbered.

Much against his better judgement and Fianna's protests, he had brought Aldfrith, now eleven, with him. The boy was thrilled and Oswiu managed to re-establish a better relationship with his son, though he was too busy to devote as much time as he would have liked to him. He took him along with him whatever he was doing in the hope that the boy would learn something about leading an army and preparing for battle. That seemed to be working as the boy asked lots of intelligent questions and was useful as a messenger.

'Cyning, Penda has camped for the night five miles south of here,' the scouts reported.

Shortly afterwards Eormenred arrived with his gesith. He had stayed in Northumbria for the winter but the last that Oswiu had heard of him he'd been visiting Oswine in Eoforwīc. Even better, he'd brought with him Hrothga, the elderly Eorl of Eoforwīc, and his warband of fifty trained warriors, all mounted.

'I'm surprised that Oswine gave permission for you join me.'

'He didn't,' the eorl replied with a grin. 'I told him that I was going to defend my lands, which is true in a way, although they lie east of Penda's line of march.'

'Well, I'm delighted to see you. Now, I have a task for you, if you're willing.'

Both men listened to what Oswiu wanted them to do and a grin spread across each of their faces as what he was planning sunk in.

When Penda reached the four fords the next morning he found Oswiu's army drawn up ready to oppose his crossing. All four crossing places were in sight of one another and Oswiu had constructed earthworks topped with a short palisade to defend the north bank. Behind each low timber wall stood his archers with the various warbands of trained warriors behind them. He had kept the fyrd and less experienced fighters with him as a reserve to go to the assistance of whichever of the four crossing points needed it.

He sat astride his horse on higher ground so that he could see all four fords. Aldfrith sat on his pony on one side of him and Ceadda on the other with his gesith, now forty strong, behind them.

Penda tried to rush all four fords at once using his unarmoured men. They had shields, which gave them some protection, but nevertheless scores were wounded or killed by the archers on the north bank before they got halfway across.

When the Mercian archers came forward to respond, they made the mistake of firing their arrows in one volley. Oswiu's men ducked behind the palisades and then sent a withering hail of arrows back which killed or wounded nearly a quarter of the enemy archers. They quickly retreated behind their shield wall.

Oswiu was just thinking how well it was all going and wondering how Eormenred and Hrothga were doing when to his amazement they and the hundred horsemen he had sent with them came galloping back.

'What's wrong? I was expecting you to be on the other side of the river by now.'

He had sent them to capture and set fire to Penda's baggage train.

'Penda's smarter than we thought,' Eormenred replied.

65

'He's sent Peada and the Middle Anglians downstream to cross at the ford we were going to use. There are eight hundred of them not far behind us,' Hrothga added.

Oswiu thought quickly and gestured to them, pointing to the low hill covered in a wood to the north of them.

'Take up a position in the front edge of the trees as quickly as you can. I'll engage them with the fyrd; we'll heavily outnumber Peada's men but they'll have experienced warriors with them. Nevertheless, I expect to be able to hold them for a while. When you see my standard lowered and raised once again that'll be the signal for you to charge them in the flank. Now go.'

After they had galloped off, he turned to Ceadda.

'Take charge here. Aldfrith you stay with him. I'm leaving ten of the gesith with you. If it goes badly I'm relying on you to get my son to safety at Bebbanburg. Utta, you make sure Aldfrith does as he's told.'

The boy was about to protest that he wanted to stay with his father, but one look at Utta's ferocious grin with its pointed teeth changed his mind.

'Barduwulf, you are to take charge of the rest of my gesith and come with me. We'll be fighting on foot so tether the horses here.'

Barduwulf nodded and dismounted, ordering the gesith to do the same, whilst Oswiu went over to brief the various eorls commanding the fyrd and others in the reserve. Nerian was left holding Oswiu's helmet and shield, which Oswiu had obviously forgotten about in the heat of the moment. After sitting on his horse indecisively for a minute or so, he kicked his heels into its flanks and trotted after his master.

Peada and his men had been too busy negotiating the ford to notice Eormenred's horsemen at the edge of the wood. The ford was not as shallow of the four being used by his father and was really only safe for mounted men to use. By the time that he'd got his army across he'd lost thirty men carried away by the current and the sun was far higher in the sky that he'd hoped.

'Your father will have expected us long before this,' one of his eorls commented.

'My father is safely on the south bank,' Peada shot back. Knowing that that the eorl's criticism was correct didn't help. 'Let's get moving, at the run.'

'Cyning, if we run for the next three miles the men will be too exhausted to fight,' another of his nobles pointed out.

'I'm well aware of that, I'm not an idiot. We run for a mile or so and then march the rest of the way to allow the men to recover.'

'Yes, Cyning. I didn't mean ....'

'I know exactly what you meant, now shut up and run.'

Peada knew as soon as he'd spoken that he'd upset an important man unnecessarily and that made his mood even worse.

Being late March, the sun would set in less than four hours and, being overcast, it would get dark before that. Peada calculated that they would have about two hours of daylight left by the time they reached the four fords.

Penda was getting anxious. His son should have been here before this. He'd launched several more attacks across the fords but only twice had they reached the palisades. Once there, his warriors had been held whilst the Northumbrian archers sent arrow after arrow at high trajectory into the unarmoured men in the rear of the attacking column.

'Surely they must run out of those bloody arrows soon,' Penda commented to no-one in particular as his warriors beat yet another hasty retreat across the fords.

Then, at last, he saw his son's column appear from the east on the far bank. They halted as those in the rear hastened to move into formation facing the Northumbrian right flank. At the same time Oswiu led his reserve forward with his gesith in the centre to face them. Peada's army had greater depth and overlapped his formation to the north but, he noticed with satisfaction, there were no more than about forty well armoured warriors.

Half of the archers left the palisades to pour several volleys into the Middle Anglians, then ran back again as Penda launched yet another assault across the river. His men, hitherto demoralised by their lack of success and heavy losses, became positively enthusiastic when Peada's men appeared and attacked with a ferocity that was lacking before. It was all that the seasoned warriors that manned the palisades could do to keep them from overwhelming their defences.

Meanwhile Peada's and Oswiu's armies ran towards one another. Suddenly Oswiu's men stopped and a shower of spears darkened the sky and fell amongst the enemy. As they were running most still had their shields on their backs and the few who had already swung them around to protect themselves had the shields facing forwards, not upwards. A hundred and fifty men fell dead or wounded: over a fifth of Peada's men.

That was unsettling enough but then, just as the two war hosts were about to meet, he was distracted by a roar from his left. He glanced that way and was dismayed to see a mass of horsemen charging at his flank.

'Face left', he yelled in panic.

That totally confused his men and a large number in his centre and right flank also turned to their left just at the critical time when Oswiu's reserves crashed into them. They might not be professional warriors like his gesith and his warband, but they knew how to kill a confused enemy, and they did so with gusto.

Large numbers of Peada's front three ranks were cut down before they could recover and by then the cavalry had charged into the flank, spearing the enemy first and then using their swords to slash and thrust at the milling footmen.

Other than the trained warriors who stood in the in first three ranks, the Middle Anglians were members of the fyrd and they fled in panic leaving Peada, his gesith and the remainder of his warband stranded.

Peada grabbed a riderless horse that had belonged to one of Oswiu's horsemen who had been killed and made his escape. Seeing this his gesith and his warband surrendered in disgust.

Oswiu looked around for either Eormenred or Hrotha but the horsemen had set off in pursuit of the routed enemy.

'I hope they remember to seize the baggage train,' he thought to himself.

Seeing his son's army routed, Penda knew that the battle was lost and withdrew from the battlefield as dusk fell. Later that evening the sky the far side of the river was lit up by flames leaping high in the sky. The horsemen had indeed remembered their orders to fire the Mercian baggage train. Oswiu was confident that they had had the good sense to remove the gold, silver and any other valuables first.

~~~

Eormenred had parted from Hrotha after looting and firing the baggage train. The elderly eorl had confessed to being exhausted and he returned to Oswiu bringing with him several chests of gold and silver, mainly items looted from churches and the odd monastery in the path of Penda's advance north through Deira.

The rest of the horsemen kept up the pursuit of Peada's fleeing army until they came across Penda's more disciplined retreat. By then most of the Middle Anglians were too dispersed to offer much sport. They followed Penda's route, making numerous pinprick attacks on the marching army and then they harassed them all night. When the exhausted and dispirited Mercian army eventually stopped the next night they set fire to the dry undergrowth upwind of the Mercians and killed quite a few more of them – some were incinerated alive, many succumbed to the smoke and others were ambushed in the woods as they ran from the fire.

Eormenred's horsemen finally gave up the chase as they neared the border with Mercia. It took them a lot longer to return through Deira as they stopped to loot all the bodies they had left in the heat of the chase. Three weeks later Eormenred set off to return to Kent a lot richer than when he had come north with his niece.

CHAPTER FIVE – THE FALL OF WESSEX

645/6 AD

'Are you sure?'

'Very sure. The wise woman said that I must be a least four months gone.'

'So the baby's due when?'

'Five months from now. Surely you know that the normal period for a woman to carry a baby is nine months?'

'I suppose so. I hadn't really thought about it.'

'And you've had three children before this? Men!'

Oswiu kissed Eanflæd and pulled her to him.

'What would you do without us?'

'Not get fat and go through the pain of childbirth for a start.'

Oswiu remembered Rhieinmelth's death and the fact that Oswald's first wife had also died in childbirth. He couldn't afford to think like that. Eanflæd was young and healthy – but so had the other two been.

'What's wrong? You shuddered as if someone had just walked over your grave.'

Not mine he thought.

'Oh, it's just that I'm going to miss making passionate love to you for the next five months or so.'

'Why? The wise woman said it was alright to do that until it got too uncomfortable for me.'

'Really? Then I think we should retire early tonight to celebrate the conception of our first child.'

In the event the birth was relatively easy and they decided to call their son Ecgfrith. He was a lusty baby and both that fact and the uncomplicated birth led Oswiu to hope that they would have many more children together. The spectre of Rhieinmelth's harrowing death was banished.

In thanks for his new son's safe delivery he decided to establish a new monastery and went to see Aidan.

'I have some land at Hartlepool which is available, if you think that's a good location.'

'Hartlepool? Just north of the mouth of the Tees?'

'Yes, I own a vill there which is managed for me by a reeve. You could draw up a charter making the abbot the thegn.'

'I was thinking of an Abbess. We already have two monasteries for men and only one – that at Coldingham – for women. It would be a good location too, being near Deira. I fear that James the Deacon has too much influence in the area.'

'You have concerns because he belongs to the Roman Church?'

'Yes, they are beginning to call themselves Roman Catholics, indicating that it is the universal church for Christians. They are a hierarchical organisation where bishops fancy themselves secular lords as well as spiritual leaders. Not like us where an abbot is superior to a bishop. Where we are humble men, they fancy themselves as princes of the Church.'

'Very well, who do you have in mind as abbess?'

'Two nuns spring to mind. Your wife's niece, Hild, who is also related to you I think, or Hieu, who is Irish like me.'

'Yes, perhaps Hild as she is my cousin. But have you thought of a combined foundation?'

'You mean one for monks and nuns? No. I know they exist but I have always thought it best to keep them apart to avoid the temptations of the flesh.'

'You seem to have a poor opinion of your fellow clerics devoutness and discipline. It seems to me that it could work well provided they have strong leadership. We don't need to make a decision now. It will be some time before work can start, given the other building work in progress at the moment, but I suppose you could start work on the plans. And I'm sure you can find a suitably chaste monk to act as prior and be in charge of the men.'

'I suspect I'm being teased but, very well. I'll write to Hild tomorrow to see if she would be agreeable in due course, and I'll think about who I could put in charge of the monks.'

'Good. Now, how are Catinus and Conomultus getting on?'

'Very well, especially the younger of the two. Catinus and Seward remained enemies until I was able to send the latter to Melrose after he took his vows. Now Catinus is old enough to do so too but he says that he doesn't wish to become a monk; he wants to train as a member of your warband.'

'Well, I certainly need some new recruits to replace those I lost fighting Penda last year. Send him to Ceadda and he can start his training. What about his brother? How old is he now?'

'Thirteen, but he'll soon be fourteen. However, he wishes to take his vows and to remain here.'

'I thought those two were inseparable.'

'They were, at first, but Conomultus is by far the better scholar and I think that Catinus became a little jealous of his brother. Conomultus had grown in confidence over the past year or so and he no longer depends on Catinus like he used to.'

'So they have grown apart?'

'To some extent; they are still fairly close, but they are resigned to following different paths in their lives from now on.'

'The same is true of Alweo and Wigmund, although Wigmund isn't the scholar that Conomultus is.'

'I assume that Alweo wants to become a warrior too?'

'So I understand. He and Catinus have become good friends.'

'Hmmm. Two Mercians who want to join my warband. I wonder if that's wise.'

'Catinus is entirely loyal to you. I'm not so sure about Alweo though. He still thinks of himself as a Mercian princeling. However, he hates Penda with a passion.'

'I only hope it's a case of whoever hates my enemy is my friend.'

~~~

Whilst Wigmund seemed to almost relish being free of Alweo's dominating presence, Conomultus found the departure of Catinus more upsetting than he had expected. Although his growing sense of independence and self-worth had brought the two brothers into conflict recently, the bond between them was still strong. However, the arrival of two new twelve-year old novices soon drove Catinus from his mind.

He was now the senior novice and, as such, one of his tasks was to help the Master of Novices to keep order amongst his charges. Mostly this wasn't a difficult task as in the main the boys were placid and devout. Untypically, all of the present crop of students seemed destined to become monks and so they were less troublesome than those who couldn't wait to become old enough to train as warriors. True, there were also a few who came for a basic education before returning to farm the land or to learn a trade, but most families didn't want their sons educated; they were needed to work as soon as they were able to.

However, two of the new twelve-year olds who had just joined - Wilfrid and Eata – were far from equable or well-disciplined. Wilfrid was the son of the Eorl of Hexham and was used to lording it over his social inferiors, whereas Eata was the son of a ceorl and had an axe to grind. Ever since their father had died and his elder brother had inherited, the family had struggled to pay the thegn the inheritance tax due. Eata blamed the family's descent from relative prosperity to poverty on his superiors and was consequently far from amenable to authority. The only reason he was at Lindisfarne was because he was lame and couldn't earn his keep at home. His minor disability was something else that made him ill-tempered. Wilfrid's arrogant attitude was inevitably going to infuriate him.

Eata wasn't the only boy to take an instant dislike to Wilfrid; Conomultus was denigrated and undermined by Wilfrid from the start. Not only was the older boy a Mercian, he was a Briton as well, which made him the lowest of the low in Wilfrid's eyes. It had started the moment that Wilfrid had arrived and Conomultus had shown the two newcomers where they would be sleeping.

'No, I'm not sleeping in the corner trapped in by a dirty, smelly Briton like you. What are you even doing here? Only decent Anglo-Saxons should be allowed to become monks.'

For a moment Conomultus couldn't believe what he had just heard. Then he grew angry.

'How dare you! I'm the senior novice and you will accord me proper respect.'

'Why? What have you done to deserve it? I'm told you're not even from Bernicia, but are a Mercian dog. Why aren't you serving that pagan swine, Penda?'

'Both my brother and I serve King Oswiu. He was the person who placed us here, with Bishop Aidan's full support. Now stop being a complete arse before I report you to Brother Tuda.' Seeing the puzzled look on the other boy's face he added, 'the Master of Novices.'

'Go on then, let's see if he will side with a pagan Briton or the son of the Eorl of Hexham.'

'I don't care whose damn son you are, as a novice you have a duty of obedience to your superiors, and that includes me.'

The two boys stared defiantly at each other. Because of Conomultus' short stature, he had to look up at Wilfrid despite being

73

nearly two years older. Wigmund and the other boys had watched this exchange with interest. They all liked Conomultus but a little bit of drama brightened up their otherwise humdrum lives. However, one of them had watched with increasing annoyance.

'In the name of God, stop being such a prick, Wilfrid. Who cares whose son you are? We're all just novices here, whatever our birth. You'd better get used to it.'

'Who the hell are you to tell me what to do? You're a serf's son; not much better that this oaf.'

It was the wrong thing to say to Eata. He was very proud that his family were ceorls – tenant farmers - not slaves, which was what serfs were. With a cry of fury he stepped forward and punched Wilfrid on the nose. The surprised boy let out a howl and fell to the ground clutching his blood covered face. Eata would have followed his punch up by kicking the prostrate Wilfrid but Conomultus and Wigmund grabbed him and pulled him away. Eata was amazed at how strong the slight young Briton was. Conomultus let go of Eata and, telling Wigmund to stop him if he tried to attack Wilfred again, he knelt by the injured boy.

'Stop blubbering like a little girl. Eata shouldn't have done that, no matter how infuriating you are and he'll be punished. However, you are going to have to be far less arrogant if you are to survive the next two years here. Now move your hands away so I can see the damage.'

When the other boy continued to wail and clutch his nose Conomultus lost patience with him and pulled his hands away, then slapped his face.

'I told you to shut up, you snivelling cur. I hope you want to be a monk because there's no way you'd ever make a warrior.'

Wilfrid stopped crying and gave the other boy a venomous look.

'You'll pay for that,' he spat at him.

'Oh, that's a pity. It sounds as if you'll live after all. Now get up and go and clean that blood off your face before Brother Tuda sees you. By the way, I've decided I don't want you sleeping next to me. Eata can have the nice warm bed in the corner. Your bed is by the door. It'll be draughty and cold I fear. Sorry about that.'

The other novices gave an ironic cheer as Wilfrid stalked out of the hut to go and wash the blood away. Conomultus had a nasty suspicion that Wilfrid was going to be trouble, not just as a novice, but later in life as well. He just didn't appreciate how much.

~~~

Cenwalh was beginning to realise that repudiating Penda's sister as his wife hadn't been his smartest move. He had married Edith to neutralise the Mercian threat, but she was very much older than him and, when he found out that she was beyond child-bearing age, he sent her back to Mercia.

Penda had been too occupied with his plans for the invasion of Bernicia at the time, but now, smarting as he was at his defeat at the hands of Oswiu, he decided to take his rage out on Cenwalh of Wessex.

'How will you manage to invade Wessex when we lost so many warriors at the battle on the Tees, father?' Wulfhere, Penda's second son asked him when his father told him of his plans.

'You don't have to remind me, boy. Cenwalh is no warrior. We'll start by invading Hwicce and getting that back. Then I'll offer him peace before attacking Wessex itself the following year. As to warriors, there are men we can hire from Frankia.'

'But to lull him into a false sense of security with a bogus treaty impinges on your honour, father.'

'No, he betrayed me by rejecting my sister; betraying him in return is what he deserves. Don't try and dissuade me, Wulfhere. My mind is made up.'

Wulfhere frowned, but there was no arguing with his father when he was in this mood.

'Who will you send to Frankia?'

'You, who else?'

He set sail the next day from a settlement on the southern bank of the River Mersey, Mercia's only access to the sea. The journey to Frankia was uneventful. He had taken two birlinns and two knarrs, trading ships propelled by a single sail with no oars. He needed the knarrs to transport the mercenaries who they recruited back to Mercia. However, this meant that their progress was dictated by the wind. Wulfhere was frustrated at the time that it was taking and once even resorted to using the birlinns to tow the knarrs, but the rowers soon tired and he gave that idea up.

Finally, after three weeks they reached the mouth of the River Seine and sailed up to the port of Rouen in Neustria. The King of Neustria and Burgundy was the six-year old Clovis II. Consequently the monarchy was weak. His nobles struggled against each other for power and anarchy reigned. This was unfortunate for Wulfhere as those willing to become mercenaries were in high demand.

'This is pointless,' Wulfhere fumed. 'We've managed to recruit five men and none of them would be worthy of a place in any warband of mine. We're going to have to try elsewhere.'

'Frisia?' the captain of the birlinn suggested.

'Yes, and further to the lands of the Saxons, Angles and Jutes if necessary.'

They set sail the next day heading north east along the coast of Neustria until they reached Austrasia in Northern Frankia. Once again they found that the Austrasians were too busy fighting Neustria or amongst themselves to have many warriors seeking employment elsewhere and they sailed on. By now they were entering the narrows that separated Austrasia from Kent and this time their passage was far from trouble free.

The four Kentish war galleys were small but fast. The inhabitants of Kent were Jutes and they were no friends of the Angles, who inhabited Mercia. It all stemmed from the fact that they were neighbouring tribes in their original homeland, the Jutland peninsular, where there were constant cross border raids.

The smaller galleys had the wind gauge and a pair made for each of the two birlinns. Wulfhere immediately gave up the futile attempt to escape and, instead, turned to face the oncoming galleys. At the last moment his steersman put the oar over and, instead of running between the two galleys, he turned so he passed one of them on the outside. As soon as they were level he came alongside and his crew threw several grappling irons aboard to tie the two vessels together.

He led his men aboard it before the second galley could react and his more numerous crew laid into the Jutes manning the galley, desperate to eliminate them before the second galley could intervene.

Warriors at sea didn't usually wear armour; a man weighed down by it sunk to the bottom regardless of how good a swimmer he was. However, the captain of the galley was wearing a byrnie as well as a helmet. He thrust his sword at Wulfhere, who deflected it with his shield before cutting at his opponent's side. It struck home but the blade didn't penetrate the chain mail.

'Prepare to die, dog,' the confident captain told him with a grin before cutting at Wulfhere's right shoulder with his sword. The Mercian twisted around so as to take the blow on his shield then pushed his sword over it aiming at the enemy captain's right eye. However, the man turned his head at the last moment and the tip of the sword glanced harmlessly off the side of his helmet.

By now the noise of battle around them had lessened and the victorious Mercian crew gathered around the two men, cheering on their prince. The captain realised that this meant that his crew were either dead or had surrendered and lowered his sword.

They were standing near the gunwale opposite where the Mercians had boarded; Wulfhere glanced behind the captain of the Kent galley before charging the Jute with his shield held in front of him. It was the last thing the man had expected and, taken unawares, he was pushed backwards until he toppled over the side and sank below the waves.

Wulfhere grunted in satisfaction before realising that his crew were hastily re-boarding their own ship. The other galley, having charged past them, had turned and come back alongside the Mercian birlinn. Now the Jutes were swarming aboard the birlinn.

It was a foolish move. Their initial success in overcoming those Mercians who had remained on board was short lived. As more and more of Wulfhere's boarding party arrived back on their own birlinn, the Jutes were pressed back towards their galley and started to scramble back on board. The first to arrive back on board cut the ropes that held the two ships together and cast off after less than half of their number had made it back aboard.

It took less than another five minutes to dispose of the remaining Jutes, most being thrown overboard. Wulfhere was about to set off in pursuit of the poorly manned second galley when he felt his arm grabbed. His steersman pointed aft to where the second birlinn was trapped between the other two Kentish galleys. The knarrs were standing off some distance away as their crews weren't warriors, and there were few enough of them anyway.

'Shit! Forget about that galley, head for the other birlinn,' he told the steersman, cursing its captain for his inability to deal with the pair of galleys on his own.

Wulfhere's birlinn pulled alongside one of the Kentish galleys and he led his men aboard. Only three men and two ships' boys were aboard and it took him and his men seconds to dispose of them before clambering aboard the beleaguered birlinn. The crew had suffered a number of casualties but they had inflicted as many deaths on the Jutes as the latter had on the Mercians. The Mercians had been outnumbered but the arrival of the rest of their compatriots had turned the tables.

Wulfhere thrust his sword into the back of an unsuspecting enemy and used his seax to beat aside a sword thrust from another. He tried to pull his sword out but it had apparently got stuck between a couple of vertebrae and he left it in the Jute's back. He picked up a discarded axe and, with that in one hand and his seax in the other, he advanced on a Jute with a dagger who appeared to be no more than thirteen. Rather than kill him, the Mercian batted his dagger aside with his sword and rapped him on the head with the pommel of his seax. The boy dropped like a stone.

He looked around for his next adversary but it was all over. His men were busy pitching the dead Jutes over the side as well as those who were badly wounded. The rest would be sold into slavery. Once the minor damage to the birlinns was repaired and the Mercian wounded dealt with, he set sail once more for Austrasia.

'How many men did you lose?' Wulfhere asked the other captain once they had docked and sent their captives to be locked in the slave pens.

'Eight dead and seven too badly wounded to be able to fight again.'

'Therefore to date our mission to recruit mercenaries has netted us five men of dubious quality at the cost of fifteen good Mercian warriors.'

'It's not all bad news, three of the dead and one of the wounded were our new recruits.'

'So one miserable recruit in exchange for eleven of your crew is good news, is it?'

The man shrugged. 'We captured two galleys as well.'

'God's teeth man, we can barely man our two birlinns with the men we have left, let alone the galleys.'

'No, but we can sell them here which, with the money for the slaves, will give us a lot more gold and silver to hire mercenaries with.'

Wulfhere grinned at the birlinn's captain.

'Perhaps you have got a brain under that mop of greasy hair after all.'

A week later the four ships arrived at the port of Hammaburg on the River Albia in Saxony. It was a good place to hire warriors as young men from Saxony and Frisia, as well as Slavs from the other side of the Albia, tended to congregate there looking for someone who could offer them riches in return for their skills as fighters. The alternative was to stay and endure subsistence living on a farm. Wulfhere managed to recruit eighty men, though most had several years to go before they'd reach twenty and none had experienced a battle. At least a few of them were the sons of fishermen and could therefore row and handle sails. However, none had armour and most were equipped with a crudely made shield and either an axe, a spear or a cheaply made seax. Wulfhere had to spend some of his gold and silver buying each of them a sword and a helmet.

The knarrs in which the majority now travelled were broad beamed but had a shallow draft. They therefore tended to roll quite a lot and the experienced sailors amongst them found the sight of their fellow recruits heaving their guts out over the side hilarious.

Two days later the small fleet landed at Esbjerg in the north of Angeln, the Mercians original homeland. Life was even harder there than it was in Saxony and he managed to sign on another forty five men varying from sixteen to thirty in age. At least some of them had fought an enemy before, usually the Jutes who lived to the north.

That made his next port of call – Hanstholm – problematical. The Angles couldn't be trusted ashore.

'Why not? They deserve a drink or two and a rut with a tavern wench before the long sail home,' his captain suggested.

'Why not?' He couldn't believe that the man could be so naïve. 'I'll tell you why not. Because our Angles are itching to rampage through the place and rape all the women. They don't like the Jutes and the Jutes don't like them. We're even going to have to keep the Angles on one knarr and the Jutes on another so they don't kill each other before we get them back to Mercia, that's why not.'

He solved the problem by anchoring the knarr with the Angle recruits on board offshore. Although there were enough Jutes here who were looking to escape to the life of a warrior, they were chary about serving with Angles and Saxons, especially if that meant that they'd be under the command of an Anglian prince. In the end it took him a week to enrol just thirty Jutes.

His instructions had been to recruit two hundred experienced warriors. Instead he was returning with a hundred and sixty youths and men, many of whom would need training before they'd be of any use in battle – and he'd lost a dozen men in doing so. He didn't imagine that his father would be exactly ecstatic.

~~~

Cenwalh had fondly anticipated that Penda wouldn't be able to invade Wessex to avenge his sister's dishonour, not after the losses the Mercians had suffered trying to invade Bernicia the previous year. In any case, he was confident that Wessex could now field more warriors than

Mercia could, should he try. Penda's invasion of Hwicce therefore came as something of a shock.

'How many men has Penda brought with him?' he asked the Eorl of Hwicce, who had fled from Gleawecastre before the Mercians could trap him there.

'Our scouts estimated there to be about six hundred, Cyning,'

'And you say that they are all warriors?'

'They are all wearing helmets and either chainmail or a leather jerkin so they don't appear to be members of the fyrd.'

'That's nearly two hundred more in his warband than we thought he had. Is there any information about Peada and his Middle Anglians?' he asked his hereræswa.

'No Cyning. He hasn't moved towards us, as far as we can tell.'

'Very well. I'll call a meeting of the Witan and you had better start to mobilise our forces.'

'What about Oswiu?'

'What about him?'

'Mercia has invaded our territory so Bernicia is honour bound to support you. At the very least he could keep Middle Anglia from being involved.'

'He might if he were King of Deira as well but, as it is, he would have to travel all the way through Deira in order to engage Peada's Middle Anglians. No, we'll manage without his help.'

At first the army from Wessex met little opposition as they entered Hwicce but, the nearer they got to Gleawecastre, the more nervous Cenwalh became. When his scouts came back to report that the Mercians were drawn up ready for battle before Gleawecastre he became suspicious.

'How many are there?'

'We estimate that there are between three and four hundred, Cyning, and they all appear to be warriors, that is not members of the fyrd,' the chief scout replied.

The King of Wessex smiled broadly. He had brought seven hundred men with him, three hundred warriors and four hundred members of the fyrd which he'd collected on his way north. His warband appeared to equal Penda's in number but he had the fyrd in addition. He planned to use them to outflank the Mercians.

He advanced until he was three hundred yards from Penda's front rank and then deployed his men with a hundred and fifty of the fyrd on each flank and a hundred in reserve. Neither side had many archers but what few they had ran to the front and, advancing to within sixty yards of each other, they sent volley after volley into the air. None injured the waiting warriors but both sides lost quite a few archers.

Penda evidently tired of this war of attrition and recalled his men first. The bowmen from Wessex were only too glad to do likewise. Both sides then advanced towards each other. The Mercians were led by Penda in the centre, easily identified by the banner flying over his head. Had Cenwalh stopped to think, he might have wondered where Wulfhere was. He was about to find out.

Once Cenwalh's men were fully committed, his flanks started to engulf the Mercians. Unlike Penda, he was watching from a small hill a quarter of a mile from the battle, surrounded by twenty of his gesith. To his horror he saw nearly a thousand men erupt from the woods behind his reserve and attack them. He recognised the banner of Wulfhere in the front rank of the Mercian fyrd. He'd been tricked.

They tore into the small Wessex reserve and either killed them or put them to flight in what seemed like a few minutes. Then they advanced towards the rear of the main Wessex army. Although Cenwalh's rear ranks were made up of trained warriors, they were the least experienced and most of them were scarcely more than boys. Nevertheless they turned to defend themselves and did considerable damage to the Mercian fyrd before Wulfhere's men managed to completely surround them. The surviving four hundred or so men of Wessex were now hemmed in and outnumbered by over three to one. There could only be one outcome and Cenwalh's hereræswa took the sensible decision to surrender.

Cenwalh took one last look at the fiasco before turning his horse and heading east. He therefore missed the one execution that Penda had ordered. His faithful hereræswa was forced to kneel and moments later the King of Mercia took his head from his shoulders.

'Are we going back to Wintan-ceastre, Cyning?' the captain of his gesith panted as they galloped away.

'No, my warband is finished and there is no time to assemble the rest of the fyrd now. I must seek sanctuary somewhere whilst I seek allies to help me take back my kingdom.'

'Where will we go, then? Bernicia?'

The king shook his head.

'That would mean crossing Deira and I don't trust Oswine. He's just as likely to hand me over to appease Penda as he is to allow me safe passage. No, we'll head for East Anglia. At least King Anna is no friend of Penda.'

~~~

'You've heard what's happened in Wessex I take it?' Oswiu asked.

Aidan nodded his head sombrely. The two men were sitting outside the bishop's hut at Lindisfarne watching the sun's reflection on the sea as it sunk over the hills to the west.

'You always said that Cenwalh was a fool, now it seems that he has proved it.'

'Yes, the only surprise is that Anna has risked the wrath of Penda by offering Cenwalh sanctuary.'

'I assume that he's taking the long view; Penda will find that conquering Wessex is much easier than holding it.'

Aidan was referring to the fact that Penda had set about subduing Wessex with a view to adding it to his domain.

'Yes, disinheriting the eorls and banishing all the thegns has merely given Cenwalh the support he needs to re-conquer his kingdom.'

Penda had set about subduing his new subjects by replacing their Saxons lords with Mercian ones.

'Have you heard of the term *ealdorman*?' Oswiu went on to ask.

'No, I gather that it's one that the Angles and Jutes use in their homeland to signify the overlord of an area. Why?'

'Apparently he has made Wulhere Eorl of Wessex and the captain of his gesith Eorl of Hwicce, indicating that he intends to incorporate both into Greater Mercia. The previous eorls have been replaced by ealdormen who rank between the new eorls and the thegns.'

'I just hope that Cenwalh times his return sensibly.'

'What do you mean?'

'Well, he needs to leave it long enough so that resentment against the new alien lords has time to fester amongst the people, but not so long that they get used to them and accept the new regime.'

'I see. Presumably you would be prepared to help Cenwalh when the time comes?'

'Provided he has a sensible plan, yes. It would be easier if I ruled Deira as well. As it is, Penda is too strong. He can now call himself Bretwalda of England; only Bernicia, Lindsey, East Anglia and Kent stand against him.'

'What will you do?'

'Build my alliances in the north so that I don't have to worry about invasion from that quarter and intensify the training of my young men. The fyrd are a useful source of manpower in time of war but their value is limited because they lack both experience of warfare and aren't very proficient with the few weapons that they do have. I plan to start training them on one day per week, increase the number of archers, train the boys who are too young to fight to be slingers and set my blacksmiths to work making swords, arrow and spear heads and helmets. I also want to breed more horses to give my warband better mobility.'

'For that you'll need money and a source of iron.'

'The Romans mined iron ore in Rheged but the deposits near the surface are worked out; however, there is plenty more if we dig for it. For that I'll need slaves.'

'Where will you get them from?'

'I can't go north if I'm trying to keep the Picts and the Strathclyde Britons as allies, and the nearest place to the south of Rheged is Wales.'

'Gwynedd or Powys?'

'It's tempting to raid Powys as they were partly responsible for my brother's death, but Gwynedd is nearer, especially Ynys Môn.'

'Ynys Môn? To me slavery is abhorrent, but at least the inhabitants of that island are pagans, or so I'm told.'

'So that makes it alright?' Oswiu was amused.

'No, but it is better than raiding good Christian folk. Will you go yourself?'

'No, tempting though it is. I need to stay here in case Penda decides to attack again. I thought of putting Dunstan in charge. It'll be good experience for him and, although he's my horse marshal, he's commanded a birlinn before.'

'You'll need more than one birlinn if you want enough slaves to work a mine.'

Oswiu laughed. 'You worry about our souls and I'll worry about organising a raid.'

'Oh, sorry. I suppose I was getting a little carried away.'

'It's fine. After all I was consulting you, as I do so often these days.' He paused. 'How is Conomultus getting on as head novice?' Oswiu asked, to change the subject more than anything.

'Having a testing time, I fear. Wilfrid seems intent on upsetting everyone. I would have expelled him before this but he is devout and, as he's the son of the Eorl of Hexham, I didn't think it sensible to upset him.'

Oswiu grunted. 'He's like his father then. I've thought of replacing him as eorl before now, but I need the support of his family. They're influential in Deira as well as in Bernicia.'

'You do know that Oswine had expelled the priests I sent him and replaced them with men recommended by James the Deacon?'

'Yes, I had heard. I gather he's acknowledged the supremacy of the Pope in Rome in preference to the Celtic Church.'

'Yes, which reminds me. Sister Heiu and your cousin Hild have approached me about establishing a new monastery near Hartlepool.'

'For nuns only?'

'Yes. We seem to have more women wanting to be nuns than we do men seeking to become monks these days.'

'The way that some men treat their wives, that doesn't surprise me.'

'Talking of which I understand that you are to be congratulated. I hear Queen Eanflæd is expecting another child.'

'You are well informed; she only told me a week ago. It's early days yet but she is certain she's pregnant again.'

'Are you hoping for another son?'

'No, I'd rather like a daughter this time. Sons can be a problem I've found. Oswald never got on with his and Aldfrith and I seem to quarrel a lot.'

'He's what? Thirteen now?'

'In two months, yes. I suppose I should have sent him here to be educated but he seems to respect Utta and he's making a good job of teaching him to read, write and about the life of Christ.'

'I'm not surprised he does what Utta tells him. One smile from him with those sharpened teeth would make any child behave.'

Both men laughed.

'What about Elhfrith?'

'He'll be seven in the summer but I don't see as much of him as I'd like. I don't want to keep reminding Eanflæd that she wasn't my first wife so I keep him away from my hall.'

Aidan thought that Oswiu was making a mistake which could alienate his second son as well as the first, but he said nothing.

'Will you stay the night?'

'No thank you, I suppose I'd better be getting back to Bebbanburg before the light goes. At least it will soon be spring when the days start getting longer.'

The king collected Ceadda and Raoul, who had escorted him there, and they rode across the sands at a canter just as the tide was starting to rush in and cut the island off from the mainland.

~~~

Dunstan steered his birlinn towards the sandy beach on the northwest coast of Ynys Môn. It was five miles north of a large sandy bay and a sizeable settlement of fishermen and their families. He prayed that the inhabitants didn't keep a lookout at the north-east point of the island as they beached their three ships for the night before settling down to catch a few hours' sleep. He wanted to launch his attack on the settlement at dawn tomorrow whilst the Welsh were hopefully still asleep.

Three hours before dawn Dunstan led the warriors from his birlinn along the coast towards the settlement. He left the ship's boys, including Catinus and Aldfrith, to guard his ship whilst Lorcan prepared the other birlinn to sail southwards accompanied by a knarr.

Dunstan had been surprised how well Catinus and Aldfrith had got on, given their very different backgrounds and the two year difference in the ages. Catinus had started his warrior training and was the senior ship's boy whilst Aldfrith, at twelve, was the next oldest. Two other twelve-year olds made up the complement of boys. They, together with the steersmen and a few sailors looked after the ship, its sail and the rigging. The warriors provided the rowers.

Aldfrith watched them go with a wistful expression on his face.

'I wish I was going with them,' he said to Catinus.

'So do I. After all, I'm meant to be training as a warrior and I don't suppose there will be much risk in rounding up a few Welshmen.'

'I can't wait to start my own training.'

'Hey, you two. Stop gossiping like a couple of old women and get up onto those rocks and keep your eyes peeled,' the steersman yelled at them.

'Shall we take our weapons?'

'If you think you can do so without chopping off something important. Yes, of course take your weapons. You should know the drill by now, especially you Catinus.'

The two boys climbed up the rocks that surrounded the beach and took over from two warriors from the other birlinn who muttered 'about time' before re-joining their crew.

An hour later the second birlinn and the knarr were shoved back into the sea and set off quietly towards the south.

Just as dawn was breaking the two ships sailed in towards the settlement. At first they weren't spotted but, when a boy emerged from one of the huts to relieve his bladder, something made him look seawards.

'Saxons!' he yelled in Welsh. He let his homespun tunic drop back into place and stuck his head inside his hut.

'Father, Saxon ships entering the bay.'

'What? Are you sure?'

The boy nodded vehemently and the man swore before kicking the rest of his family awake.

'Get moving. The bloody Saxons are here. Grab anything of value and follow me.'

The Welsh couldn't differentiate between the various Germanic tribes who had conquered England and called them all Saxons. He picked up a spear and his son grabbed a small axe they used to chop firewood. By the time that they emerged the rest of the settlement was like a disturbed ants' nest. They fled, following the stream that led inland and the rest of the families followed them, the single men bringing up the rear intending to delay any pursuit as long as they could.

By now the crew of the birlinn were leaping into the shallows and wading ashore. The Welsh had a good start on them and were just beginning to think that they had escaped when over thirty armed men appeared from the undergrowth that lined both banks of the stream, blocking their escape. Some gave up, resigned to their fate, whilst others raced off to the side, only to find their escape barred by more warriors.

The boy with the hand axe gripped it firmly and ran at the centre of the line of warriors. Several of the braver men followed him.

'Don't kill them, knock them out,' Dunstan called to his men.

He waited until the boy tried to stave in his head with the axe, then batted it aside contemptuously with his shield before bringing the pommel of his sword down on the boy's head. Seeing his only son fall, his father gave a cry of rage and thrust his spear at Dunstan's throat. Oswiu's horse master was unprepared for the frenzied attack and only realised the threat when the spear point was inches from his throat. There wasn't time to bring up his shield and so he ducked. The spear glanced off the top of his helmet and he shoved his shield forward so that the boss collided with the man's rotund belly. The air whooshed out of his lungs and he collapsed winded. Dunstan brought the edge of his shield down on the man's forehead, knocking him out.

The rest of the Welshmen who had bravely attacked the raiders had been dealt with by the time that Dunstan looked around. Only one had been killed and that was after he'd managed to wound the youngest warrior in the arm. The lad was only fourteen and had acted instinctively after being wounded.

'I'm sorry, Dunstan. I didn't mean to kill him.'

'Don't worry, we're lucky that only one was slain. Go and get that arm bound up by your friends. It's only a flesh wound and you'll be getting plenty more of those.'

By now the other crew had joined them and they shepherded their hundred or so captives back to the settlement. Oswiu's instructions had been clear. He only wanted men and boys old enough to work in the mines. However, Dunstan's eyes had been drawn to a raven haired girl who looked as if she might be quite pretty under the grime covering her face. He had yet to marry and he decided to take the girl back as his slave, intending to make her his bed companion.

As soon as he singled her out for loading onto the knarr, several other single warriors asked if they could choose a girl as a slave too. He agreed but drew the line at the boy who'd been wounded. His choice looked to be barely eleven and, in any case, the lad needed to live in the warrior's hall for several more years before he'd be allowed a hut of his own.

The women wailed when all the men except the greybeards were pulled from their families and a few had to be cuffed before they'd let their menfolk go. Dunstan then separated out the boys and inspected them, choosing all those who he thought could be useful, if not as miners, then to lead the ponies and carts once they were laden with ore.

The women fought even harder to keep their sons by their side and a few had to be beaten unconscious before he'd finished his selection. Just as the slaves were being led towards the beached knarr, his other birlinn sailed around the headland and Dunstan was startled to see boys on the prow and up the mast waving frantically. Evidently something was wrong but he couldn't imagine what.

~~~

Aldfrith struggled to keep his eyes open after the second birlinn and the knarr had disappeared out to sea until Catinus poured half the contents of his water skin over his face.

'They'll whip you, if not worse, if you fall asleep when you're on guard duty,' he whispered to his friend as the other boy spluttered and cursed. 'Shut up for Heaven's sake. Haven't they taught you anything yet?'

'Sorry. It won't happen again.'

'It had better not. You fall asleep when it matters and men will die because of you.'

'I said I'm sorry, now belt up. You watch inland and I'll watch the sea.'

Catinus could see across the sea to the shadowy mountains of Gwynedd as the sun slowly illuminated the earth. At first he couldn't make out any detail as everything seemed to coloured in shades of grey but, as the sun cleared the tops of the mountains to the east, he thought he saw something moving far out from the shore. He nudged Aldfrith and pointed to where three small dark shapes sat on the lighter grey of the sea.

'Shit, they look like boats of some sort. If they are, then they've probably either come from the northern shore of Gwynedd or from the estuary of the Mersey. Either way, they're not friends. We'd better tell the rest,' Aldfrith said.

'You go. I'll stay here and keep an eye on them. If you want me to come down to the beach jump up and down.'

'Jump up and down? Oh, I see. Very funny. Quit trying to make me look like an idiot. I'll wave.'

Catinus sniggered. They were good friends but they were always trying to score points off one another. He watched Oswiu's bastard son keep low until he was below the skyline and then get up and run towards the beached birlinn before he looked back towards the three ships. The light was improving all the time now that the sun was well above the horizon. He shaded his eyes and studied the three shapes. He could see that they all had a large square sail and were heading on a north westerly course, then the sail was quickly furled and they started to row due west against the wind. He couldn't make the oars out but he could see the occasional splash as the blade entered or left the water. He could also see the white bow waves quite clearly now.

He tried to estimate the number of oars on each galley and had just come to the conclusion that two had ten oars a side and the other twelve when he noticed Aldfrith waving frantically. He climbed down the rocks and ran towards his friend, who was now helping the sailors and the other boys push the birlinn back into the water. He added his meagre weight to their efforts but the birlinn wouldn't budge.

'Did you manage to make out any more?' the steersman asked him as soon as they took a break.

'Three galleys of some sort, either birlinns or perhaps large currachs. I think two had twenty oars and the other twenty four.'

'Probably small birlinns or perhaps one or more pontus. How long before they get here?'

Catinus thought carefully. 'They are well over the horizon but we can't see them from here yet. So more than three miles away. From up there we could see perhaps ten miles to the horizon and they appeared to be over half that distance away, so perhaps six miles away, but they'll be nearer now.'

'So we have less than an hour before they arrive. Right, Catinus, you're our best swimmer. Although this beach is sandy, there are rocks here and there. I'm hoping that there are some further out behind our birlinn. Swim out and dive down and see if you can find one. Don't just stand there with your mouth open, strip off and go and find me the most substantial underwater rock you can.'

'And when I have?' asked the puzzled ship's boy.

'Come back for a rope and go and secure it to the rock. Maybe, with all our weight aft we can pull her off.'

Catinus had never swum until he arrived at Lindisfarne but one thing that all novices were taught was how to swim. He had taken to it like the proverbial duck to water and had learned to dive to harvest the oysters from the offshore beds. The sea off Ynys Môn was crystal clear and he found what he was looking for on his third dive. There was an outcrop of rock about a hundred yards out with a projection pointing away from the shore. It was ideal as an anchor point. Twenty minutes later the rope had been secured and he clambered back on board, dripping water and with chattering teeth in the cold offshore breeze. However, there was no time to dry himself and warm up.

The crew had put the rope around the mast and they pulled with all their might to try and pull the bows off the sand.

'Move further towards the stern,' the steersman told them after the first failed attempt.

They did so and then one of the younger boys spotted a sail on the horizon.

'Come on heave, put your backs into it lads.'

Just when they thought they'd fail and the steersman was considering abandoning the ship and fleeing down the coast on foot to warn Dunstan, Catinus felt the birlinn move slightly as an incoming wave lifted the bows before setting it back down again on the sand.

'Wait for the next incoming wave then pull for all you're worth.'

This time the ship moved a foot backwards and then, after the next wave had lifted the bows again, they were afloat.

'Quick, man a couple of oars and back paddle to get us clear.'

As four of them did so they heard a splash as Catinus dived overboard.

'Release the sail to push us further backwards,' the steersman yelled, grasping the steering oar to keep the ship going in the right direction and looking over the side for Catinus.

Suddenly the boy's head bobbed up with a knife between his teeth. He held up the severed rope in one hand and the man realised that he had gone to save the rope. Once they were far enough away from the beach he pushed the steering oar away from him and slowly it turned until it was heading south east. The sail, which had been pressed back against the mast, went slack and then filled with a sudden crack which shook the mast. Slowly it began to pick up speed. Then he remembered Catinus. He cursed and brought the birlinn head to wind.

'Quick, pull Catinus aboard.'

A few minutes later the shivering boy was back aboard spewing up seawater.

'I thought you'd forgotten me,' he spluttered.

'I left you there to teach you not to be so stupid in future. Believe it or not, you're slightly more valuable than a length of bloody rope,' the man told him whilst pushing the steering oar over again. For a minute nothing happened, then slowly the prow turned and the sail caught the wind.

Catinus rubbed himself dry with his tunic and then dressed in his damp clothing.

'Boy, you need to think before you act in future. Because of you we were delayed and those Mercians, or whoever they are, are only a mile away.'

Catinus looked and saw the three ships were heading to intercept them.

'Sorry,' he muttered almost inaudibly.

'So you should be. Now get up that mast and keep an eye out for our other ships.'

They were relying on wind power alone whilst the other three ships had rowers as well; consequently they were closing fast.

By the time they reached the bay in which Dunstan's birlinn and knarr were beached the three ships, whose sails Catinus could now see displayed the Mercian wyvern - a mythical winged two-legged dragon with a barbed tail - were barely half a mile away. As they came in sight of the settlement everyone on board started to wave frantically to grab the attention of the warriors on the beach.

~~~

It took Dunstan less than two seconds to realise what the sudden arrival of his birlinn meant.

'Ten of you stay here to get the rest of the slaves aboard. Kill anyone who tries to interfere or to run. The rest of you, come with me. Lorcan, get your birlinn back afloat. Quickly now. There must be Mercian or Welsh ships chasing my birlinn.'

Catinus' ship headed into the bay and ran towards the other birlinn, which had just backed off the beach and was now turning to row out of the bay. The two birlinns came alongside each other a few minutes later and Dunstan and his crew piled aboard their ship. By the time that the leading Mercian birlinn had rounded the headland both Bernician birlinns were being rowed towards it. Dunstan and Lorcan had decided not to use sails, although the wind was in their favour, as birlinns were more manoeuvrable when rowed.

The leading Mercian obviously didn't know what to do. By the time the other Mercian ships caught up with him, the two ships rowing towards him could have boarded him and, as they were larger and had many more warriors on board, they would have plenty of time to kill him and his crew. The leader decided to seek the protection of his other two ships and started to turn about.

He was too slow. By the time he was facing the other way and starting to get underway the other two birlinns were fast approaching. In his panic he forgot to order his rowers to bring their oars inboard in time and the two Bernician ships ran down both sides, sheering off the enemy's oars as they went. The inboard end of the oars were wrenched out of the rowers' hands and struck the back of the man in front with great force, smashing spines, breaking bones and crushing skulls. The

Mercian ship was left in their wake, drifting helplessly with most of the crew out of action.

Now the advantage lay with the Bernicians. They sped towards the other two Mercian craft and, although the rowers were beginning to tire from keeping up the relentless pace, the prospect of capturing the two Mercians fired them up.

This time the Mercian captains both shipped oars before the Bernician birlinns came alongside. Grappling irons snaked out from both of Dunstan's ships and they hooked onto the smaller birlinns. With the drag of the other ship the Bernician ships lost way rapidly but the effect on the Mercians was more dramatic. The sudden loss of forward momentum had caused some on board to lose their footing, causing chaos.

Before they'd recovered, the Bernician warriors were jumping aboard and a fierce but one-sided fight followed. The Mercians were outnumbered, dismayed by what had happened to the leading ship, and disorganised. For the loss of two men from Rheged, Dunstan's warriors had killed or incapacitated twenty two Mercians and captured the remaining twenty eight. They then returned to accept the surrender of the other Mercian birlinn.

Dunstan put the captives in chains with the slaves on the knarr and two days later he sailed into the Solway Firth and up to Caer Luel with a knarr full of slaves and three more birlinns than he had started out with.

CHAPTER SIX – RETURN TO ARDEWR

646 AD

Oswiu gazed down at his new daughter and smiled.

'What shall we call her?'

'I'd thought of Osthryth,' Eanflaed replied, smiling back at him.

'Strength of God? Yes, it's a good name. Osthryth it is.'

It had been a difficult birth and, although her women had assured him that she would quickly recover, given time to rest, he was worried about her. Since the raid on Ynys Môn and the capture of the three Mercian birlinns, things had been quiet. Too quiet. He'd tried to find out what Penda was up to but all he could find out was that the Mercians were having trouble holding onto Wessex. There had been a series of small uprisings which had been put down with brutal force, but that just seemed to make the West Saxons even more determined to throw off the Mercian yoke.

Oswiu had a strong feeling that, were Cenwalh to return to lead his people, he could regain his kingdom fairly easily. However, the King of Wessex seemed content to hide in East Anglia. Of more immediate concern was the situation in the north. Talorgan and Bishop Ròidh had been forced out of Dùn Dè by Talorc, the High King of the Picts. Talorgan had made the mistake of releasing the large warband he'd assembled to make Talorc recognise him as King of Prydenn; something that the former hadn't been slow to take advantage of, despite his treaty with Talorgan.

There were rumours that they had fled north into Cait in the far north where the High King's influence was minimal. Now Talorc was making raids into both Strathclyde and Dalriada.

'Talorc is either mad or he has an ego the size of the German Ocean,' Oswiu told his Witan two days later. 'We have agreements for mutual protection with King Guret of Strathclyde and Domangart of Dalriada, not to mention my nephew, Talorgan. Admittedly King Oswald and I had made the treaties more to keep the peace in the north so we could concentrate on our enemies in the south than with any expectation that we would become involved in a war, but I will not be foresworn.'

'What do you intent to do, Cyning?' Eorl Kenric asked.

'Go to their support.'

'How? As soon as you take your army north surely Penda will take advantage of the situation and invade Bernicia?' Iuwine, Eorl of Hexham and father of the obnoxious novice Wilfrid, asked, a trifle too smugly Oswiu thought.

'Not with his current preoccupation with Wessex,' Oswiu retorted rather more tersely than he had intended.

'Which will you tackle first? The restoration of Talorgan to the throne of Prydenn or attack Talorc's own kingdom of Hyddir?'

'Thank you, Ceadda. A good question. My own preference is to find Talorgan first and restore him to his kingdom. Then we can use his men to help us to besiege Talorc's stronghold at Stirling. However, I'm open to suggestions.'

'I think that's sensible, Oswiu. Perhaps we can use the time it takes to find Talorgan to ascertain the exact situation in Mercia and Wessex,' Kenric said.

'Yes, though I'm not sure we'll find out any more than we know already.'

'Perhaps Oswine knows more?' Iuwine put in, seemingly not at all put out by Oswiu's brusqueness earlier.

'If he does I'm sure he wouldn't tell me, Iuwine. Are you on friendly terms with him? Perhaps you could ask him?'

'What, no, not at all. It was just a thought.'

'Good. Then it just remains a matter of who to send to find Talorgan.'

'Perhaps you should send your nephew? He has the right status to speak with the King of Cait,' the irrepressible Iuwine suggested.

'Really? Œthelwald?'

'Yes, he is Talorgan's cousin after all.'

Oswiu was tempted to dismiss Iuwine's suggestion as stupid, but then he thought that the man might actually have had a good idea for once. Such a mission did require someone of status to lead it so it would have to be a member of the royal family or one of his eorls. Bran, King of Cait, was a pagan barbarian and he could afford to lose Œthelwald rather than one of his eorls, except perhaps Iuwine, if it all went wrong.

'Excellent idea, Iuwine. Thank you.' Then he had another thought. 'And I'd like you to go with him to guide and assist my nephew.'

'Me? No, I couldn't possibly....'

'No, I insist. You'll be invaluable to young Œthelwald.'

It would almost be worth failing to locate Talorgan if those two disappeared, he thought, but was then ashamed of wishing them ill, however aggravating they might be.

~~~

Talorgan and Ròidh were a long way from Cait so Œthelwald and Iuwine were destined to have a fruitless search. When they had fled with Ròidh's priests and Talorgan's gesith they had indeed headed north and told everyone they met that they were headed for Cait. However, once they reached the land over which Ròidh's father had once been king, they headed for the River Oich that connected the loch of that name and Loch Ness. Two weeks after evading Talorc's army as it closed on Dùn Dè, they reached the crannog on Loch Ness that was the home of the present king – Ròidh's younger brother, Fergus. Their arrival didn't start well.

As they approached the crannog they were met by Fergus' war host. Fifty men armed with spears and shields barred the path along the lochside. It was fortunate that they didn't have any archers as the warriors were obviously nervous. There were thirty men in Talorgan's gesith and ten of those did have bows. Each man quickly nocked an arrow to his bow string and began to draw it back.

'Wait!' Talorgan commanded before things got out of hand. 'Lower you bows and put your arrows away.'

He turned to the band of Picts.

'We come in peace. I'm Talorgan, King of Prydenn and this is Ròidh.'

'Ròidh?' the man who appeared to be their leader asked incredulously. 'I thought you long dead. Why have you returned? And why are you dressed like a priest?'

'It's good to see you too, Fergus,' Ròidh replied, a trifle ironically. 'I look like a priest because I'm the Bishop of Prydenn.'

'You haven't come back to claim the throne then?'

'No, I didn't want it when I left over twenty years ago and I don't want it now. I'm a churchman and my only desire is to serve God and my people.'

Fergus relaxed and smiled.

'Welcome home, brother. I was only eight when you left but I seem to remember that we were friends then and I hope we can be again.'

'That is my desire too, Fergus. Is Mother still alive?'

'Yes, very much so. You broke her heart when you left. I'm sure she'll be overjoyed to see you again. She's much changed, of course; she's an old woman now.'

'Are you a Christian, Fergus?'

'Of course. Though our bishop is now bedridden and likely to die soon. I've been meaning to send to Iona for a replacement.'

'Aren't any of your priests fit to succeed him?' he asked as, with Fergus on one side and Talorgan on the other, they started to walk along the track that ran beside the loch leading their horses.

'There are priests in Ardewr, of course, but only one has the ambition to be a bishop and I don't think he's the right person.'

'Well, I'm here now. Perhaps I can help until a proper replacement arrives, even consecrate a replacement.'

'Thank you. I'd be grateful. I still haven't got used to the idea of you being a bishop. But the fact remains that I don't think that there's anyone suitable to succeed Bishop Keiran amongst my priests.'

When they reached the crannog Ròidh noticed that not much had changed, except the size of the settlement that had grown up on the side of the loch. It covered twice the area it had over two decades ago, and the church was much larger than the one that Brother Finnian and he had built.

An old woman with grey hair stood with two guards at the end of the walkway that connected the crannog that stood on stilts in the loch and the shore. Ròidh still recognised Genofeva, despite the passing of twenty three years. For a moment he was tempted to rush to greet his mother, but then he remembered that she had betrayed his father with the king's younger brother. Ròidh's uncle had then killed his father, albeit in a fair fight, so that he could become king. He didn't believe that his mother had been party to his father's death, but the fact remained that she had been conducting an affair with his uncle behind his father's back and later she'd married him. In the past he had had difficulty in forgiving her betrayal, but he knew that it was his Christian duty to do so and eventually he'd managed to put it behind him.

'Mother,' Fergus called out, 'prepare a feast for our guests, Talorgan of Prydenn and his bishop.'

He turned to Ròidh and spoke to him quietly.

'She won't recognise you, her eyesight isn't what it was. If you don't wish to be known to her after what happened to father, I'll understand.'

'No, it's alright. It was long ago now and one thing I have learnt is how to absolve the sins of others. Did you find it easy to live under our uncle's rule?'

'Of course not, but I learned to hold my tongue and hide my true feelings. Mother never forgave him for killing father, you know. It was not a happy marriage. I know she took a potion to make sure she didn't have his children.'

'How did he die?'

'He took me fishing out on the loch when I was fourteen. Perhaps I didn't hide my true feelings as well as I thought as he tried to push me over the side. I was ready for him though and threw myself flat into the bottom of the boat. He was taken by surprise and stumbled over the side. In my panic to rescue him I accidently hit him over the head with an oar and he sunk below the waves, never to reappear. We never did find his body.'

'Accidently? Most fortuitous. And you've been king ever since?'

Fergus nodded as his mother joined them.

'Mother, this is King Talorgan. Talorgan, this is my mother, the Lady Genofeva.' But she wasn't paying him any attention.

'Ròidh? It is you isn't it? Oh Ròidh, you've come back after all this time.'

So much for her not recognising me, he thought. He smiled, realising for the first time that he had not only forgiven her, but he was glad to see her again.

'Yes, mother, it's me. I'm sorry it's been so long.'

She held his shoulders and looked into his eyes before pulling him into an embrace.

'Forgive me,' Genofeva whispered.

'I have. I only feel love for you.'

She started weeping and Ròidh took her arm as they walked along the walkway towards the king's hall on the crannog. Suddenly he looked down and realised that this was the spot where he'd been fishing the day that Brother Finnian and Aidan had arrived and changed his life. How long ago that seemed now.

Fergus stopped to give instructions for the gesith to be taken to the warriors' hall and Ròidh's priests to a guest hut near the church before he and Talorgan followed them.

The next day, nursing something of a hangover from the welcome feast that his mother and brother had laid on, Ròidh went into the church to visit the grave of Finnian, the Irish monk who had brought Christianity here. He had been murdered by a druid called Uisdean, who had been shackled and thrown into the depths of the loch in retribution. Finnian had been laid to rest beneath the altar of the old church. That had been replaced but the new altar was in the same place as the old one. As he got up from his knees he noticed that there was an engraved stone next to the altar and he saw that it was the resting place of the first bishop who had arrived from Iona just before he left. The present bishop, Kieran, was presumably his replacement.

Next he went to see Kieran. His hut next to the church was primitive with a floor of beaten earth, a central hearth, a bench and table, and a small bed. The bishop lay in the bed being fed some broth by a boy of about ten or eleven, who got up a bowed when Ròidh entered.

'Bishop Kieran, I'm Ròidh, Fergus' brother and Bishop of Prydenn,' he said with a smile.

The frail old man slowly turned his head and looked at him for a few moments before replying.

'I'm honoured to meet you at last, Bishop Ròidh. I have heard a lot about you and your missionary work with Aidan of Lindisfarne.'

He paused and lay his head back on the sack stuffed with heather that served as his pillow. The few words had obviously taken a lot out of him.

'Don't tire yourself out, bishop. I merely came to pay my respects.'

At that moment a priest entered. He hadn't been at the feast the previous evening but Ròidh knew that his name was Damhnaic and he had arrived with the bishop from Iona. It was too dark in the hut to see much but Ròidh sensed the animosity of the man without being able to see his face clearly. Instinctively he knew that Damhnaic hoped to become the next bishop here and saw him as a threat.

'Father Damhnaic, I'm Ròidh...,' he started to say before the priest interrupted him.

'I know who you are, bishop. I hope you have a pleasant stay with your brother, the king.'

The man might just have well have said 'make your visit a brief one.'

'Stay? I've come home, Damhnaic.'

He turned back to the frail old bishop.

'I hope you'll give me permission to celebrate mass in the church this coming Sunday.'

'Of course,' Bishop Kieran replied before coughing and bring up some blood, which the boy deftly wiped away with a cloth.

'You're tiring him out! Leave him to rest now,' the priest barked at him.

'You forget yourself, Father Damhnaic. I'll thank you to show me some respect.'

Ròidh was not normally a man to stand on his dignity, far from it, but this priest had made the hackles rise on his neck the moment he'd entered the hut. The man abruptly turned on his heel and stalked out of the hut without another word.

As Ròidh took his leave of Kieran and went to leave himself the boy came over to speak to him quietly.

'Watch your back around Damhnaic, bishop. He's a nasty piece of work and he's been bullying my master to ordain him as his replacement before he dies. However, the king doesn't like him and so a little while ago he sent to Iona for a replacement. Unfortunately the messenger was found murdered at the side of the loch five miles away. No-one has been caught but everyone suspects Damhnaic.

'The king was about to send another one, this time with an escort, but your arrival has driven it from his mind, I think. Damhnaic has become desperate to get himself ordained before the new messenger can leave. No doubt the purpose of his visit just now, was to try yet again to bully Bishop Kieran into consecrating him'

'Thank you. That's helpful to know. What's your name boy?'

'Morleo, bishop.'

'Look after him Morleo. I'll come back to visit him again tomorrow, if that won't tire him.'

'He knows he has only a short time left on this earth and he is eager to leave it for the next. I know he enjoyed seeing you, especially as it kept the wretched Damhnaic away.'

Ròidh made his way back to the king's hall on the crannog where he told Fergus and Talorgan what Morleo had told him.

'I'll put a sentry on the hut,' Fergus said. 'I wouldn't put it past Damhnaic to creep in and later claim that he'd been consecrated as the next bishop.'

'I think that Morleo would soon refute that.'

Ròidh was surprised that Fergus looked uncomfortable as soon as he mentioned Morleo, then he noticed that his mother was staring at him, her face a mask of fury.

'We don't mention his name,' Fergus said quietly.

Both Ròidh and Talorgan were intrigued but didn't pursue the matter. Ròidh decided to ask the boy why his name seemed to be anathema the next time he saw him.

~~~

'And you're certain that Talorgan isn't in Cait?' Oswiu asked Œthelwald.

'Completely sure. We didn't exactly get a friendly reception but they seemed genuinely surprised that we thought that Talorgan might have fled there. Of course, Cait is a large kingdom and he might not be at the king's hall, but other settlements are small, scattered and primitive, even by Pictish standards.'

Iuwine had returned to Hexham without even having had the courtesy of calling on his king to report on their mission. It was the final straw as far as Oswiu was concerned and he'd sent a messenger after him to order his immediate return to Bebbanburg.

'Well, if he's not in Cait, he wouldn't have fled to one of the southern Pictish kingdoms. So that leaves Pobla, Ardewr or Penntir. It wouldn't be Pobla as the king is a cousin of Talorc's and probably supported his invasion of Prydenn.'

He said no more, aware that he couldn't trust his nephew's discretion. He had, however, just remembered that Ròidh had originally come from Ardewr and he had a vague feeling that his father had been the king there at one time. He decided to send someone to find out. He thought of Œthelwald but then remembered that Aidan had spent some time in Ardewr as a youth. Cait was a pagan land whereas Ardewr was Christian. Perhaps a monk might make a suitable emissary.

Two days later he set off for Lindisfarne but when he got there he found that Aidan was away visiting Goddodin. He therefore told Dunstan he would need forty horses and Ceadda that he should inform his gesith to get ready to set off the next morning. Apart from the gesith he took Aldfrith and a few servants, including his body slave, Nerian. The boy was now nearly seventeen and, although Oswiu had offered to free him so that he could train to be a warrior, the boy had refused, much to his surprise, saying he'd prefer to continue to serve the king.

He'd found Aidan at Dùn Èideann and, after exchanging the usual pleasantries with his host, the eorl, and his wife, he took Aidan aside.

'I think that Talorgan and Ròidh may have taken refuge at the crannog on Loch Ness. Talorc is proving to be something of a nuisance and I need Talorgan to re-establish himself in Prydenn. If I can enlist the aid of Fergus of Ardewr we can do that and depose the King of Pobla as well. That will enable Talorgan to challenge Talorc for the leadership of the Picts.'

'It's not without its risks, Oswiu. Even if you succeed, I suspect that Talorc might still be supported by Uuynnid opposite us across the Firth of Forth and Penntir between Prydenn and Ardewr.'

'I know, but I can't allow Talorc to become too strong. He is a pagan and he's destabilising Strathclyde and Dalriada. I don't need enemies on both my northern as well as my southern border.'

'How can I help?'

'I need to remain in Bernicia in case Penda is planning anything. I'm looking for someone with sufficient status who I can trust implicitly to travel to Fergus' crannog to see if Talorgan is there and, if so, to see if we can forge an alliance against Talorc.'

'And I take it that man is me?'

'If you are willing, that would be ideal, but if not, can you suggest someone else?'

'I'll go, if you can furnish me with a ship to take me to the mouth of the River Ness; preferably one that can transport horses. I'm happy to walk from there but it would be quicker on horseback.'

'You'd go alone?'

'It wouldn't be the first time, but perhaps I should take a monk with me.'

He thought for a moment.

'Perhaps Conomultus. He's only recently taken his vows as a monk but he has a sensible head on his shoulders and, as a Briton, he comes from similar stock to the Picts.'

~~~

Ròidh was restless. He and Talorgan shared a guest hut with the latter's body slave. The fugitive king was snoring softly but it wasn't loud enough to mask someone moving stealthily near the door. At first he thought that the slave had got up to relieve himself but, as his eyes adjusted to the gloom, he saw someone kneeling beside the slave with what looked like a knife in his hand.

To his horror he saw the knife slash across the slave's throat before the shadow arose and headed across the small hut directly for him. Ròidh gripped the staff with the cross on top that he always carried and waited until the assassin was in range, then he swung the staff as hard as he could across his body and cracked it across the wrist holding the knife. He heard the radius bone crack and the person screamed in pain, the knife dropping from his hand to the earthen floor.

Talorgan awoke and grabbed his sword but, before he could get up, the would-be assassin fled through the door clutching his arm to his chest. Talorgan ran after him with Ròidh hard on his heels but the king tripped over the dead slave's body. By the time the two men had got out of the hut the assailant had disappeared. The next morning they weren't surprised to discover that Father Damhnaic was nowhere to be found.

Ròidh went to see the elderly bishop the next day and told him about the incident in the night. He added that Damhnaic seemed to have disappeared and of his suspicion that he might have been the assassin. Kieran seemed to listen but didn't respond.

'I think that his body is still here but his mind had left him,' Morleo said in a whisper. 'I don't think it'll be long now. If Damhnaic had succeeded in killing you it wouldn't have done him any good. My master is too far gone to have ordained him as his successor.'

'Did he really think he could have killed me and no-one would have suspected him?'

'His mind is warped and blinded by ambition. He probably didn't think about the consequences. He just saw you as an obstacle to be removed.'

Ròidh nodded in understanding.

What will you do when Bishop Kieran dies?'

The boy didn't reply; he just sat and wept.

'I love him like a father; no, more than a father. My own father made me a slave rather than acknowledge me. Kieran took me in and has looked after me ever since I was a baby. I don't want to live after he dies.'

'Who was your father, Morleo?'

The boy looked at him sharply.

'Has no-one told you?'

Ròidh shook his head.

'When I mentioned your name to the king he looked uncomfortable and my mother gave me a filthy look. Apparently mentioning you is forbidden.'

'That should tell you something, bishop. I think Fergus would recognise me as his son if he could, but his mother wanted me drowned out in the loch when I was born. Bishop Kieran stopped her and took me in, hiring a wet nurse to look after me until I was old enough. When I was six his old servant died and I took his place.'

Ròidh thought about what the boy had said and suddenly comprehension dawned.

'Fergus is your father?'

The boy nodded and looked down at the ground.

'Do you have something to do with the fact that he is still unmarried?'

'I suppose so.'

Just at that moment the old man stirred and tried to reach the beaker of water beside his bed. Morleo rushed over to him and gently helped him take a few mouthfuls before the dying man lay his head down again and went to sleep.

'Do you mind, bishop? I think the end is near and I'd like to be with him when he goes.'

'Of course, I'll leave you now. Come and find me when you're ready. I'll be fishing from the walkway to the crannog.'

The boy shook his head. 'I'm not allowed on it, or anywhere where the Lady Genofeva might catch sight of me.'

'Very well. I'll come back in a few hours' time.'

As he sat on the lochside with a borrowed rod and line he tried to piece together what he'd learned. Fergus was Morleo's father but he'd never married. Obviously the boy was the son of someone who his mother considered unsuitable, probably a slave girl. But plenty of men had children with a slave, why did she seem to hate him so?

He was still trying to puzzle out the mystery when there was a commotion at the far end of the settlement. He went and gave the rod back to the man who'd lent it to him, together with the two trout he'd managed to catch, and went to investigate. He was astounded to discover the identity of the new arrivals – one was a young monk of no more than fourteen or fifteen but the other was his old mentor and friend, Bishop Aidan.

'Aidan! What on earth….'

He got no further before the older bishop smiled broadly and spoke.

'I had a feeling I'd find you here, or at least King Oswiu and I did. I assume that King Talorgan is with you?'

'Bishop Aidan?'

At that moment Talorgan had arrived accompanied by Fergus and several of his gesith.

103

After the welcome and introductions Fergus was about to arrange for another feast when Ròidh felt a tug on his sleeve. Looking behind him he saw that it was Morleo. The boy was hiding behind him whilst trying to gain his attention. Ròidh knew that could only mean one thing.

The welcome feast for Aidan was consequently something of a muted affair with several men standing to pay tribute to the late Bishop Keiran. He was buried the next day with Aidan and Ròidh conducting the service jointly. The latter noticed that the one person who should have been there appeared to be absent; then he noticed Morleo watching from the shadows at the edge of the trees that surrounded the settlement. As soon as he was free, Ròidh took Aidan with him and went to Kieran's hut.

When they entered the boy jumped up like a startled rabbit and tried to hide the knife in his hand behind his back.

'Morleo, this is Bishop Aidan, my friend and mentor.'

The boy bowed towards Aidan but continued to look frightened and wary.

'I know that you are well aware that taking your own life is a mortal sin so I suggest you put all thoughts of it from your mind. You can put the knife down now. We are here to help you.'

'What can you do? The Lady Genofeva wants me dead and forgotten and Keiran can no longer protect me.'

'No, but we can.'

'But in a few days you'll be gone.'

'Possibly but, if so, I'll take you with me, if you're prepared to serve me that is,' Ròidh told him.

'You would?' The boy's whole demeanour changed and, for the first time, he started to think that he might have a future after all.

Aidan sat down on the solitary bench in the small hut and invited Ròidh and Morleo to join him.

'But first you'd better tell us why Genovefa hates you so much.'

'The king fathered me on a pretty slave girl he thought he was in love with. I think he would have married her if he could. However, his mother wanted him to marry her niece and she was brought here for him to marry. Just before she arrived my mother told King Fergus that she was pregnant. He refused to marry his cousin and I'm told that he and his mother had a blazing row and they ended up not speaking for ages. The girl was sent back and that caused another rift, this time between Lady Genofeva and her brother – the girl's father.

'Anyway, Lady Genofeva had my mother killed just after she'd given birth to me and told a fisherman to take me out into the centre of the

104

loch and throw me in. King Fergus was only nineteen at the time and was used to obeying his mother; however, he was determined that I should live and went to consult Bishop Kieran. The rest you know. He rebuked my mother and promised her she would end up in Hell if she harmed me, then he took me in.

'My father never forgave his mother for killing my mother and vowed not to marry or have other children. I think his plan was to acknowledge me after his mother died and make me his heir. However, over time they have become reconciled and he is now promised in marriage to one of the daughters of Maelgwr, King of Penntir.'

The two bishops exchanged a glance. If Ardewr was allied through marriage to Penntir would they be strong enough to stand up to Talorc? Of the seven Pictish kingdoms, Talorc's writ as high king didn't really extend to Cait in the north, although its king, Bran, had taken part in his election and sworn an oath of loyalty to him. In practice Cait was too remote and Bran only acknowledged the high king's rule when it suited him.

Talorc ruled his own Kingdom of Hyddir, which bordered on Strathclyde and Dalriada, in addition to being high king. Uuynnid in the south-east bordered Goddodin and its king walked a tightrope trying not to upset either Oswiu or Talorc. Prydenn and Pobla were now ruled by Talorc's cousins. If Talorgan could regain Prydenn, with the support of Fergus and Maelgwr of Penntir, he could challenge Talorc, possibly even without Oswiu's help. Ròidh dragged his thoughts back to the unhappy eleven-year-old boy.

'You're not to worry, Morleo. Your devotion to Bishop Keiran will not go unrewarded. Stay here for the moment and I'll ask King Fergus if I can move in here for the time being and take over as his bishop temporarily until a more permanent replacement is available.'

'What about Bishop Aidan?' Morleo asked, looking much happier.

'I'll be leaving in the morning with King Talorgan to go and meet King Oswiu.'

He turned to Ròidh.

'But first I think you, Talorgan and I need to talk to Fergus.'

CHAPTER SEVEN – THE LAND OF THE PICTS

647 AD

At fourteen Aldfrith was wrestling with a decision about the rest of his life. Ever since the birth of Ehlfrith he had known that his chances of succeeding his father as king were minimal. The appearance of Ecgfrith two years ago meant that the odds against him were now even worse, even though he was the eldest, provided his father lived long enough for his two half-brothers to grow to maturity.

As a bastard, he would need the patronage of his father to make anything of himself but, having started to take an interest in him when he was a few years younger, recently the king seemed to have little time for him. It was almost as if he'd become invisible.

When his mother, Fianna, had become ill the previous winter and had died, he sank into depression. She was the only person who really cared for him and now he felt as if he was alone in the world. Aldfrith had accompanied Aidan to the funeral and was grateful for his superior's comfort and support. It was more than he got from his father. Oswiu, who had once loved Fianna with a passion, didn't seem at all upset by her death. His mind was probably pre-occupied by the situation in the north, but that was no excuse.

'He's probably more concerned by the fact that he'll now have to find someone else to look after Elhfrith and Alflæd,' he commented bitterly to Aidan. Fianna had looked after the two children of Oswiu and Rhieinmelth ever since the latter's death.

Aidan rebuked him but secretly he thought that the novice probably had the right of it. The king's children by his former wife were now eight and five and Oswiu seemed to evince as little interest in them as he did in Aldfrith. All his love was lavished on Eanflaed and her children, Ecgfrith and Osthyrth.

The more he thought about it, the more determined Aldfrith became not to be beholden to his father, even if the king was minded to offer him a position suitable to his rank, which was far from certain. He therefore told Aidan that he wished to become a monk, but he wouldn't remain at Lindisfarne.

'Where do you want to go then? Are you not content here?'

'It is too near Bebbanburg and my father; I would prefer somewhere where he doesn't have to be reminded of me.'

'Are matters that bitter between you, then? I am aware that he probably pays you little attention, having other things to concern him, but I wasn't aware that your relationship had grown that acrimonious.'

'It hasn't, at least not yet. Perhaps I'd feel happier if it had. At least then I'd know that he was aware that I existed. I confess that I'm jealous of the love he lavishes on Queen Eanflaed's children and I need to distance myself so that I can overcome my sinful feelings towards them, and him.'

'Would it help if I had a word with Oswiu?'

'No, I don't want his affection just because he feels it's his duty. It wouldn't be genuine and I think that would be even worse than ignoring my existence. No, my mind is made up, father abbot; I'd like to go to Melrose, if my uncle, Abbot Offa, will have me.'

Aidan smiled. 'I'm sure he would welcome you, but don't expect to be treated any differently to the other young monks.'

'It would only make me unpopular if I were. Thank you father abbot.'

~~~

That had been in January. Oswiu had been surprised when he'd been told of his son's decision. He was well aware that he should have done more to strengthen the relationship between him and Aldfrith; he didn't want them to become estranged in the way that Oswald and Œthelwald had become, though he suspected that his brother and his nephew would never have become close, whatever Oswald did. They were too dissimilar and Œthelwald was too self-interested. Aldfrith was different; he had the makings of a good ruler and the king berated himself for not doing more to foster him.

He sighed; well, it was too late now. His thoughts turned to Elhfrith and Alflæd. He would speak to Eanflaed about bringing them into his hall to be brought up with their children. However, the moment to broach the matter never seemed to occur and, in the end, he left the two in their own hut to be looked after by slaves.

Four months later Oswiu went north to meet Aidan and Talorgan at Dùn Èideann. They had travelled down from the Moray Firth with Aidan on the birlinn that had taken him north. Oswiu knew that his friend was uncomfortable with politics and warfare and wasn't surprised when Aidan elected not to stay, but to return to Lindisfarne. Both Guret of Strathclyde and Domangart of Dalriada travelled overland to join Oswiu, having received the necessary safe-conducts, and arrived just after Aidan had left. After the usual pleasantries, Oswiu got down to business.

'As I said in my letter inviting you here, Talorc can cause us a great deal of trouble individually, but together we can defeat him.'

'Are you planning a major war to dethrone him then? It would be huge risk. Apart from his cousin, Garnait, who rules Pobla, another cousin, Drest, is now King of Prydenn.'

'Talorgan, where does Fergus of Ardewr stand?'

'Fergus is betrothed to the daughter of Maelgwr, the King of Penntir, a match arranged by his mother. However, he has yet to meet the girl and so the match isn't certain. If he goes ahead then an alliance between Penntir and Ardewr would be powerful enough to oppose Talorc' rule. Fergus certainly doesn't approve of the way the high king deposed me so that his cousin Drest could take the throne, especially as he feels that this places too much power in Talorc's hands. The high kingship is meant to be for one of the seven kings elected by the rest. With three of the kingdoms ruled by one family there is a danger that Talorc's family would become the rulers of all of Pictland in perpetuity.'

'So is Fergus willing to join us in opposing Talorc?' Guret asked.

'He is worried that, if he does, he would be vulnerable unless Maelgwr supports him. Penntir, Prydenn and Pobla all lie along his southern border.'

'Does he think that Maelgwr will join us?' Domangart wanted to know.

'He suspects not, unless he agrees to marry the girl. All we can hope for is that he will remain neutral for now.'

'You presumably have a plan, Oswiu?' Guret said.

'Yes, if Fergus will join us, then I would ask the two of you to invade Hyddir and besiege Talorc in Stirling. I will pressure Uuynnid to remain neutral by threatening to invade from Goddodin. With Penntir neutral as well, Fergus might be persuaded to raid Pobla to keep Garnait occupied, leaving Talorgan free to reclaim his throne back from Drest with a little help from me.'

'So it all depends on Penntir? What happens if Maelgwr doesn't agree to Fergus' request?'

'Let's wait and see what they decide first, shall we?'

'Co-ordinating attacks by four different kingdoms will be difficult. I see scope for disaster here.'

'What's your solution, Guret?' Oswiu asked.

'To elect you as our leader or, as you Anglo-Saxons term it, Bretwalda.'

~~~

Conomultus had learned a great deal from accompanying Aidan to Ardewr, in particular he discovered that he had a natural interest in the complex relationships between one kingdom and another. Of course, it wasn't his place to make any contribution to the various discussions, but he'd been present when Aidan, Talorgan and Ròidh had deliberated on the strategy for reclaiming the throne of Prydenn. Officially he'd been present to record the decisions made so that there could be no argument later about the agreement reached and the commitments made.

Aidan was impressed with the accuracy of the young monk's record and had asked him to perform the same function at the various meetings between the kings at Dùn Èideann. When someone was needed to act as the messenger between Oswiu as Bretwalda and Fergus, despite his youth, it was agreed that the young monk should act as the go-between.

In March of 647 AD Conomultus set out to sail back into the Moray Firth to see Fergus, taking with him a letter signed by Oswiu and the other kings. He was also tasked to ascertain, with Ròidh's help, the outcome of the negotiations with Maelgwr of Penntir. He was escorted by his brother, Catinus, now a warrior in the Bernician warband and Leofsige, a member of Oswiu's gesith.

The arrival of the three aroused some interest in the settlement beside Loch Ness as they made their way through it but nobody challenged them. Conomultus wanted a private word with Bishop Ròidh before he asked for an audience with King Fergus, so he made for the hut beside the church.

'As far as I know Fergus has managed to get an assurance from the Maelgwr that he will remain neutral but, like Aidan, I take little interest in these matters. As a servant of God my concern is for the safety and well-being of my flock, not the struggle for power.'

'But you were happy to attend the meeting where these matters were discussed with King Talogoran, King Fergus and Bishop Aidan,' Conomultus replied without thinking.

'You've a lot to learn, boy, if you want to be a negotiator. Impudence won't serve you well.'

'I apologise, bishop. You're quite right, it wasn't my place to ask such a question. It was merely that I was puzzled.'

Ròidh sighed. 'Yes, I suppose it must seem a trifle odd to you. Kings like to consult their bishops about important matters. They like to feel that what they are about to do has the blessing of God and his Son, Jesus. We can hardly refuse, but both Aidan and I are simple men and so we tread a careful path between not upsetting the men of power, on who we depend for assistance to promote Christianity to the people, and getting too involved in temporal matters.'

'I see. I feel even more foolish now.'

'Don't be. I see a great future ahead of you, but not as an abbot or a bishop. Oswiu's kingdom and the lands over which he is now bretwalda are likely to grow. He is a great man, greater than his brother Oswald I suspect, and he will need assistance to govern. Nobles can help to some extent, but he is going to need clerks to deal with the detail: keeping records, writing charters and the like. That is where I see your future.'

Conomultus blushed and glanced at Catinus, who was looking at his brother in a new light. Leofsige had remained outside to ensure that they weren't interrupted and so hadn't heard the conversation.

'Thank you, bishop, for your advice, as well as your kind words. You've certainly given me something to think about.'

'God bless your mission, Brother Conomultus. Don't be in too much of a hurry to make a name for yourself. You're still very young and you'll make mistakes until you gain experience.'

When Conomultus arrived at the start of the walkway leading to the king's hall on the crannog the two sentries denied him entrance until Leofsige stepped forward with his hand on his sword and told the older one that, if he didn't announce the arrival of the emissary of King Oswiu, Bretwalda of the North, immediately he'd throw him in the loch.

'Emissary? This boy? You are jesting,' he began to say when he was interrupted by Ròidh.

'Let them through, you oaf, Brother Conomultus is who he says he is.'

Grumbling under his breath the sentry stepped aside but stopped Catinus and Leofsige from following him.

'Not you. You're armed. The bishop said nothing about you two.'

Catinus looked behind him and saw Ròidh disappearing back towards the church. By the time he'd turned back Leofsige had used his shield to barge into the obstreperous sentry and the hapless man tottered backwards before falling off the walkway into the shallows at the side of the loch, dropping his spear in the process. The younger sentry stared open-mouthed and made no attempt to stop the two warriors from following Conomultus along the walkway.

Fergus looked surprised when the sentry guarding the entrance to his hall announced that there was an emissary from King Oswiu to see him. The man was still smirking at his fellow sentry's ducking. He was known for being officious and wasn't popular amongst the rest of Fergus' warband. He was even more surprised when a monk who looked to be about thirteen or fourteen walked in followed by a warrior who looked like a slightly older version of him. Behind him came another warrior, but this was a giant of a man with a lived scar across his face which gave him a permanent snarl. He vaguely remembered the monk as having accompanied Aidan six weeks previously. Conomultus bowed.

'Brenin, I bring greetings from King Oswiu, Bretwalda of the North and from Guret of Strathclyde and Domangart of Dalriada,' the monk began in a version of the Brythonic tongue that was very similar to that spoken by the Picts.

'Welcome, brother monk. You look and speak like us but I suspect you are not a Pict.'

'No, Brenin, I'm a Briton from Mercia originally. Now I'm a monk of Lindisfarne. This is my brother Catinus and a member of King Oswiu's gesith, Leofsige.'

'But you are the emissary?'

'Yes, Brenin.'

'Very well. I suggest we speak in English so that Leofsige can understand us.'

'Of course, Cyning. But perhaps we could speak in private?' Conomultus replied, switching to English.

The nobles and warriors in the hall and his mother looked upset but didn't say anything as Fergus led the monk into his bed chamber.

'Now what is it that's so secret?'

Conomultus handed Fergus the letter from Oswiu and waited until the king had finished reading it.

'You know the contents?'

'Yes, Cyning.'

'And you are authorised to do what?'

'Answer any questions you may have which I am competent to answer and to take back your reply.'

'Oswiu doesn't say when he plans to launch these co-ordinated attacks.'

'No. He thought it best not to in case the letter fell into the wrong hands. The first new moon in June.'

'And I'm expected to attack Pobla and ensure the neutrality of Penntir, the kingdom ruled by my betrothed's father?'

Conomultus looked a little uncomfortable. 'King Oswiu thought that might be possible, provided you still intend to marry her, of course. It might be difficult otherwise.'

Fergus looked at Conomultus sharply and the monk wondered whether he'd overstepped the mark again. Then the king started to laugh. Conomultus relaxed and began to grin.

'I like you, monk. Are you as clever as you are witty?'

The young monk shrugged, embarrassed.

'Modest too. Very well, yes, I'll raid into Pobla in June to keep Garnait too busy to come to the aid of Drest or Talorc.'

'Thank you, Cyning. Do you wish me to communicate your reply verbally or should I take back a letter?'

'Very clever. If you report back verbally I can always deny what I've promised, but a written reply commits me. I'll hand you my sealed letter in the morning.'

'That way I won't know what you've said. It would be helpful to know what's in it just in case I can spot any queries that the Bretwalda might have.'

Fergus laughed again.

'Very tactful. Alright, I'll show you the contents before I seal it.'

'Thank you, Cyning, I'm most grateful to you.'

When he told his mother after Conomultus had left, she was pleased.

'I assume that you will now agree to marry the girl?'

'No mother, not necessarily. It's you who has given your word, not me.'

'But I'll be foresworn if you don't.'

'You had no right to make a promise on my behalf without my agreement.'

She glared at him, then changed tack.

'You'll risk everything if you go ahead without the support Maelgwr of Penntir. You can only be certain of that if you ally yourself to him through marriage.'

'I only need his neutrality.'

'If you spurn his daughter he might well turn into an enemy. And suppose Oswiu and the others let you down?'

'Does Oswiu have a reputation for breaking his word?'

Not that I'm aware of, no but....'

'Are Guret and Domengart likely to let me and Oswiu down?'

'No, I suppose not, but you don't know them.'

'Mother, I came of age years ago. I'm grateful to you for your help when I was young and inexperienced but I'm perfectly capable of ruling without your support now. I'm told that there is a monastery for women where Oswiu's sister is the abbess not far from Lindisfarne. Perhaps it's time you thought about spending the rest of your days in prayer and service to God?'

She glared at her son, but said nothing further. Instead she went to find the warrior who Leofsige had humiliated.

What Fergus hadn't told her was that he had decided to go to Penntir himself to see Maelgwr and discuss the treaty. He could make his mind up about the girl at the same time. It was a pity that his annoyance with his mother prevented him from confiding in her; he might have saved a few lives.

~~~

The Pictish warrior who Leofsige had shoved into the loch rode his pony at a canter towards the isolated farmstead where his family lived. Damhnaic had taken refuge there after his failed assassination attempt and, now that his broken forearm had mended, he worked for his keep tending the family's small field of barley, milking their two cows and looking after their sheep. Half an hour later the warrior set out again, this time accompanied by his father, two of his brothers and Damhnaic.

Genofeva's instructions to him had been clear. He was to catch up with Conomultus, kill him and his escort and hide the bodies; then bring the letter the monk carried back to her. Conomultus, Catinus and Leofsige had a two hour start on their pursuers but they were in no particular hurry. They had all day to reach the birlinn that was waiting for them; and it couldn't set sail before the dawn in any case.

113

Only the warrior and his father rode. Damhnaic and the man's younger brothers had to run behind them. The fugitive priest was beginning to tire when, at long last, they saw Conomultus and the other two half a mile ahead and several hundred yards below them. At that point the steep hills that lined the loch were covered in trees. Damhnaic spotted an animal trail leading through the wood and the undergrowth and the five men followed it, slowly converging on their quarry.

The narrow track emerged from the trees onto a stretch of bare hillside. It had been hard work following the overgrown trail through the trees and they had fallen further behind the monk's party, who were just entering another patch of trees. As they were now hidden from those they sought, the five men made their way across the hillside above the loch as quickly as they could. After two miles they calculated that they should now be level with the other group and they again began to descend the hill at an angle.

Leofsige was leading the way as they walked their horses along the road that led to the north end of the loch and the start of the River Ness. He had been a warrior in Oswald's warband but he had broken his left wrist in training just before the fatal battle where Oswald was killed. He had joined Oswiu's warband and then, two years ago, he'd been selected to join his gesith – the king's personal bodyguard. He was now twenty eight and had been a warrior for a dozen years; years in which he had gained a great deal of experience. Despite the fact that they were in friendly territory he kept scanning the land ahead and to the left of him. Occasionally he would stop and listen for a minute before carrying on.

Behind him rode Conomultus who was getting impatient with Leofsige's caution. Catinus brought up the rear and, like Leofsige, he kept his eyes roving to his left and occasionally glanced behind him. However, he lacked the older warrior's skill and didn't spot the group of Picts charging towards then from above through gaps in the trees. Leofsige did, however.

He dismounted and signalled for the other two to do the same. Handing the reins of his horse to Conomultus he gestured for Catinus to follow him into the trees and to bring both his bow and the javelin that they carried on horseback instead of a spear.

Leofsige reached the edge of the trees when the two mounted men were a hundred yards away. The three on foot were a little distance behind them.

'You take the old man on the left and I'll take care of the one on the right,' he said quietly.

Catinus wasn't sure that the Picts meant them any harm and was about to protest when he recognised the man he was to take care of. It was the sentry from the walkway. If any further doubt remained, it was dispelled by the man's drawn sword and the venomous snarl on his face. He took careful aim and, when his target was thirty yards away, he let fly. The arrow was aimed too low to hit the man but it struck his mount squarely in the centre of its chest. It collapsed with a whinny of pain and its rider was catapulted over its head to land, badly winded, twenty yards away from Catinus.

Without a thought about the danger he might be in, he ran forward and cut the man's throat. When he looked up he saw that Leofsige had killed his man cleanly with an arrow in the centre of his chest. He was nocking another to his bow as Catinus whirled around only to see that the priest Damhnaic was about to crush his skull with a heavy cudgel. He cursed himself for not taking the time to put his helmet on when Leofsige's second arrow took the priest in the leg. He dropped the cudgel and went down on one knee, clutching at the wound.

Catinus dropped his bow and pulled out his seax, thrusting it into Damhnaic's neck, severing both his carotid arteries. He let go of the hilt of his seax and pulled his sword out of its scabbard ready for the next assailant. He needn't have bothered. The last two were heading back up the hillside as fast as their legs could carry them. Leofsige took careful aim but the distance was too great and his arrow fell short.

At that moment Conomultus burst out of the trees leading the other two horses. Men on foot struggling up a bare hillside are never likely to outrun riders on horseback on a hillside covered in grass and heather. They had only gone a quarter of a mile when they stopped, their chests heaving with the exertion and their mouths sucking in great lungfuls of air. They turned to face their former quarry holding their spears firmly, determined to sell their lives dearly.

Leofsige had learned long ago not to risk his life in pointless acts of heroism and, dismounting, he drew back his bowstring. When the two remaining brothers realised that they weren't even going to be given a chance to fight, they rushed at him yelling defiance. An arrow took care of one of them but the remaining Pict, scarcely more than a boy, thrust his spear at Leofsige. The warrior had pulled his shield around from where it hung on his back so he was never in any danger, but Catinus' javelin took the youth in the chest before he could complete the thrust.

Leofsige smiled.

'Not a bad throw from the back of a horse,' was his only comment.

An hour later they had thrown the bodies into the loch, including that of the dead pony, and they took the other one with them. None of the Picts had anything on them worth taking, except the warrior who Leofsige had pushed into the loch when they arrived. He had a pouch containing several scraps of silver.

'Payment from Genofeva no doubt,' commented Leofsige laconically.

He divided the silver between the three of them. At first Conomultus declined, until Catinus pointed out that he could give it to Bishop Aidan for the monastery at Lindisfarne.

~~~

Cuthbert was in something of a quandary. He was thirteen and enjoying life as at novice at Melrose. However, the life was predictable and mundane. During his first year he had learned to read and write, mainly in Latin but also in English. He had enjoyed studying the life of Jesus Christ and learning about the Celtic Church. Now he was putting that knowledge into practice, helping to copy documents whilst continuing his education. He was beginning to learn Greek whilst continuing to improve his Latin and English.

In a few months he'd be fourteen and it would be time to decide whether he wanted to take his vows as a monk or to leave to train as a warrior. He was drawn to the latter. A life of adventure and fighting had an attraction for a restless boy. The humdrum round of prayers, never having enough to eat, prayers, lessons, copying in the scriptorium, prayers, working on the monastery farm and more prayers failed to satisfy him.

He was a devout boy but he wanted more out of life. Therefore, when Abbot Offa sent for him to ask him what he wanted to do when he finished his noviciate, he didn't know what to say.

'I'm not sure, Father Abbot. I'd like to experience the exciting life of a warrior but I'm drawn to a life of quiet contemplation and prayer as well. Whatever I do, I want to serve God and His Son.'

'I can't advise you, Cuthbert. I've always wanted to be a monk and have spent much of my life as a hermit in prayer and meditation; I've never had a craving for adventure and excitement, though, from what others have told me, a warrior's life is one of boredom interspersed with short periods of intense terror.'

'That may well be the case, Father, but I think I need to experience that for myself.'

'I see. One thing I can say which might help you decide is that several warriors, even the odd king, has become a monk later in life. However, if you choose the path that Bishop Aidan and I follow, then you cannot then decide to become a warrior later. Learning to fight is a young man's game. Does that help?'

'Yes, Father Abbot. I hadn't thought of it that way before. In that case I think I should opt for the life of a warrior when I reach fourteen.'

'Good, I'm glad I've helped you reach a decision. Now, there is another matter I need to discuss with you. As you know the present senior novice takes his vows next week and the Master of Novices and I need to decide on who to appoint to succeed him. I know that you're the eldest, but there is a new novice arriving tomorrow.'

'A new novice? How does that affect your choice of the senior?'

Cuthbert would never have spoken so impolitely had he not suspected that his expectations were about to be dashed.

'Don't take that tone with me, boy!'

Offa never spoke sharply to anyone and Cuthbert was astute enough to realise that he'd only done so now because he was about to do something he wasn't happy about.

'This boy, Wilfrid, is slightly older than you,' he continued more calmly.

'If he's a new novice, he won't be experienced enough to guide the others.'

'He is experienced. He's coming from Lindisfarne.'

The look Offa gave him didn't encourage him to ask any more questions, but he was left wondering why a novice nearing the end of his training would be moved from the main monastery to a daughter house. For Bishop Aidan to get rid of him he must have either committed a heinous sin or be persona non grata with his fellow novices. Either way he couldn't imagine him being a good leader of the younger novices at Melrose.

'Will he be the senior, Father Abbott, rather than me, even though he doesn't know any of the others and, more importantly, they don't know him?'

'Pride is a sin, Cuthbert.'

'Forgive me, Father. I am not being proud. I'm thinking of the smooth running of the school.'

Offa sighed. He genuinely didn't know what to do for the best. The Master of Novices was little help. He saw Wilfrid as an intruder and wanted Cuthbert as the senior. It wasn't as simple as that though. Wilfrid was a devout novice, extremely so, and there was no doubt about him taking his vows in a few months' time. The problem was he was a prig who could never see anyone else's point of view. Aidan felt that taking charge of the novices might teach him how to manage his fellow human beings better. Offa didn't agree. He suspected that being given a little power was likely to make Wilfrid more intolerant, not less.

Offa was correct. As soon as Wilfrid arrived he started throwing his weight around, or at least trying to. The decision to make him senior novice hadn't been popular, even before he arrived. Cuthbert was respected and well-liked. As soon as Wilfrid entered the hut they all shared he ordered Cuthbert to move so that he could have the best space for himself. Cuthbert didn't like it but he did as he was bid until a few of the other boys picked his straw mattress and his few belongings up and, throwing Wilfrid's possessions into the centre of the hut, they put Cuthbert's back in his original space.

Unsurprisingly Wilfrid was furious and started yelling at them. Whereupon two of the other boys picked up the sack containing Wilfrid's spare clothes and his small chest and threw them out of the hut into the mud.

'If you can't behave yourself, you can find somewhere else to live. We don't want you here,' a small red-haired boy told him belligerently.

He was nearly as old as Cuthbert but he was a Briton and they tended to be smaller. This boy was short for his age, even by their standards.

Wilfrid made the mistake of thinking the boy was younger than he was; in fact he was only two months younger than Cuthbert. When Wilfrid tried to cuff the red-haired boy, he ducked and punched Wilfrid hard in the stomach. The air left his lungs with a whoosh and he doubled over in pain. Whilst he was incapacitated the other novices grabbed hold of him and threw him out to join his possessions in the mud.

Half-an-hour later they all stood with heads bowed in the presence of Offa.

'I will not allow brawling in my monastery. You should be ashamed of yourselves. I am particularly displeased that you all ganged up on poor Wilfrid. He is your senior and is entitled to your respect.'

'Excuse me Father Abbot, but Wilfrid brought this upon himself,' Cuthbert said, looking the abbot in the eye.

'I'm especially surprised at you, Cuthbert. You've disappointed me.'

'But Cuthbert didn't touch Wilfrid,' the red-haired boy blurted out. 'It was because of Wilfrid's high-handed manner in chucking Cuthbert out of his bed space that we all took against him. It was only when he tried to hit me that we threw him out. Cuthbert didn't play any part in that.'

'But he didn't stop you, did he?'

'He tried to, but we ignored him,' said another novice.

What Offa had feared had come to pass, just rather more quickly than he'd anticipated.

'Well, Wilfrid, is this true?'

'No, of course not. They just ganged up on me for no reason as soon as I walked in the door. They should all be whipped.'

Cuthbert picked up a beautifully illuminated copy of the Bible from the abbot's desk.

'Would you please place your hand on this Bible and swear before God that what you have just said is the truth,' the novice said in a commanding voice that no-one had heard him use before.

'I don't need to swear. My father is an eorl and my word is not to be doubted.'

'Very well. So is my father, but I hereby swear before God, Jesus Christ and all the angels that what you have just said is false.'

Offa took a deep breath. The room was deathly silent. Then the abbot spoke again.

'Well Wilfrid, Cuthbert, who I have known for nearly two years as an honest, trustworthy and honourable boy, has sworn on the Bible that you are a liar. Will you now take the oath that what you have told me is the truth?'

Wilfrid turned crimson and glared at the abbot and all his fellow novices in turn.

'You will all regret this,' he spat at them, before turning on his heel and stalking out of the room.

'Very well, so be it. Cuthbert, you'd better take over as senior novice. Tell Wilfrid to come and see me when he's calmed down. Don't worry he won't be staying here.'

The next day Wilfrid left carrying a letter for the abbot of a monastery in Frankia. It would be many years before he returned to England but, when he did, he soon made it clear that he'd hadn't forgotten his promise of retribution.

~~~

Talorgan and Oswiu watched the first part of the army disembark from the fleet of birlinns, pontos, currachs and knarrs that Oswiu had managed to borrow or hire to supplement his own ships. They had ferried several hundred men from the southern shores of the Firth of Forth to the beach on the north shore of the Firth of Tay. Once they had unloaded they would return for the second half of Oswiu's army. He was taking something of a gamble as, in addition to the warbands of Rheged, Goddodin and Bernicia, he had mustered the fyrd from the first two and that of the northern eorldoms of the latter. That would leave both Rheged and Bernicia vulnerable should Penda decide to move against him.

At that moment two of Talorgan's scouts returned and rode up to where the two kings sat on their horses.

'Brenin, there are no signs of anything out of the ordinary at Dùn Dè.'

'Did you see any signs of patrols?' Talorgan asked.

'Ten mounted men rode out of the fortress shortly after dawn today but they headed north. Two of our scouts are shadowing them but it looks as if they are heading for the border with Ardewr.'

Talorgan nodded his thanks and was about to dismiss the scouts when Oswiu suddenly asked them a question.

'The shipping in the harbour; did there seem to be less craft than usual?'

'Yes, Brenin. There was hardly any ships tied up alongside.'

'Thank you, go and get something to eat and some sleep.'

'Why did you ask him about the harbour?'

'Because I don't think Drest is still at Dùn Dè. I think he's taken his warband up the Firth of Forth into Hyddir to go to the aid of Talorc. You'll remember the reports two days ago that there was an unusual amount of traffic moving along the far coast of the firth. My guess is that Guret and Domengart have launched their attack against Hyddir early. It isn't good news for our allies but, if Drest has gone to their aid, it does mean that fewer warriors will be left to guard Dùn Dè and, hopefully, the fyrd that are left will have divided loyalties.'

'Well, I suppose we'll find out soon enough.'

Oswiu glanced at him sharply. He didn't sound very certain.

The next afternoon all of Oswiu's men had landed and they camped above the beach for one more night. His scouts had brought in several

Picts who lived nearby in case they went to warn the garrison at Dùn Dè, but it was far from certain that others hadn't evaded the net.

Shortly after dawn the army packed up the camp and the column of sixteen hundred men started to wind its way along the coast. The inhabitants of the first fishing village they came to started to flee, some by boat, some inland and some along the coast. The pontos and currachs of Oswiu's fleet rounded up the fishing boats and horsemen were waiting to intercept those who had fled on foot.

Talorgan rode up to the sixty or so men, women and children who huddled together, fearing for their lives.

'Don't be afraid. I'm King Talorgan come to reclaim my throne. All I ask of you is that you stay in your huts until you are told that it is safe to continue with your daily lives. If you do this no-one will be harmed. I'm leaving a few men behind to make sure you do this.'

'You don't need to do that, Brenin. We don't like Drest and we welcome your return. We will do as you ask.'

'Very well, but if one of you should disobey me then you will all pay for his or her disobedience. Your men will die and the women and children will be sold into slavery.'

'We understand Brenin. God speed you in your battle to re-take Dùn Dè.'

'Leave men to watch the village secretly. If anyone leaves kill them and round the rest up as captives. Kill anyone who resists,' Talorgan told the leader of his warband.

The man nodded and went to select a few men he could rely on to do what they were told.

By mid-morning the scouts and the vanguard had reached a vantage point overlooking Dùn Dè. The gates to the fortress stood open and carts laden with produce were entering the settlement for the weekly market. Then a knarr arrived from the east bringing wounded men who were unloaded and taken into the fortress on carts.

Oswiu thanked God that he had had the foresight to send his fleet to anchor in a deserted bay further up the coast. The knarr must have sailed along the Firth of Forth from near Stirling, northwards along the coast and thus into the Firth of Tay. Had he left his fleet near where his army was camped to the east of Dùn Dè, the knarr would have reported their presence.

'They must have come from the fighting around Stirling. I wish we knew how the siege is going.' Ceadda, the commander of Oswiu's gesith, said.

'Perhaps we should send a few scouts to find out?' Talorgan said to Oswiu.

'Perhaps, though our priority is to recover your kingdom. I'm sure that the combined armies of Strathclyde and Dalriada can cope for now. However, there must have been fifty or so casualties on that knarr. Drest's men have been badly mauled, which is good news for us.'

They watched the knarr load up supplies, obviously for Drest's army, and then cast off again before turning around and heading seawards again. As he watched it disappear Talorgan had an idea.

The following day another knarr appeared from the east and about sixty wounded warriors disembarked. This time, though, they were all able to walk. Some had head wounds, others had arms in slings or bandaged limbs. A few were only able to walk with the aid of crutches crudely fashioned from the branches of trees.

Like most Picts, few wore armour or a helmet, but they all still had a sword, seax or leant on a spear. As they approached the open gates into the fortress the custos appeared with two monks. The latter were infirmarians who rushed down to help the walking wounded. It wasn't until one of the monks recognised the leading warrior as a member of Talorgan's gesith that he came to the belated conclusion that these weren't members of Drest's warband. As he went to cry out a warning one of the pseudo walking wounded jabbed him in the stomach with the end of his crutch and then hit him over the head with it as the monk doubled over.

The assault hadn't been seen by the custos or the guards on the gates as he was hidden from sight by the straggling mass of supposedly injured men. The second monk was new to Dùn Dè and didn't recognise the Picts as members of the deposed king's gesith; however, he suddenly realised that the man he went to examine with a bandaged head wasn't a Pict as soon as he opened his mouth to reply to his questions. The dialect spoken by the men of Rheged, where the warrior hailed from, was somewhat different to that spoken by the Picts – though both were Brythonic languages.

He too was felled before he could shout out, but this time it was seen from the gate.

'It's a trick,' the custos yelled, running back inside the fortress. 'Shut the damned gates!'

One of the men with a bandage around his upper arm drew back the spear he'd been leaning on and threw it at the retreating custos. It was a long throw but the man had powerful arms. It was too far for him to hit the custos, but the spear struck the ground between his legs and tripped him up. He went sprawling in the middle of the gateway.

The two sentries were struggling to push the gates to. It was a task normally undertaken by three men to a gate. Others were running to help but one of the sentries made the mistake of abandoning his gate in order to help the custos to his feet.

'Never mind about me, you fool! Get back to the gate.'

The man ran back to it just as another member of the garrison arrived to help him. Two more were now pushing the other gate to and it slammed shut with a bang. Talorgan had been hiding in the midst of the attackers with a bandage around his head but he had run forward to lead his men as soon as their deception had been uncovered. Now he was desperately sprinting towards the gates. If they were barred against him his plan would fail and he'd be trapped between the fortress and the settlement. Oswiu was standing ready with his army to come to his aid but it would take him time to reach him. He had to get inside the fortress and capture it with the men he had with him.

Just as the second gate swung shut, he and several of his men reached it. They flung themselves against it and, before the defenders could lower the bar to lock it in place, they managed to force it open a few inches. Talorgan thrust his sword through the gap and was rewarded by a scream as it bit into the flesh of one of those trying to hold it closed. The pressure against the attackers eased slightly and now more men had arrived to help Talorgan and the first arrivals to push.

Slowly their combined weight inched the gate open but more defenders had now arrived to help close it again. Furthermore defenders had now appeared on the ramparts above them and were starting to loose arrows at them and throw down rocks.

'Come on, men. One last shove and we're in,' Talorgan urged them.

Just as the gate started to inch open again he heard the sound of men yelling as they ran up the road between the settlement and the fortress. He prayed that they were Oswiu's men and not Drest's warriors from the settlement.

CHAPTER EIGHT – OVERLORD OF THE NORTH

647 AD

He didn't have the time to worry about the approaching warriors though; the fight for the gate demanded all Talorgan's attention. He thrust his sword towards an opponent who was trying to drive his spear past Talorgan's large circular shield. The spear slid off the shield leaving the man's bearded face exposed. Suddenly he arched his back just as Talorgan's sword entered his mouth and penetrated his brain. As the dead man dropped to the ground another wild-eyed Pict took his place.

The exiled King of Prydenn realised that he was a boy no more than twelve years old – too young to be fighting grown men at any rate. However, compassion had no place in a desperate fight like this and Talorgan batted aside the youngster's feeble attempt to stick his spear into him and knocked him backwards with his shield. As the boy stumbled, nearly falling to the ground, Talorgan brought the bronze rim of his shield down on top the lad's head, knocking him out cold.

He realised that the few remaining members of the garrison had drawn back to regroup. When his battle rage had receded somewhat he suddenly recalled the men running up the path from the settlement to attack his rear and he turned in alarm. He needn't have worried. The new arrivals were his former subjects. They had endured heavy taxation and unfair judgements in the time he'd been gone and were only too glad to be rid of Drest's rule. They thrust their motley assortment of weapons in the air and yelled his name over and over again.

His gesith and his other warriors pushed their way into the fortress and quickly surrounded the sixteen survivors of Drest's garrison. Sensibly they surrendered and were tied up ready to be sold as slaves later. At that moment Oswiu arrived with his mounted gesith.

'I see that you managed without me,' he said, grinning down at his sweat and blood covered nephew.

'Just as well since you took your time.'

Oswiu laughed then the expression on his face changed to one of alarm and he pressed the point of his spear into the nape of the neck of the boy who Talorgan had knocked out.

'Careful, boy. Let go of the spear and get to your feet very slowly.'

The lad did so and stood looking at the ground.

'What's your name and why were you fighting alongside this scum?' Talorgan wanted to know.

'I'm Eógan, Brenin, my father forced me to fight alongside him.'

'Who's your father?'

Eógan pointed to dead warrior lying a few feet away.

'He was Drest's custos.'

Talorgan nodded as Oswiu dismounted.

'And do you support Drest?

The boy shook his head vehemently.

'My mother was ever loyal to you, Brenin, and scolded my father for turning traitor. He beat her for that and when I tried to intervene, he knocked me out. When I awoke my mother was dead. I never forgave him and he made me a kitchen boy to teach me a lesson. Then when we were attacked he sent a warrior to fetch me and told me that I was to protect his back. I didn't. I thrust my spear into him just before you struck him. When you knocked my spear aside, I wasn't trying to kill you. I was pulling it out of my murdering father's back.'

Talorgan nodded. His instinct was to send the boy to be sold with the other captives, but he hesitated. The lad's tale rang true; it wasn't the sort of story a twelve year old would make up.

'Very well. Do you have any other relatives?'

The boy shook his head sadly.

'Just a distant cousin but he's in Drest's warband now and I don't know where they've gone.'

'Why don't you hand him over to Bishop Ròidh when he arrives? I'm sure he could use another novice.'

Talorgan nodded but Ròidh never did arrive. Two days later most of the priests and monks who had fled with Ròidh reached Prydenn to take up their old positions, but the bishop wasn't with them. The senior priest told Talorgan that Ròidh sent his regrets but he had decided to stay with his mother and brother and become the Bishop of Ardewr. A few of his priests had elected to stay as well. Talorgan sighed. He had liked Ròidh and had got on well with him. Now he would have to write to Aidan and ask for a replacement. It was a problem he could have done without.

Two days later he bade Oswiu and his army farewell as they sailed away heading for the Firth of Forth and Stirling. Eógan stood by him holding his helmet. Far from being a novice, he was now Talorgan's new body servant.

~~~

The Kings of Dalriada and Strathclyde were both feeling frustrated and each had started to blame the other for their failure to make much progress with the siege of Talorc's fortress at Stirling. Guret and Domangart might be allies, but that didn't mean that they were friends, or even that they trusted one another. Both wanted the stronghold of Stirling for themselves. It would give whoever occupied it control over the valley of the River Forth to the west as well as over the four major routes through the mountains that surrounded it – to the south into Strathclyde, to the north west into Dalriada, to the north east into Cait and to the south east into Goddodin.

Talorc had taken refuge inside the fortress with his warband, leaving the rest of his kingdom of Hyddir to be ravaged by the invaders. Uuynidd had remained neutral and Pobla was busy dealing with raids from Ardewr, but Drest of Prydenn had come to his aid. A battle to the south-east of Stirling between some of the besiegers and the Picts had proved inconclusive but the Picts had withdrawn to the east as darkness descended. It was Drest's wounded from this battle which Oswiu and Talorgan had seen arrive back at Dùn Dè.

'We should deal with the Picts from Pryden before renewing the attack on Stirling,' Guret told Domangart the day after the battle.

'I don't agree. Our commitment to Oswiu was to besiege Talorc in Stirling.'

'But, if we do that, we leave ourselves vulnerable to attack by the Picts outside the fortress. If Talorc sallies forth whilst we are engaged with the Drest's men, we'll be trapped between two armies.'

'We've given Drest a bloody nose and together we outnumber him several times over. His men won't be in a hurry to fight us again if we strike now. Talorc will stay bottled up where he's safe.'

'You don't know that. It's too big a gamble to take.'

'Scared are we?' Domangart sneered at the younger man, whose hand went to his sword hilt as he began to lose his temper.

Just at that moment a sentry popped his head inside the tent.

'There's a messenger to see you, King Domangart.'

Both men relaxed as a young man entered the tent. He bowed to Guret before addressing his king.

'Brenin, my father has sent me to tell you that a large contingent of warriors is approaching from the north east.'

Domangart recognised the eldest son of one of his chieftains who he had sent to watch that approach.

'How many men and how far away are they?'

'Probably ten miles and my father's scouts thought that there were probably a thousand warriors. They appear to be half naked and many of them have either painted their faces blue or have white spiked hair.'

'Sounds like a warband of Picts from Cait,' muttered Guret. 'I don't like the sound of this.'

'We have over two thousand men between us. I thought that would be sufficient, but we'll be outnumbered if the Picts combine against us.'

'I wish I knew where Oswiu is and whether Talorgan has recaptured Dùn Dè.'

'Perhaps if we send a message to Drest to inform him that Talorgan has returned that might take him and his warband out of the equation,' Domengart suggested.

'But that risks Drest re-appearing suddenly in Prydenn just when Talorgan might be about to succeed.'

'I'm certain that he and Oswiu will be able to take care of him, and it means that we can then leave one of our armies here to contain Talorc whilst the other marches to block the approach of this relief force.'

'We don't know that's what it is yet,' Guret objected.

The messenger had stood quietly by the entrance during the conversation between the two kings.

'May I make a suggestion?' he asked diffidently.

'No!' Domengart barked just as Guret said 'go ahead, what's on your mind?'

The two glared at each other before the King of Dalriada shrugged.

'Go on then, let's hear it; but it better be good.'

'Send me as an emissary to find out if it is indeed King Bran of Cait and what he wants here. At best you'll have more information and at worst it will delay their arrival a little.'

'They'll have you for breakfast and return your head on a platter,' Domengart scoffed.

'It's a risk I'm prepared to take, Brenin.'

'You're a brave lad. What's your name?'

'Bridei, Brenin.'
'Well, good luck Bridei.'

~~~

Ricbert was the first to spot the approaching fleet. He was a ship's boy aboard the Sword of Jesus, Oswiu's birlinn, and he had drawn the short straw to act as lookout. He was sitting with one arm around the mast and his legs dangling from the yard from which the mainsail hung. He moved in response to the wild lurching of his perch as the ship ploughed its way through the choppy seas off the coast of Pobla. The motley collection of ships carrying the combined force of warriors from Bernicia, Goddodin and Rheged was about to turn into the Firth of Forth when he saw the other fleet sailing towards them.

'Ships ahead, lots of them,' he called down.

'How many, Ricbert, what sort and is there any emblem on their sails?'

'Over a dozen, I'd say, Cyning. Mainly large currachs with a couple of birlinns and three knarrs. No device; they're rowing against the wind. No, wait. The knarrs are under sail but they're tacking and I can't see the front of the sails yet. Right. Two of them don't have a device but the third has a black sail with some sort of symbol on it.'

'Does it look like a horizontal crescent with a stylised V superimposed on it?'

'Yes, that's it,' Ricbert cried excitedly.'

'That's Drest's symbol,' Oswiu muttered to himself, then he turned to his shipmaster.

'Dunstan, signal the other birlinns to form an attack line. Two birlinns are to stay in the rear of us to sweep up any of the enemy who get past the line.'

As Oswiu's warships moved into formation across the northern exit from the forth, Drest's fleet started to edge to the south to try and outflank them. It was a waste of time and effort as Oswiu's ships merely changed course to intercept them. Drest's best tactic would have been to split his fleet up. There was plenty of sea room and some of his ships would inevitably have escaped. As it was Oswiu's and another large warship headed for Drest's two smaller birlinns and the rest of his fleet prepared to ram the plethora of currachs.

The stout wooden prows of the birlinns crushed the light frame of the currachs over which waterproofed skins had been stretched and six of them were destroyed, leaving their crews floundering in the water. Three managed to escape but two of these received the same treatment as the other currachs from the birlinns following the main fleet. Only one managed to escape but one of the birlinns set off in pursuit, lowering its sail and unshipping its oars as it turned.

It was a heavier craft but it was powered by twenty four oars instead of the currach's eight; and its rowers were fresh. They soon began to gain on the other ship and their quarry quickly realised that they couldn't escape. Rather than be sunk, they ceased rowing and surrendered.

Meanwhile Ricbert had a bird's eye view as the Sword of Jesus crashed alongside one of the two Pictish birlinns. The enemy rowers managed to ship their oars before they were smashed but they were still sitting unarmed on their benches as the grappling irons snaked out and Oswiu's men lashed the two ships together.

He watched as Oswiu and his gesith jumped down into the smaller ship and started to fight their way towards the stern where the steersman, several warriors and a man dressed in a scarlet tunic, yellow trews and a blue cloak stood. The colourfully dressed man wore a sword but he made no attempt to draw it. As Oswiu's men slaughtered the Picts the man started to pace up and down yelling at his men. At first Ricbert thought it was words of encouragement, but then he realised, without understanding a word he said, that he was cursing the failure of his crew to defeat the attackers.

The boy tore his eyes away from the fight below him and glanced over at the other Pictish birlinn. It was now sandwiched between two Bernician warships and the outcome of that encounter was never in any doubt. He looked back just in time to see Oswiu and three of his men dispatching the last of the warriors guarding the brightly dressed man. As Oswiu advanced towards him, he pulled his sword from its scabbard but, instead of defending himself, he threw it down on the deck.

It was all over. Oswiu had destroyed Drest's fleet but the bulk of his warband had escaped on the three knarrs. Oswiu prayed that his nephew had managed to weed out those loyal to Drest and would be ready to defeat the warriors on the three knarrs. It might help that the popinjay he'd captured turned out to be Drest himself.

In the event the three knarrs didn't go anywhere near Prydenn. Many of Drest's warriors were mercenaries from Cait and the Orcades and that's where they returned.

~~~

129

Bridei waited three miles north-east of Stirling with six mounted warriors that his father had sent as an escort. He'd tried to convince his son not to go ahead with what he regarded as utter folly but the boy wouldn't be dissuaded. He was convinced that his son had as much chance of persuading Bran not to go to the aid of Talorc as he had of learning to fly. After all, several of the dead and badly wounded left behind after Drest's army had withdrawn had been Picts from Cait. Even if they were being paid by Drest, they wouldn't have been so stupid as to fight for another king if Bran hadn't given permission.

The first of the army from Cait appeared over a rise in a disorganised mass that filled the space between the trees and undergrowth that lined the muddy track. They stopped uncertainly when they spotted the seven stationary horsemen until a man mounted on a small pony rode forward from somewhere behind them accompanied by several other riders similarly mounted.

The men who rode towards Bridei wore a simple piece of cloth wrapped around their loins and thrown over one shoulder. A short sword in an elaborately decorated scabbard hung from a wide leather belt around the leader's waist and the steel helmet he wore on his head displayed four eagle feathers on the crest. Incongruously, compared to the simplicity of the woollen plaid, the calf length leather boots he wore on his feet were made of the finest leather and had been elaborately hand-tooled.

The dozen other men who rode behind him looked to be in two distinct groups. Five were dressed similarly to their leader but wore either two or three feathers on the crest of their helmets or, in two cases, stuck through the side of a leather cap. The other half dozen were either naked or wore a scrap of cloth around their waists. None wore a helmet but several wore a woollen cap. They were armed with a long dagger, a spear and a targe – a small round shield. Evidently they were the leader's gesith.

'What do you want, boy? Get out of my way before my men kill you and make your skull into my drinking cup,' the leader barked.

'Do I have the honour of addressing King Bran of Cait?' Bridei asked politely, seemingly unfazed by the man's threat.

'Perhaps. Who wants to know?'

'I come as the emissary of the Kings of Dalriada and Strathclyde and of King Talorgan of Prydenn.'

He had added Talorgan's name to make it seem to Bran as if he represented a fellow Pict.

'Don't you mean the lickspittle of Oswiu of Bernicia, who has the nerve to call himself Bretwalda of the North?'

'The title of bretwalda was awarded to him by the three kings I've mentioned and by Fergus of Ardewr and Maelgwn of Penntir.'

Again he was stretching the truth somewhat. Fergus had agreed to help by raiding Pobla and Maelgwn had remained neutral; it was some way from accepting Oswiu as Bretwalda and therefore their superior.

'The last I heard Drest was King of Prydenn and both Fergus and Maelgwn acknowledged Talorc as our high king.'

'Things change, Brenin.'

Bran no longer seemed so certain of himself. He had crossed into the south-western part of Ardewr in order to reach Talorc's Kingdom of Hyddir and to return he'd either have to traverse that part of Ardewr again or enter part of Dalriada. Both supported Talorgan. He began to feel a little vulnerable.

'Very well. We will camp here for now. Return to your masters and say that I want to meet my fellow Pictish kings here in order to resolve this business. Needless to say, Oswiu, Guret and Domengart, being invaders, are not invited.'

Bridei couldn't believe his luck. Despite the dire warnings of his father and the scepticism of Domengart, he'd succeeded in delaying Bran. Now all he needed was for Oswiu to arrive with his army. As it would take some time for the other Pictish kings to arrive, he was certain that by then Drest would have been ousted, not knowing that had already happened. Perhaps now there was a chance for a negotiated peace, and it was all thanks to him. Not bad for someone who was only seventeen.

~~~

Despite the protests of both Talorc and Bran, Oswiu was invited to attend the meeting of the seven Pictish kings, as were Guret and Domangart. As Oswiu pointed out, this wasn't just about who ruled what in the land of the Picts; it concerned the whole region.

The first bone of contention was over who should preside. Talorgan, Fergus, Guret, Maelgwn and Domengart supported Oswiu whilst the other four kings opted for Talorc. However, when Oswiu pointed out that Talorc was forsworn by failing to abide by his arrangement with Talorgan, all but the King of Pobla withdrew their support.

'To my mind the matter is simple,' Oswiu began, 'Talorgan's grandmother was the matriarch of the ruling house of Prydenn. With the death of her son, Edwin, the heir became Talorgan. So when she died Talorgan inherited. Talorc as high king didn't accept that and drove Talorgan out, placing himself on the throne. Many young Picts felt that this was dishonourable and joined Talorgan's army which invaded Prydenn. Talorc retreated and agreed a treaty with Talorgan whereby he took his rightful place as King of Prydenn. Talorc then broke the treaty and placed his cousin Drest on the throne. Talorgan has now recovered his kingdom and Drest is my prisoner. Is that a fair summary?'

'No, it is my prerogative as high king to resolve disputes between rival claimants to one of the seven kingdoms,' Talorc stated as if that was an end to the matter.

'That may be true, but there was no dispute and no rival claimants,' Oswiu countered. 'You acted to put one of your family with no connection to Prydenn on the throne there. It was merely a ploy to strengthen your domination of all the Picts. No doubt in time you plan to unite all the Picts under your rule.'

'That's a lie!' Talorc blustered. 'Talorgan seized Prydenn by force. I was defending its inhabitants by exiling him and putting a fair and just ruler in his place.'

'If Drest was so fair and just why did he need mercenaries in his warband to control his subjects? Why did the fyrd rise up to support Talorgan and help him take the fortress at Dùn Dè? Why have his loyal people petitioned me to hand Drest over to them so that they can execute him? Is this how subjects normally regard a fair and just ruler?'

Talorc seemed lost for words and merely glared at Oswiu.

'Is this true?' Bran asked.

Taking Talorc's continued silence as acquiescence, Bran then formally withdrew his support for Talorc as high king. That was enough for Oswiu to table a motion depriving Talorc of the high kingship. Only one Pictish king objected, but as he was Talorc's cousin that was only to be expected.

Bran then proposed Talorgan as the new high king, but insisted that Talorc be allowed to remain as King of Hyddir.

'I agree, but on one condition.' Fergus said. 'Oswiu should be given possession of Stirling. It cannot remain in Talorc's control, otherwise he'll use it as a base to cause discontent in the kingdoms around it.'

'But that's my capital; it's been in the ownership of my family for generations,' Talorc bellowed in outrage.

'Just be thankful that you've been left in possession of anything,' Oswiu told him quietly.

'What about Drest?' Talorc asked after a pause.

'When you vacate Stirling and hand it over to Talorgan so that he can hold it on my behalf, I'll release Drest into your custody; but first you must swear to live peaceably with your neighbours.'

Grumbling, Talorc so swore but Oswiu didn't set much store by his word. He'd broken it in the past and the Bretwalda of the North had no doubt that he'd do it again.

CHAPTER NINE – WAR CLOUDS GATHER
648/9 AD

'Bretwalda of the North?' Penda said incredulously.

'So I understand,' his son Wulfhere replied.

'How did you hear this?'

'From a master of a merchantmen who'd arrived at Legacæstir from Caer Luel. He said that Talorc has been deposed as High King of the Picts and Oswiu's nephew, Talorgan, now rules in his place. Oswiu is now Bretwalda of the Picts, Strathclyde and Dalriada in addition to his own kingdom.'

'I wager it won't be long before he challenges Oswine for the throne of Deira as well. He already appears to have Lindsey in his pocket. We need to curb his power before he gets strong enough to challenge me for leadership of the south.'

'What will you do? The damned insurrection throughout Wessex ties us up down here. You can hardly set off to confront Oswiu at the moment.'

'No, I'm going to have to reach a compromise with Cenwalh. I'm fairly certain that he'll be prepared to accept me as his overlord if it means he can return as King of Wessex. If not; well, I'm sure I don't have to spell it out to you.'

Wulfhere thought that killing Cenwalh was the better option in any case. The man had no sons, no brothers left alive and only distant cousins to succeed him. With Cenwalh dead Wessex would be divided into factions and would no longer pose any sort of threat to Mercian supremacy. However, Penda was averse to having an anarchic realm on his borders; he preferred one he could control.

Penda gave more thought to the problem over the next few weeks and eventually he decided to send his eldest son, Peada, to negotiate with Cenwalh. Peada started by negotiating a safe conduct so that he could travel into Suffolk to meet both Anna of East Anglia and Cenwalh. Even with Anna's permission he still took a warband of one hundred warriors with him in addition to his personal gesith. Understandably Anna was wary of such a show of strength and mustered his own warband as a precaution. It was not an auspicious start.

~~~

Oswiu travelled back to Bebbanburg by sea but, keen as he was to return to the arms of Eanflæd, he decided to stop at Lindisfarne en route. Aidan displayed his usual pleasure at seeing his old friend but Oswiu could tell that there was something wrong.

Aidan was now in his mid-forties but he moved with the agility of someone ten or more years older. The privations he had undergone whilst travelling and preaching, coupled with his austere life style which resulted in him not eating enough to keep his body healthy, were taking their toll. Oswiu in contrast was the picture of rude health at thirty six.

'You look as if you've got the weight of the world on your shoulders.'

'Not the world, just Prydenn,' Aidan replied.

'Why?' Oswiu asked, somewhat alarmed as he thought that he had left the north subdued and under the control of his nephew.

'Ròidh has decided that he wants to remain as Bishop of Ardewr now that he's been reunited with his brother. I suppose I should have expected it but I now need to find a replacement for Prydenn, and also more priests as some of those who accompanied Ròidh into exile want to stay with him. Consequently, I need to find more priests for Prydenn in addition to the bishop.'

'Surely Ròidh doesn't need them in addition to those who were there before?'

'You might think so, but he's unimpressed with their quality and their debauched lifestyle, as he puts it. By that he means that most have married and even had children. He's defrocked them.'

'I see.'

Oswiu did his best to hide a smile. It was not unusual for Celtic monks and priests to marry - celibacy was a Roman rule – but dedicated churchmen like Aidan and Ròidh deplored the practice. Oswiu was as devout a Christian as the next man, but he couldn't understand how a real man could forgo the pleasures of the flesh.

'Furthermore, he's decided that the heathen Picts of Cait need to be converted.'

'Does he have any idea how big Cait is? From what I've been told, it's the biggest of the Pictish kingdoms by some margin.

'Yes, you're right. I've tried to explain that to him, using Conomultus as an intermediary, but now the wretched boy has asked to remain with Ròidh to help with his mission.'

'Have you anyone in mind as the new bishop?' Oswiu asked after a pause.

'Yes, but you won't like it.'

'Go on, tell me,' Oswiu said with a sigh.

'Utta.'

'Utta? Do you really have no better source of abbots and bishops than my chaplains? First Offa and now Utta. No, you'll have to find someone else.'

'Can you think of anyone better to keep the Picts in line? He'll be ideal.'

'Very well. Who do you intend to inflict on me as my new chaplain?' he asked after a pause.

'Conomultus, if only to stop him being killed by the barbarians who live in the wild highlands of Cait.'

'Isn't he a bit young?'

'In years maybe, but he is wise and has some experience after his time in Ardewr.'

'Very well; however, I don't suppose he'll be delighted to exchange the adventurous life of a missionary in Cait for the somewhat more tranquil existence as my chaplain.'

'Tranquil? Life with you is never tranquil, Oswiu. Besides the boy worships you. You're his hero in many ways.'

'Really? I'm not sure I want to be the object of my chaplain's veneration. I'd hate to shatter any illusions he has about me.'

He grinned at Aidan but the bishop gave him a sour look.

'At least you know what your faults are, Oswiu, and you do try and repent; not always successfully.'

'They are calling my brother a saint, you know.'

'Oswald was as fallible as the rest of us,' Aidan replied, 'but he's been blessed by Christ. Many miracles are attributed to his name.'

'Yes, I know. Pilgrims are starting to travel to Bebbanburg to worship the casket containing the arm I recovered from the apple tree near Maserfield. They say it has healing properties.'

'Not only that, they've renamed the settlement near there Oswald's Tree in his honour. I hear that Penda is furious about it.'

'I can imagine. Well, I can't conceive that anyone would regard me as a saint when I'm dead.'

Aidan chuckled. 'Nor me.'

At that moment one of the novices brought in a platter of stale bread and a pitcher of water and set it down on a side table. The boy bowed to Oswiu and left.

'I suspect you had something else on your mind when you called here instead of rushing back to your family.'

Oswiu grinned again.

'You know me too well. As you know, Eanflæd was baptised by Bishop Paulinus and brought up as a Christian, but one who follows the Roman Church. Therefore we keep having ecclesiastical arguments. The one before I sailed north was about the date of Easter. She insists that it should be observed on the first Sunday after the first full moon following the vernal equinox. I don't need to tell you that we set the date to coincide with that of the Jewish Feast of Passover, which is on the actual day of the full moon following the equinox. We therefore end up celebrating Easter twice.'

'In 325 BC the Council of Nicaea was convened by the Roman Emperor Constantine to regularise Christian worship throughout the Empire. Amongst many other things, it established that Easter should be held on the Sunday following the full moon. Unfortunately, the Irish Church decided to stick with the original link to the Passover.'

'What do you think?'

'I follow the teachings of the mother house on Iona. Whilst I live I shall do my best to observe our traditions.'

'I see.' Oswiu sighed. 'Then it seems that my wife and I will continue to celebrate Easter on different days. It's very confusing for the children though and a pain for everyone else.'

Aidan shrugged.

'Why don't you celebrate Easter officially on the correct date and then allow your wife to hold her services on the other date as well, but insist that your children and everyone else does as you do?'

'It's easy to see that you've never been married, Aidan.'

'I've found that the easiest route to conversion for a community is through its womenfolk, but I've never pretended to understand them.'

~~~

Cenwalh waited with King Anna and the latter's warband hidden in one of the few woods that dotted the bleak, flat landscape at the edge of the Fens. If there was trouble they would fade away along the secret paths that ran through the vast area of bog interspersed with open water that surrounded the settlement at Ely where Anna had based himself for this meeting. The King of the East Angles had chosen the meeting place with care. It wasn't an area that belonged to him, or to the Middle Angles. It was a wasteland whose inhabitants were fiercely independent. However, they were quite happy to take payment for their co-operation and to provide guides.

Anna would only allow Peada and his gesith into Ely for the talks, therefore it didn't really matter how many warriors he brought along as escort. Once in Ely Peada would be cut off and Cenwalh hoped to intimidate him into agreeing to his terms. He was well aware that Penda wouldn't recognise the treaty if it wasn't exactly what he wanted, but then he'd be foresworn and his reputation would suffer.

His failure to put down the insurrection in Wessex had already done considerable damage to his standing and, coupled with the growing prestige of Oswiu as Bretwalda of the North, repudiation of his son's agreement would further undermine Penda's efforts to make himself overlord of the south.

Finally, a day late, Peada appeared leading a number of horsemen. It was a day of torrential rain, which rather spoilt his grand entrance. The drenched riders were followed by a horde of muddy warriors on foot and a baggage train that stretched back a long way. Carts kept getting stuck in the morass that had been a road and so it was spread out for over a mile.

Cenwalh did a rough count and estimated the mounted contingent at around thirty men – presumably the gesith of the King of the Middle Anglians – and the footmen seemed to total just over a hundred, though it was difficult to count them as the squally conditions hid some of them from view at times.

What neither Anna nor Cenwalh had anticipated was Peada's refusal to go to Ely for the meeting. Anna's gesith and warband came to eighty – far less than Paeda had brought - and Cenwalh didn't have more than a handful of followers. Both men began to feel extremely vulnerable, not without reason. Penda's instructions to his son were quite clear: he was to get the man to agree to become Penda's vassal or he was to be killed.

When Peada arose the next morning sunshine had replaced the rain but the East Anglians had disappeared into the Fens. He sent some scouts to follow their tracks but, after three had sunk into a bog and disappeared, he gave that idea up. He was now in something of a quandary. He daren't go back to Penda and tell him he'd failed to solve the Wessex problem, but he didn't know how to proceed.

'We can't just sit here,' one of his eorls told him. 'Every time we send out a forage party it gets ambushed by the Fens people and we can't follow them and kill them because they disappear into the marshes. Our warriors are getting demoralised and some of my men have already deserted. I don't suppose that they will be the only ones to slip away.'

'Yes, I'm well aware of the situation,' Peada replied testily. 'You know damned well what my father's reaction would be if I slunk away now without securing peace in Wessex. He's desperate to attack Oswiu before he gets too powerful and to do that he needs quiescent neighbours in the south.'

He regretted baring his soul like that as soon as he'd finished speaking. It was a symptom of how frustrated he felt.

'Well, then. It looks as if you'll have to go to Ely and negotiate, doesn't it?'

It was the reluctant conclusion that Peada had come to himself but it didn't help to hear it from the lips of one of his nobles.

The next day he rode forward with his gesith and waited where Anna and Cenwalh had been encamped. An hour later an elderly guide and three surly looking locals armed with spears appeared and the guide spoke to him in a language he didn't understand.

'He's asking you to dismount and follow him on foot, Cyning,' one of his gesith who spoke Brythonic helpfully explained.

Grumbling under his breath Peada did as he was bid and his gesith also dismounted. However the three spearmen barred the path after Peada had passed them. His men were incensed by this and would have slain the spearmen had Peada not told them to stop. Eventually he managed to negotiate with his guide, via the interpreter, and five other men were allowed to accompany the fuming Peada.

He arrived on the island of Ely that arose out of the surrounding fens like an inverted bowl. The headman of the settlement greeted him and he was shown to a primitive circular hut, bare apart from a fire in the central hearth and beds of cut reeds around the wall. Young boys brought bowls of water for him and his men to wash most of the mud and slime off themselves and then brought them a simple meal of eel stew. It wasn't until he lay down to sleep that Peada realised that he was now effectively the prisoner of King Anna and these strange fishermen.

'My father is prepared to allow you to resume the rule of Wessex provided that you swear to accept him as your overlord,' Peada told Cenwalh the next morning.

He'd decided to skip the usual formalities and preamble and get straight down to the crux of the matter. He couldn't wait to get out of this place and didn't want to spend another uncomfortable night there if he could help it.

'In other words he wants me to be his sub-king.'

'I suppose so, yes.'

'My great great great grandfather, Cerdic, conquered what is now Wessex and it has been an independent kingdom ever since. I would rather die than betray my heritage.'

'Perhaps that can be arranged,' the captain of Peada's gesith muttered in his ear, causing the king to smile mirthlessly.

'It is only a way of ensuring that Mercia and Wessex become, and remain, friends from now on.'

'Perhaps your father would like to become my vassal then? It would achieve the same purpose.'

Peada gave him a pained look.

'I think we both know who holds the whip hand here.'

'I'm not so sure. Penda has failed to subdue Wessex and, from what I hear, the revolt against his rule and the cruel taxation of my people is growing.'

'That's true and Penda's patience is exhausted. So far he has treated the Saxons of Wessex leniently, but no more. The next vill that refuses to pay its taxes will be burnt to the ground and its people executed. That'll continue until the wretched Saxons learn their lesson.'

Cenwalh's face paled and Anna gasped in disbelief.

'He wouldn't dare. His name would be anathema throughout England. He would be regarded as a barbarian,' Anna almost yelled.

'But he is a pagan barbarian, or had you forgotten. He isn't bound by your Christian mores and morals and doesn't need to confess his sins to a priest. He will do what is necessary to achieve his ends.'

In fact Peada was bluffing. He knew full well that a scorched earth policy in Wessex might well subdue the West Saxons, but it would also alienate his father's present allies. The threat had had its desired effect on Cenwalh, however.

'Very well. I'll do as you ask, up to a point. I'll become Penda's ally and repudiate my alliance with Oswiu, but I won't become his vassal, his sub-king. If I did I doubt I'd be accepted back as King of Wessex. My people would say I'd betrayed them, and they'd be right.'

Peada nodded slowly. It might just be enough to appease his father.

'I'll take you proposal back to Penda. I suggest we meet again at the edge of the Fens the day after the next full moon. This time I'll only bring my gesith, if I have Anna's safe conduct, and you are to bring no more than thirty. I'll trust you not to have more men hiding in those damned marshes.'

Anna nodded and Cenwalh assured him that he would bring no more than thirty men. He would have to borrow some of the East Anglians even then; only nine of his own gesith had survived to flee into exile with him.

~~~

'You've heard I suppose?'

Oswiu was sitting in his chamber off the king's hall at Bebbanburg with Eanflæd. In front of his chair three year-old Ecgfrith played with a pair of carved models of warriors armed with sword and shield whilst his daughter, six year-old Alchflaed, was learning embroidery from her step-mother. The baby, Osthryth, was sleeping in a cradle beside his wife's chair.

'Heard what, Oswiu?'

'Cenwalh has made peace with that bloody man, Penda, in return for Wessex. Not only does that mean the Mercians will be freed from the insurrections within Wessex but he is now effectively bretwalda of southern England. He's even managed to get Anna to accept what he likes to call an emissary to the East Anglian court.'

'You're forgetting my cousin, Eorcenberht. Kent will never ally itself with Penda whilst he rules.'

'That's true, but he may well be forced into a position of neutrality now that he has the East Saxons across the Thames estuary, Wessex and the Middle Saxons all arrayed against him along his borders. He's not in a strong position.'

His wife didn't reply but her body language betrayed her feelings. She thought Oswiu was wrong and Kent would stand firm against Penda and his allies. Oswiu knew that Eocenberht was vulnerable, especially since Penda had seized Lundenwic which stood on the north bank of the Thames just where the north-east tip of Kent met the north-west corner of the Kingdom of the South Saxons. From there Penda could threaten either kingdom. The South Saxons had remained neutral over the past few years but they were unlikely to support Kent, given their vulnerable situation.

Wisely Oswiu decided not to argue with his wife. There was no point in falling out with her when there was nothing to be gained. Instead his thoughts turned to his children. Elhfrith was now nine and he was glad that he had listened to Eanflæd and brought the boy into his hall to be brought up. He was out at the moment playing with his friends but he had taken an interest in the boy and they now had a good relationship. The same couldn't be said of Aldfrith. He had now been a monk at Melrose for the past year and Offa had written to him recently saying that the boy was doing well. He had shown an aptitude for administration and he was being trained by the monk in charge of the books of account to record the rents paid to the monastery by its tenants. He regretted his estrangement from his eldest son but the feeling was transitory. Oswiu might have regrets but he had too many current concerns to devote much time to the past.

Even the growing power of Mercia wasn't his primary worry at the moment. It was Deira. Oswine had been stirring up trouble for him in the south of Bernicia. Iuwine, Eorl of Hexham and father of that unruly young monk, Wilfrid, had obviously been taking bribes from Oswine to ignore Deiran raids across the border. They had only been minor affairs so far but it was Iuwine's duty to put a stop to them.

After his failure to report to Oswiu after his abortive mission to Cait, Oswiu had warned him that he was in danger of losing his earldom. After that the man had kept his head down and, with his son studying abroad, Oswiu had rather forgotten about him. Now he was causing Oswiu problems again and this time he wouldn't get off so lightly; neither would that fool Oswine. However, he needed to act swiftly before Penda was in a position to attack him.

The next morning Catinus found himself as a member of a group of mounted warriors led by Dunstan heading for Hexham with instructions to escort Iuwine back to Bebbanburg. Oswiu had sent twenty men; more would seem too threatening and less wouldn't be enough if there was trouble.

When they arrived Dunstan found the gates in the palisade around the eorl's hall shut.

'Open up in the king's name. I have an urgent message for the eorl.'

The sentries standing on the parapet looked down at the group of horsemen and began debating amongst themselves.

'Come on, hurry up. I haven't got all day. You know who I am – Dunstan, the master of the king's horses.'

Five minutes later the right hand gate swung open sufficiently to allow a man wearing a byrnie and a helmet to squeeze through, then it clanged shut again. Dunstan recognised the man as one of Iuwine's gesith.

Greetings Sighard.'

'Good morrow, Dunstan. I apologise for the less than effusive welcome but no one is quite sure what is happening. The Deirans have ben raiding near here recently and four days ago Eorl Iuwine rode out for a meeting with King Oswine, but he hasn't returned.'

'Where was this meeting?'

'All I know is that it was at a small settlement one day's ride to the south.'

'In other words just over the border into Deira?'

'So it would seem; I can't see Oswine coming north into Bernicia.'

Dunstan grunted his agreement.

'Well, if no-one knows where they are meeting, I suppose I'll have to stay here and await his return.'

The other man shifted uncomfortably from one foot to the other.

'The thing is, Eorl Iuwine left strict instructions that no-one was to be allowed into his hall whilst he was away.'

'Why am I getting the distinct impression that Iuwine is about to turn traitor?'

At this Sighard looked even more uncomfortable. He was faithful to Oswiu and Bernicia but, as a member of the Eorl's gesith, he'd taken an oath of loyalty to him. He had a nasty suspicion that Dunstan was correct and Iuwine was about to do something that could cost him his head, but an oath was an oath and he couldn't break it.

'Very well,' Dunstan sighed. 'We'll camp outside the settlement whilst we wait, but you can supply us with food and ale just the same.'

Sighard looked relieved.

'Yes, of course. If I may I'll come and join you and your men tonight and I'll bring a few of my warriors with me.'

'That's more like it. I was beginning to think that you were acting more like an enemy.'

Sighard gave him a sharp look and prayed silently that Iuwine would come to his senses before irreparable damage was done to his position. He had little doubt that Oswiu would replace Iuwine as eorl, given sufficient excuse, and he was worried where that would leave him and his family.

~~~

143

Oswine was enjoying Iuwine's discomfort. He'd quickly come to the conclusion that the eorl wasn't very clever. He'd asked for the meeting in the hope of persuading Oswine to halt the raids across the border into his territory. The money he'd been paid to turn a blind eye hardly made up for what he was now losing in revenue. Oswine was getting greedy and the plunder he was taking and the crops he had burned recently reduced what Iuwine could collect in taxes.

However, there wasn't much in the way of an incentive he could offer Oswine. He daren't even complain to Oswiu. He was well aware that his king would seize on any excuse to replace him and failure to defend his lands might well be just the excuse he needed.

Oswine wasn't in such a quandary.

'It's quite simple, my dear Iuwine. I want your support when King Penda and I invade Bernicia. You, your warband and your fyrd will join us as we sweep north. In return, I'll stop raiding your border territory and we won't pillage your lands as our armies move through them.'

Both men knew that Oswine had just made a promise he couldn't possible keep. An invading army had to forage to feed itself; and it was almost impossible to stop men looting, whether the territory was friendly or not.

Iuwine's mind worked furiously. He was slow witted but even he could see that allying himself with Penda and Oswine was unlikely to bring him any rewards. On the other hand, rejecting Oswine's demands was unlikely to solve his problems. Instead he temporised.

'We both know that, even if you can keep the Deirans in check, the Mercians and Middle Anglians are likely to plunder and rape at will. My fyrd will stay at home to protect their lands but I'll gladly join you with my gesith and my warband.'

Oswine thought for a moment.

'That's acceptable, but I'll need a hostage to ensure your promise to join us is made in good faith.'

'Who do you have in mind? My eldest son, Wilfrid, is studying at Cantwareburg at the moment.'

'You have other children do you not?'

'Yes, but Rægenhere is only eight and my daughter is a babe in arms.'

'Rægenhere will suffice. You do as you have sworn and he'll come to no harm. I'll send a few of my men back with you to collect him and escort him safely to Eoforwīc.'

144

Iuwine knew that he'd ben outsmarted. Instead of negotiating a deal whereby Oswine respected his territory he'd been forced into supporting Penda of Mercia; not something that Oswiu would ever forgive if he got to hear of it. Apart from the captain of his gesith, who he trusted implicitly, no-one else knew of his dealings with Oswine. Provided he could kill the ten men being sent with him to take young Rægenhere as a hostage, he could deny ever have made a deal with the Deiran king. The problem was how to kill them without raising suspicions about the reasons for their presence amongst his own people, especially as his gesith only numbered a dozen men.

He decided that he would wait until they reached Hexham where he had a lot more men before acting, but he was in for a shock when he got there. As he approached his hall Dunstan and his twenty men rode to intercept him.

Dunstan was puzzled by the number of men accompanying the eorl. They looked similar and at first he assumed that Iuwine had taken some of his warband with him in addition to his gesith until one of the riders swung his shield round from where it was being carried on his back and held it in front of him with his left arm, as he would in battle. It was emblazoned, not with the eorl's red cross on black, but with the gold cross on blue of Deira. One of the other riders yelled sharply at the man but it was too late.

Dunstan pulled his men to a halt and ordered them to prepare to engage the enemy. It was unexpected and there was a moment's confusion until Dunstan yelled that they were Deirans surrounding Iuwine. Almost as one the Bernicians swung their shields around and lowered their spears. The other group came to a halt ten yards from Dunstan as Iuwine held up his hand.

'What are you doing Dunstan? Why are you here?'

'Why are you being escorted by King Oswine's men, my lord?'

'That's my business,' he snapped.

'No, it's King Oswiu's business. Now explain yourself.'

'You haven't yet told me why you are here in my territory.'

'It's the king's territory, now stop prevaricating and answer my question.'

Iuwine looked unhappy and didn't answer. Then the senior warrior of his Deiran escort, a man noted for his short temper, decided that he had enough.

'Come on Iuwine, ignore this oaf. Go to your hall, hand over Rægenhere and then we can be on our way.'

145

'What's this about your son?' Dunstan asked.

For a moment he was confused but it didn't take long for him to realise what was happening. If Iuwine was handing Rægenhere over to Oswine as a hostage that could only be as surety for some deal he had done. Whatever it was, he was willing to gamble that it involved the betrayal of Oswiu.

'My lord, King Oswiu requires your immediate presence at Bebbanburg. He has sent me to escort you there without delay.'

'He goes nowhere until he's handed over the boy,' the Deiran told him, reaching for his sword.

It was a mistake. What the man couldn't see behind the screen of horsemen in front of him was that six of Dunstan's men had dismounted and unhooked their bows and quivers from their saddles. Now three ran out to each side of their comrades until they had a clear shot at both the Deirans and Iuwine's gesith. As soon as the Deiran leader started to pull his sword from its scabbard he was hit in the chest by two arrows. Both failed to kill him, merely penetrating his chainmail byrnie and his leather undercoat. Although the points didn't pierce his flesh by more than a fraction of an inch and no vital organs were hit, the force of the double blow knocked him backwards. He toppled from his horse and lay on the ground winded.

With a roar the rest of the Deirans charged forward. This time three weren't so lucky. They only had leather jerkins to protect them and they fell to the arrows before they had closed on Dunstan's men. The remaining six stood no chance against the fourteen spears of those Bernicians still mounted and they were quickly killed.

Iuwine's men waited for their eorl to tell them what to do, but he seemed paralysed and just sat there as Oswine's men were dispatched. Now Dunstan's warriors outnumbered his and the six archers were aiming their bows at him. He hung his head in defeat as Dunstan rode forward, gave him a contemptuous look, and thrust his spear into the neck of the Deiran leader.

An hour later the eorl and his son rode off to the east escorted by Dunstan and his men. His gesith didn't go with him. They were busy burying the Deirans in a nearby wood and hiding all traces of the brief conflict. Iuwine's wife was left behind to deal with the inevitable enquiry from Oswine; she told his messenger that her husband had never reached his hall at Hexham, which was true in a way.

~~~

146

Oswiu was sitting at the high table with Queen Eanflæd, Caedda – who he had just appointed as his hereræswa – Romuald, the Custos of Bebbanburg and Redwald, Ceadda's replacement as captain of the king's gesith, when Dunstan and Catinus escorted Iuwine into the king's presence.

'Ah, I'm glad you could spare the time to answer my summons at last, Iuwine. Why did it take three invitations and a personal escort for you to come?'

Iowine didn't say anything; just scowled.

'Dunstan tells me that you were on the point of handing Rægenhere over to Oswine when he found you. Now why would you do that?'

He turned to his wife.

'How is the boy, by the way?'

'Bewildered and unhappy. He's been told that his father wanted to surrender him as a hostage and now he hates him.'

The queen gave Iuwine a hard stare and the man had the grace to blush and look at the floor.

'I gather his father didn't pay him any attention before and so it's not a surprise that the boy says he never wants to see him again.'

Oswiu nodded. 'Well, you had better add him to your household then. He'll be a playmate for Elhfrith.'

'But he's my son!' Iuwine protested. 'He'll be my heir now that Wilfrid has become a monk.'

'Heir to what?'

Oswiu seemed amused and both Ceadda and Redwald smirked.

'Why to the Eorldom of Hexham, of course.'

'That will rather depend on the outcome of your trial, won't it?'

'Trial, Cyning? What trial?'

'Why for treason, of course. You've been plotting with Oswine of Deira behind my back.'

'You can't prove that. I deny it.'

'Deny it all you want, I have enough witnesses to hang you.'

'Hang me! You can't do that! I'm one of your senior nobles. The Witan would never agree.'

'You think you have friends in the Witan, do you? Well, I hate to disillusion you but I can't think of one eorl, bishop or abbot who would support you. They had a low enough opinion of you before but your secret meeting with Oswine and your agreement to back Penda's invasion of Bernicia will have them howling for your blood.'

147

Iuwine hung his head, realising that somehow his king knew all about his secret pact with Oswine. It was obviously useless denying it any further.

'What will you do with me, Cyning?'

'I should kill you, but that might upset the other eorls. I'm going to banish you.'

'Where to?'

'You'll become a monk on Iona. Your wife may be innocent but I can't take that risk. She will take the veil and join my sister's priory at Coldingham.'

'I see. And if I decline?'

'Then you'll both hang.'

'Very well, you give me little choice. I accept. Who will replace me as eorl?'

'That's no concern of yours. Your possessions will be sold off and the proceeds distributed by Aidan amongst the poor.'

'I see. And what will become of my son?'

'Rægenhere? He'll stay here until he's old enough to go to Lindisfarne to be educated then presumably he'll either become a monk or a warrior. Now get out of my sight before I decide I've been too soft on you.'

When the former eorl had been hustled out of the hall and locked up until he could be put aboard a ship bound for Iona, the meal continued and no more was said about Iuwine until Eanflæd had finished her meal and retired to leave the men to their drinking. Then they turned to the king and Ceadda asked the question that was on all their minds.

'What are you going to do about Oswine?'

Oswiu didn't say anything for a moment. He took a long swig of ale from his drinking horn and put it down for a boy to refill it. The lad had returned to stand behind his chair holding the half-full pitcher but Oswiu told him to go and top it up and not to come back until he beckoned him. He didn't want inquisitive ears spreading what he was about to tell them.

'I can't wait for Penda and Peada to join with Oswine and invade. I need to act first. My instinct is to deal with Oswine first and become either king or overlord over Deira. A united Northumbria might dissuade Penda from taking the offensive.'

'So you are planning to invade Deira?' Redwald asks.

'No, my quarrel is with Oswine, not his people. After all, I don't want to alienate the nobles who I expect to elect me as their next king. I need

148

to be more subtle. I want to undermine him as king so that he gradually loses support and the Deirans look to me for salvation.'

'How are you going to do that, especially with Penda intent on invasion?'

Oswiu turned to Ceadda, who had asked the question.

'I need to draw Penda in so that he besieges Bebbanburg. He'll fail to take it, of course, and all the time we'll attack his forage parties and his supply trains. That'll weaken him and reduce his men's morale. Then I'll persuade Wessex to throw off the Mercian yoke so Penda has something else to worry about instead of me.'

'It all sounds very complicated to me,' Romuald told him.

Oswiu laughed. 'That's why you're the Custos of Bebbanburg and I'm the king.'

CHAPTER TEN – TWO INVASIONS

649/650 AD

The Eorl of Elmet read the letter that Catinus had brought him and scowled. Arthius had succeeded his father, Rand, as eorl the previous year. His father had been strongly opposed to Oswiu but his son had a more pragmatic approach to life. Nevertheless he put the interests of Elmet first and Deira second; Northumbria as a united kingdom came a long way down his list of priorities.

'Why should I believe this?'

'You don't have to my lord. Wait until King Oswine summons you to join him to attack Bernicia, then you'll know that he has allied himself with Penda.'

'Why has he done that?' the eorl asked, suspecting that Oswiu was telling the truth in his missive.

'Because your king fears both Penda and Oswiu, but he sees the latter as the greater threat. He's convinced that Oswiu is after his throne.'

'And is he?'

'What do you think, my lord? Oswiu has never made a secret of the fact that he believes that only a united Northumbria can defeat Penda and maintain its independence.'

'I'm beginning to think we've elected a fool to rule us,' he muttered to himself, then waved a dismissal at Catinus.

'What reply should I take back to my king?' Catinus asked, standing his ground.

'None. I need to think. Now get out.'

Catinus bowed and did so. So far he'd visited three other eorls; two had responded the same way as Arthius, but the third, whose earldom lay on the Mercians line of march through Deira, had told him that he was Oswine's man and he'd do what his king told him. Catinus had left immediately, certain that he'd either be detained or killed once the eorl had time to think.

A month later Penda invaded but by then Oswiu's campaign to oust Oswine was well under way. Coincidentally the agents of the Deiran king's downfall were all originally Mercians – Catinus was a member of his gesith whose job was to sow dissention amongst the nobles whilst two monks - his chaplain Conomultus and his friend Wigmund - preached against Oswine to the common people. Oswiu had chosen them because they weren't Bernicians, and therefore had more credibility, but there was a certain pleasurable irony in using two Mercians as part of his scheme to spread rebellion.

When the warbands and the fyrd were called out most men were well aware by then that they would be expected to support Penda. Consequently, many of the thegns, the freemen who made up the fyrd and several of the eorls refused to comply with the muster. However, some of those through whose lands Penda would march decided that they had better obey or see their property destroyed. Their thinking was flawed. The Mercians and the Middle Anglians needed to forage and they raped and burned a swathe through the centre of Deira in addition to stealing the recently harvested grain and the livestock.

Oswine found himself accused of betrayal by many of his subjects and only the fact that he was travelling with Penda saved him from assassination. To make matters worse, Penda derided him for failing to bring the promised army to support him; in fact fewer than a hundred men had answered the muster and, even with the sixty members of his gesith and permanent warband, it still amounted to less than the numbers that many of Penda's eorls had brought.

All told, an army of nearly four thousand began to besiege Bebbanburg as autumn began. Oswiu had kept a mere hundred men inside the fortress, half of them archers, but he was so confident of the place's impregnability that he was sure he could have held it with half that number. He had prepared well and the storage huts were full of grain and dried meat. Furthermore, he had more ships than Penda and so resupply by sea wasn't too much of a problem either. Meanwhile the rest of his warriors roamed the countryside in small groups, attacking the Mercian forage parties and supply columns.

'Father, we can't just sit here, especially with the approach of winter,' his son Wulfhere told him one evening. 'The men are starving and morale is sinking lower and lower. Disease is starting to take its toll – dysentery is rife and typhoid is now spreading. Unsurprisingly, desertions are also becoming a growing problem.'

'Do you want to tell me anything else that I'm already well aware of?' his father sneered. 'Instead of reciting a list of woes, perhaps you would like to make some constructive proposals?'

'Perhaps train some young warriors to scale those cliffs?' suggested Peada, who had stood quietly in a corner of the tent up until now.

'And then what?'

'Lower some cord so that they can haul a rope ladder up. Once you have some warriors inside the fortress they can open the gates and let the rest of us in. It wouldn't take us long to kill the small garrison he has inside the place.'

Peada let his father and brother think that he'd had an original idea, but he knew that was how Oswiu had managed to capture Dùn Èideann years ago.

'Hmmm, it might work. Nothing's lost except a few more lives if it doesn't. Very well, select your climbers and go and find somewhere where they can train.'

~~~

Oswiu looked over the parapet at the besiegers' camp to the west of Bebbanburg and smiled grimly.

'There seems to be about a thousand less than there was three months ago,' he remarked to the two members of his gesith who had accompanied him on his morning stroll along the walkway around the fortress.

As they walked on a few flakes of snow fluttered down from the steel coloured clouds above and the wind picked up. Oswiu drew his fur cloak closer about him to keep the cold out. He was now approaching forty and the icy blast off the German Ocean affected him more than it had done when he was a young man.

He stopped to talk to the sentries on top of the southern gate and to warm his hands on the brazier they used to thaw themselves out after patrolling their part of the defences. It was now snowing heavily. The three of them continued along the walkway along the east wall. There were no enemies along this stretch of the coast as it was within arrow range from the fortress but Oswiu enjoyed watching the waves crash the shoreline. He found it therapeutic. Suddenly one of his escort halted and pointed out to sea.

'Cyning, a boat is approaching,' he cried excitedly.

'You've got sharp eyes, Baugulf,' he told the warrior and the young man smiled, pleased at the compliment.

They watched as the fishing boat appeared out of the swirling blizzard and dropped its sail and glided onto the sandy beach.

152

'You've got better eyes than me, Baugulf; can you see who it is yet?'

'It looks like Catinus, but I can't be sure.'

The man made his way across the sand towards the base of the rocky outcrop on which the fortress stood and then made his way along it to the sea gate. The Mercians kept an outpost two hundred yards from the gate but they either weren't keeping a lookout in this weather or they didn't try and stop the lone man, probably because they were well aware that the sentries on top of the gate included bowmen. Oswiu was waiting to greet him when the gate opened a fraction to allow him to slip inside.

'Welcome back, Catinus. I'm indebted to you for the work you've done in turning his nobles against that wretch, Oswine. But why have you returned now? Is there news?'

'Yes, Cyning. Perhaps we could go somewhere warmer first through. It was bloody freezing on that boat and I can't feel my hands or feet.'

'Yes, of course. Come with me.'

Oswiu started to lead the way towards his hall when a slave – a boy of about ten or eleven – came running up to him and knelt respectfully in front of him.

'Cyning, the queen's ladies sent me to inform you that she is in labour.'

'Thank you.' It wasn't unexpected news; in fact the queen was late in giving birth this time and he hoped the baby wouldn't be too big. 'Come and tell me when the baby is safely born.'

'Yes, Cyning.'

The boy darted away and the four men entered the hall, shaking the snow from their cloaks.

'Right, Catinus, let's have it,' the king said as he stood facing the other man as they warmed themselves in front of the central hearth.

'Penda's in trouble. Cenwalh has declared Wessex as independent of Mercian domination and Anna has killed Penda's emissary and his men.'

'Excellent news.' Oswiu's eyes sparkled with delight. 'You were quite right to return and let me know. He'll have to break off the siege and return to deal with the revolt. I must get a message to Ceadda. I want his men harried all the way back into Mercia. Now I can deal with Oswine without interference from Penda.'

A little later he sent for Romuald, his custos.

'Double the sentries from now on. Penda will have to abandon the siege soon and I've a nasty suspicion he'll try something before he has to leave. It could be an all-out assault using scaling ladders or it could be something else.'

'I'll have stones and oil ready to throw down on the attackers in case he tries an assault and I'll get every container filled with water in case he uses fire arrows to burn us out; mind you, I don't think that stands much chance of success with all this snow covering the roofs.'

As soon as Romuald left he noticed the slave boy from earlier standing nervously just inside the door.

'What is it boy? Do I have another son?'

'No, Cyning. I'm afraid not.'

'Oh! A daughter then?'

The lad shook his head. 'No Cyning. The baby was born dead.'

Oswiu should have known by the way that the lad was trembling in fear that something was amiss.

'The queen? Is she alright?' he asked more harshly than he'd intended.

'Yes, Cyning. I was told to say that she's weak but they've staunched the bleeding and she's asleep.'

Oswiu nodded. 'So the cowards sent you to tell me the bad news.'

He strode towards the door to go and see how his wife was for himself and to give the midwife and the queen's attendants a piece of his mind but he stopped when he reached the boy.

'What's your name lad?'

'Ansgar, Cyning.'

'An Angle or a Saxon?' he asked in surprise. 'Never mind, you can tell me later why you're a slave. For now come with me.'

Thankfully, apart from a tear which the old midwife has stitched with catgut, Eanflæd was suffering from nothing more serious than exhaustion. The baby had been a boy but Oswiu thought that perhaps, given the strange bulbous head, it was probably just as well it had been a stillbirth. He got his chaplain to christen the child and then he was immediately buried beside the timber church.

He'd forgotten about Ansgar until the boy came to stand by his side at the brief funeral service. The boy had been terrified when he was told go and tell the king about his dead son but he'd done so bravely and Oswiu was impressed with his courage. Most slaves his age, or any age, wouldn't have dared go anywhere near the king, let alone be the one to break the dreadful news to him.

'What's your story Ansgar? Briefly, I haven't got all day.'

'My parents were villeins but one bad harvest after another left them in debt. They sold themselves, my elder brother and me to the thegn. He kept them as slaves to work his land but I was too young to be of any use so he sent me to the slave market. The custos bought me and I became a scullion and worked in the kitchens. I happened to be passing when one of the queen's ladies came out of her hall looking for someone to take a message to you. That's it really.'

Oswiu looked at the boy's ruddy complexion and grease stained tunic and smiled.

'It's your lucky day, lad. My body servant wants to become a warrior, though he's taken long enough to decide that's what he wants. Unlike you he's a freeman, but you can replace him - if that's what you want.'

'To serve you as your personal servant, Cyning? But I don't know what to do.'

'You'll understudy him for a month and then, if he thinks you're good enough, you can take over.'

'I don't know what to say, Cyning.'

'Then say nothing. I don't employ my servants to make conversation with me. You'll only speak if you've something important to tell me or in reply to a question. Clear?'

'Yes, Cyning.'

'Right now go and have a bath and get dressed in something more suitable for your new role.'

Oswiu might not want his new body slave to talk to him, but keeping quiet wasn't something that Ansgar was very good at. He always had an interesting bit of gossip to relay to the king and Oswiu found that he knew more about what was happening in his court now than he ever had before. Such information wasn't only useful, Oswiu quickly learned that it gave him a great deal of knowledge he wouldn't otherwise be privy to and knowledge was power.

~~~

Two nights after Catinus' arrival Penda made his move and sent his climbers to scale the western cliff and palisade. It was a still night without a cloud in the sky, not the sort of night to remain unobserved. It was also extremely cold and the water on the rock had frozen. The climbers did their best to scale the cliff but it was too slippery. When one of them fell to his death he didn't do so quietly and the sentries soon spotted the

155

other climbers. A few arrows were aimed at them but it was an impossible shot at that angle. Just so long as they remained clinging to the rock face they were safe from the archers.

They weren't protected from oil though and several pitchers of the stuff were poured over the parapet, soaking them. Flaming torches followed and the climbers screamed in agony as their flesh quickly charred in the flames. Seconds later they were smashed to death as they fell onto the rocks below, mercifully putting an end to their suffering. A silence descended on the scene as the flames died down and those on both sides who had witnessed their deaths sombrely turned away.

It was the end of Penda's attempt to take Bebbanburg, at least for now.

Gamanulf lay in wait with his men as the dispirited column of Mercians and Middle Anglians trudged past along the frozen path covered in hard packed snow. As more and more feet passed along it the slippery surface melted and the rear of the despondent army had to cope with mud instead. The snow continued to fall to add to their woes.

Suddenly thirty arrows shot by the archers hidden in the trees hit the centre of the column and several men fell dead and wounded. Another thirty followed and more men fell. The Mercians howled with rage and ran into the trees to take their revenge on their attackers. This was about the twentieth time that they had been ambushed like this and they were desperate to get to grips with their persecutors.

Once in the trees there was no sign of the archers. Instead men rose up behind them and cut their throats or speared them in the back. Less than half of the hundred who had darted into the trees made it back to the column.

By the time they camped for the second night they had lost over two hundred men to the Bernicians hit and run tactics. They weren't entirely unsuccessful in finding those who attacked them, but only a dozen had been caught and killed in the first two days.

They camped along both banks of the River Aln that night and set sentries every fifteen yards around the perimeter. Fires blazed all along the river bank as the frozen warriors tried to thaw out and dry their sodden clothing. Penda seemed oblivious to the fact that the fires would silhouette his sentries to those outside the camp whilst keeping them in shadow from inside.

Gamanulf and his ten most experienced scouts slithered on their bellies through the snow and slush towards the ring of sentries. The scouts wore undyed woollen cloaks that blended into the snow and carried bows. When they were forty yards from the ring of sentries they cautiously rose to a kneeling position behind a bush or tree and aimed at the silhouetted figures. Every arrow struck true but, even with the light of fires and the moon reflected from the snow, the visibility wasn't good enough to ensure a kill and about half of the sentries aimed at were only wounded.

Their screams and cries of alarm woke the camp and the scouts sent one more volley towards the Mercians who were now streaming out of the camp before they retreated in a hurry. Their pursuers lost them in the trees but those that got separated from the bulk of their fellows never returned to the camp. Shadowy figures dropped from trees or appeared from behind bushes and cut their throats. All told the Mercians and their allies lost another fifty men that night for the loss of four of Oswiu's.

The next morning the camp woke up to more falling snow. Few had slept well and tiredness coupled with low morale made them listless. The column made its way along the Aln to a crossing place but, when they got there, they found Oswiu had beaten them to it and was holding the far bank.

The army ranged behind him wasn't large, which surprised Penda, but it was large enough to make crossing the river an expensive business in terms of casualties; particularly given the low morale of his men and their evident reluctance to contest the crossing. As he sat there wondering what to do for the best, a rider urged his horse though the press of warriors on foot surrounding the king

'Cyning,' he cried, trying to get his breath back. 'There is a large army behind us and coming up fast.'

That explained where the rest of the Bernicians were he thought grimly. No doubt they had been reinforced by the Angles of Goddodin and the Britons of Rheged as well, perhaps even the Britons of Strathclyde and some of Talorgan's Picts had joined Oswiu too. He was well aware that they could have attacked him whilst he was besieging Bebbanburg, and he had expected it, but Oswiu evidently thought he didn't need them at that stage. He knew he was trapped.

Oswiu rode forward accompanied by his nephew, Œthelwald, and the captain of his gesith, Redwald. Catinus followed them proudly bearing Oswiu's banner aloft and Ansgar followed on his pony carrying the king's helmet. Oswiu was bareheaded to show that he wanted to talk, not fight. Ceadda wasn't present because he was commanding the army that had trapped Penda's forces between him and the river.

Penda called his two sons to his side, gave his helmet to his servant and rode forward to meet Oswiu, splashing into the middle of the ford to do so.

'I suppose you think you've got the better of me this time?'

'I don't think, I know. You're surrounded Penda. You must be getting senile to have walked into this trap.'

Wulfhere's hand went for his sword but his father put out an arm to stop him. He was well aware of the hundred archers on the opposite bank, even if his hot-headed younger son wasn't.

'Not so, our numbers are evenly matched. I'll leave a small force here to stop you crossing and take the rest to slaughter the ragged collection of farmers, sheep fanciers and barbarians behind me.'

'I might just let you, if only to have the pleasure of seeing you eat your words.'

Penda had had enough of trading insults and idle banter.

'What is it you want, Oswiu?'

'Not too much, just the head of the traitor Oswine.'

Penda laughed. 'He and his pathetic excuse for an army deserted me last night, just after you attacked my sentries. I suspect that he's halfway back to Eoforwīc by now.'

'If he is, he's a fool. The eorl will bar the gates against him.'

'That's not my problem. Now, anything else?'

'Yes, you and I are going to sign a truce. You are going to swear an oath before whatever peculiar gods you believe in not to attack me again and, furthermore, to recognise Wessex as an independent kingdom.'

At that both Peada and Wulfhere started to whisper urgently in their father's ear. Eventually he nodded.

'Very well. I agree, but no truce is infinite. Shall we say for a year?'

Oswiu laughed. 'You must think I'm stupid. Five years at least.'

Penda laughed. 'How will you ensure that I keep my word? Come to that, how do I know that you will keep yours?'

'I have never been foresworn; you know that. However, I will lodge two chests of silver in your keeping as evidence of my good intent. If I break the treaty it will be forfeit. In five years it will be returned to me.'

'Really?' Penda's greedy little eyes lit up at the prospect of so much money. 'You trust me to keep it safe?'

'Of course not. I want a hostage from you in return.'

'Who?'

'Your son Æthelred.'

'But he's only just five!'

'It's a good deal, father. You've got two other sons; you don't need a third,' Peada whispered loudly enough for Oswiu to hear.

For a moment he thought Penda was going to strike his eldest son. Instead he hissed something at him quietly and Peada went puce with rage. Oswiu smiled to himself when he saw it. Perhaps he could drive a wedge between the two. It seemed that Penda was rather fonder of his youngest son than he was of the eldest.

'I agree, provided you swear to treat my son as you would your own.'

'Of course. He will be brought up with my younger children. One more thing.'

'Haven't you extracted enough blood from this particular stone for one day? Well, what is it?'

'Æthelred is to be brought up as a devout Christian and he must be baptised.'

For a moment Penda was silent and Oswiu wondered whether he'd pushed him too far. He breathed a sigh of relief when he replied.

'Very well. It makes no difference to me.'

~~~

'Oswiu might have forced me into a truce with him and Cenwalh, but he said nothing about East Anglia. I have a score to settle with King Anna. Peada, you can have the honour of leading the invasion.'

Penda was sitting in the king's hall at Towcester with his two sons and several of his eorls. After concluding the truce he had returned to Mercia, whilst Oswiu had immediately started a search for the unfortunate Oswine. It was now late August and Penda hoped that Anna wouldn't expect him to invade in the middle of harvest time. He planned a swift campaign against the ill-prepared East Anglians which would be over before the season became too cold and wet for campaigning.

He didn't anticipate any interference from either Wessex or Bernicia. Cenwalh was still re-establishing his rule over part of his kingdom and Oswiu was busy hunting Oswine.

The first Anna knew of the invasion was when a messenger arrived with the startling news that Peada and his Middle Anglians had invaded and burned the settlement at Thetford to the ground. They had crossed the River Little Ouse and were now heading for his capital at Dunwich. By striking between the lands of the Northfolk and the Southfolk he had effectively cut Anna off from the majority of his people in the south of the kingdom. He was unprepared and his fyrd were busy gathering in the harvest.

By the time that Peada reached Dunwich, Anna had fled with his family and his gesith by ship heading for the south coast and Wessex.

Oswiu wasn't altogether surprised by the news, unwelcome though it was. Thanks to the chaos in Deira, East Anglia had been more or less isolated. Had there been more warning, Lindsey might have been able to help but now, with the subjugation of the East Angles, they were the obvious next target for Penda's expansionist ambitions.

It made it all the more urgent to bring Deira under control but while Oswine lived he couldn't insist that the Witan appoint a replacement, however much many of his people detested their king. He decided that it was time to stop chasing Oswine like a fugitive and lure him into a trap. But, before he could put his plan into operation, tragedy struck.

CHAPTER ELEVEN – REGICIDE
651/2 AD

The unthinkable had happened. Aidan had been frail for some time but he had insisted on carrying on as if he was indestructible. True, he had been spending longer living in the beehive shaped hut on one of the Farne Islands as an anchorite than he had been wont to previously. Consequently he now left tramping the highways and byways of the North, preaching the gospel and checking that there was no apostasy, to others. Nevertheless his death, when it came, was a shock to everyone.

Brother Finan, the prior, and Brother Wigmund had rowed out with provisions for the week and found the bishop kneeling in prayer in the centre of the small domed hut. Although it was summer, it was chilly inside the hut made of stones piled in every decreasing circles until they met at the apex. Aidan had evidently died on his knees and slumped against one wall. Because rigor mortis had set in, probably days ago, Finan realised that they would have to break his bones to get him into a coffin. Thankfully, his body hadn't yet started to decompose, probably because of the low temperature inside the hut. This later gave rise to the story that his body was incorruptible.

Finan took the opportunity to do what was necessary to put the body in a prone position whilst Wigmund rowed ashore to break the news and to fetch a simple wooden coffin. By the time he returned with several other monks Aidan was lying on the floor of the hut with his feet facing towards the door. Finan had left his hands in the position of prayer, however. The monks reverentially placed him in the coffin, nailed the lid in place and rowed it ashore.

'Who will you chose to replace him, Cyning,' Conomultus asked him as they rode towards Lindisfarne for the funeral. His wife rode on his other side with her own chaplain, a Jute from Cantwareburg, beside her.

'I hope that whoever it is you choose will be a follower of the true faith and not an Irish heretic,' the chaplain said with some passion.

'Hold your tongue, you impertinent rogue,' Oswiu retorted sharply. 'In the unlikely event that I want your opinion I'll ask for it.'

Eanflæd gave her husband a reproachful look. Religion was the one thing they argued about; she refused to abandon the teachings and practices of the Roman Church whilst the rest of the North followed the Celtic Church, which had originated with Saint Patrick in Ireland and later been spread to the people across the sea in Caledonia by Saint Columba. One of the main differences between the two was the lack of structure in the Celtic, or Insular, Church. There was no head, such as the Pope in Rome, and each bishop and abbot was free to run their diocese or monastery in accordance with general principles, but without firm direction from a spiritual leader. The closest they came to a head of their Church was the Abbot of Iona.

Oswiu knew that, whilst his opinion carried a lot of weight, the choice of abbot lay with the monks of Lindisfarne themselves. Inevitably the next abbot would also become the bishop and Aidan's former acolyte, Bishop Ròidh, would consecrate whoever was chosen as he was attending the funeral.

In the event the prior, Finan, was the unanimous choice of the monks. Oswiu had hoped that either Ròidh or his brother, Offa, would accept the post of Abbot of Lindisfarne and Bishop of Northumbria but Ròidh was adamant that he wanted to return to his own people and Offa's reaction was even more disappointing.

'I don't enjoy being Abbot of Melrose, Oswiu. I'd far rather be an ordinary monk and I dream of becoming an anchorite again. However, I accept that God had other plans for me and I've got used to leading my brother monks, but I have no talent as a missionary, nor as the spiritual leader of your people.'

'I can't pretend that I'm not disappointed, Offa, but you always were the most unworldly of all of my brothers. Very well, I'll accept Finan as bishop as well as abbot. I don't know him that well but, if he was Aidan's choice as prior, he should be equal to the task.'

'He's a good man, Oswiu. He's virtuous and well educated. Like Aidan, he's an Irishman who served his noviciate on Iona and he's an eloquent orator. The only drawback as far as I can see is that he's quite elderly.'

'How old is he?'

'I'm not sure but nearly as old as Aidan I would guess, but he seems to be in good health. Of course, he's not suffered the privations that Aidan had.'

Oswiu nodded and determined to get to know his new bishop better.

Two days later Ròidh consecrated Finan as bishop before returning to Ardewr.

~~~

'Why is Oswine proving so difficult to catch?' Oswiu was not in the best of moods.

For nine months now the King of Deira had evaded capture and Oswiu's patience was running out. Deira was more or less under his control but he couldn't achieve his ambition to incorporate it into Northumbria again whilst the Deiran Witan were adamant that Oswine was still the elected king.

Eanflæd sighed. Her husband was becoming obsessive about the hunt for his cousin; so much so that he was neglecting other matters.

'Have you been to see Finan since his consecration?'

'No, why?'

'Because Conomultus has and he says that Finan is worried about you committing regicide.'

Oswiu glared at his wife but she stared back at him, refusing to back down.

'That's what you plan to do isn't it, when you catch him I mean?'

'He refuses to meet me in open battle, instead he skulks around in the moorland wilderness hiding from me. There's only one way to end this and that's by his death.'

'Finan says that, if you do that, your immortal soul will be in peril.'

'Finan says, Finan says,' he mocked. 'Why hasn't Conomultus told me this face to face? Better still, why hasn't the bishop had the courage to come and face me himself?'

'Finan has gone to consecrate the new Bishop of Rheged, as you well know. Conomultus told me instead of you because he hoped that I'd be able to talk some sense into you. You'd just shout at him.'

A timid cough interrupted him and he turned to tear a strip off whoever had had the temerity to interrupt. He bit back the profane oath he was about to utter when he saw it was his body servant, Ansgar.

'What do you want, boy?'

'There's a messenger to see you, Cyning. He says he's from Eorl Humbold.'

Oswiu narrowed his eyes. The only Eorl Humbold he could think of was the noble who ruled Ryedale in Deira.

'Humbold? I wonder what he wants,' he muttered. 'You'd better show him in.'

163

'Cyning, my lord sends you his felicitations and greets you in the name of Christ.'

'Yes, yes, you can skip the flowery stuff. What does Humbold want?'

'He is holding King Oswine captive at his fortress in Ryedale. He thought you might be interested in taking him off his hands. If so, a small reward would be appreciated.'

'Does he now? I presume that you are trying to say, once all the coded ambiguity is stripped away, is that he's captured Oswine and he now wants to sell him to me.'

'That's about the size of it, Cyning, though I wouldn't have put it quite like that.'

'Very well. How much is this small reward likely to be?'

'The eorl thought that a medium sized chest of silver would be appropriate, Cyning.'

Coins had been used by the Romans but as yet the Anglo-Saxons didn't have the skills to mint new ones, so their usual way of bartering was to use scraps of silver and, more rarely, gold. A medium size chest would hold around half a ton.

'Are you empowered to negotiate?'

'Wait! Husband, what are you going to do?'

'Kill him in single combat, as you and Finan are squeamish about just executing him.'

'What happens if he kills you instead?'

Oswiu laughed. 'I don't think that's very likely but, if he does, you better take the children and sail for Kent.'

Three weeks later Œthelwald, who Oswiu had sent to Ryedale with Caedda and a small warband, arrived at Tynemouth, where the king was at the time, leading a horse on which sat a despondent Oswine.

The weather the next morning was dismal. Sea fog hung over the settlement and fine droplets of water penetrated everything. The grassy area where the hand to hand combat was to take place was slippery and, because it was on a slight slope, the two combatants knew that they would have difficulty in staying on their feet.

Oswiu wore a mail byrnie that came down to his knees, leather boots with steel strips sewn into the front to protect his shins and his battle helmet; made from a single piece of steel beaten into shape and to which a piece of steel with eyeholes had been riveted so as to protect his eyes and nose. His shield was red with a yellow cross painted on it. His sword and seax hung from a leather belt around his waist.

In contrast Oswine wore a shorter byrnie that only covered half his thighs and an open faced helmet. His shield was plain black and he had chosen an axe and seax as his weapons. His gesith had been killed in their beds by Humbold's men, as had his servants. However, Oswiu had sent one of his own slaves to help Oswine dress and arm himself.

Conomultus celebrated mass with the two kings and prayed that God gave power to the more righteous man. Of course, Oswiu assumed that this meant him. After the chaplain had blessed them both the two men turned to face each other. The ring in which they were to fight was delineated by the throng of Bernician warriors who had come to watch; the boundaries were therefore somewhat fluid. This didn't bother Oswiu because he knew his men wouldn't dare crowd him, but it did somewhat intimidate Oswine, who wasn't the bravest of men at the best of times.

The two kings circled each other warily. Oswiu was supremely confident of victory and had only staged the contest to avoid condemnation for murdering Oswine, but he wasn't a fool. He knew that many a brave warrior had lost his life needlessly because he was arrogant. Suddenly Oswine made a move. Oswiu wasn't expecting it and had to hurriedly move his shield to block his opponent's blow.

The man had moved too quickly and his feet slipped on the wet grass. Consequently the axe head glanced off the shield but it still had force behind it when it connected with Oswiu's right boot. Luckily the reinforced boots stopped the blow but it had badly bruised his shin and he felt a trickle of blood beginning to fill the inside of the boot. He tried not to hobble as he moved back to plan his next move, but he knew from the gleam of triumph in the other man's eyes that he was well aware that he'd wounded his opponent.

He closed with Oswine and thrust the point of his sword towards his face. As anticipated, Oswine raised his shield and Oswiu brought the bronze clad rim of his own shield down hard on his opponent's leather shoes. He heard the bones break; Oswine was almost incapacitated, both by his broken toes and by the pain which threatened to unman him.

He shuffled backwards slowly to try and gain enough room to swing his axe but Oswiu stayed close to him, making alternating thrusts and cuts to keep him moving on his crippled feet. Throwing away his axe, Oswine drew his seax and, ignoring the pain, he stepped closer to Oswiu and banged his shield against the other one. Once again, Oswiu had been surprised. Now his shield was of no use, neither was his sword. One had been knocked out of the way and Oswine was too close to him for him to use the other.

Oswine thrust his seax towards his cousin's belly. Had he been able to follow the thrust through with his weight behind it the point would have probably parted the links of Oswiu's chain mail and gone on to penetrate his leather jerkin and his flesh. As it was, Oswiu did the only thing he could do. He head butted Oswine hard in the face with his helmet, breaking both his nose and his right cheek bone.

He howled in pain and instinctively recoiled. The force went out of his thrust and, although a few of the chain mail links had parted, the point of his seax hadn't even penetrated as far as the tunic under Oswald's leather jerkin.

As Oswine stepped back Oswiu drew back his right arm and thrust his sword at his adversary's blood covered face. It went into his cousin's gaping mouth and emerged from the back of his neck, severing his spinal cord on the way. The King of Deira fell to the ground and Oswiu finished him off. Dropping sword and shield and, picking up the man's own axe, he brought it down to sever his head from his body to the resounding cheers of his men as the head rolled away down the slight slope.

Oswiu was in an excellent mood until he limped back to his chamber and Ansgar couldn't get the boot off his right foot. When he tried Oswiu had to bite back a cry of agony and he cuffed the boy around the ear quite hard.

'That hurts like the devil, you fool.'

Not in the least put out by the blow, the boy grinned up at his master.

'Then I'll have to cut the boot off so I can see what the problem is.'

'No, they were very expensive. There must be some other way.'

At that moment Œthelwald, Ceadda and Redwald came to congratulate the king. Although they had never been close – far from it at times – Oswiu had started to rely on his nephew a little more recently and their antagonism had developed into a grudging acceptance of one another.

'What's the problem?' he now asked as he watched Ansgar gingerly trying to inch the boot down the king's leg.

'My bloody leg's swollen up where Oswine struck it and now this useless wretch can't get it off,' Oswiu complained through gritted teeth.

It was obvious that he was in agony but he clamped his lips together and squeezed his eyes shut. Eanflæd pushed her way past the three men standing by the door and went to her husband.

'I couldn't watch but I'm told you won. However, I'm not going to congratulate you for being a fool,' she told him with some asperity. 'What's wrong with your leg?' she asked, her anger turning to concern.

'The boy can't get the wretched boot off,' he replied, wincing.

'Ceada, cut it off, carefully mind.'

'No! These boots cost a fortune!'

'Don't be an idiot, Oswiu. Your leg is more important than any stupid boot!'

Ceada knelt down and pushed Ansgar out of the way. He carefully cut the stitching at the back of the boot until he could pull it off.

'There, now you can get it stitched up and it'll be as good as new.'

The grin disappeared when he saw the condition of Oswiu's leg. The metal strips might have saved the king's leg from being severed by his opponent's blade but one bar had been bent so badly that it had removed the skin covering his shin and broken the bone. It was a clean break and the two ends of the bone showed through the flesh. It was a wonder that Oswiu had managed to hobble back to his chamber, it can only have been possible because the tight boot acted as a splint; even so, it must have required indomitable willpower. Now, however, the pain was too much for him and he fainted.

The next day he woke with an excruciating pain in his leg to find that it had been tightly bandaged and splinted. Ansgar came running when Oswiu roared for him, closely followed by Eanflæd.

'Get this blooding bandage off me,' he told them.

'It needs to stay there to staunch the bleeding and hold the bones together so they can mend,' his wife told him.

'Fine, but it's too tight. It's cut off the blood supply to my lower leg and foot; look it's gone blue.'

Ansgar immediately removed the splint and the bandage and blood started to flow down his leg again.

'Now put the splint back and bandage the gash, but not too tight.'

He grimaced and bit his lip sufficiently to draw blood as Ansgar did as he was told.

'Which fool did this?' he asked after the boy had finished.

'The wise woman who attended me for the birth of our stillborn child,' she replied, looking worried. 'I'll send to Finan and ask for the infirmarian from Lindisfarne to come and attend to you.'

'I don't suppose that he's well-disposed towards me. After all, he warned me against killing Oswine.'

167

'He's a Christian, Oswiu. He's not going to leave you here to suffer and perhaps end up as a cripple, is he?'

'I don't know, he might think it's God's way of punishing me.'

'I'm sure he'll impose a hefty penance on you, but you are his king. If he refuses I'll send your gesith to bring the infirmarian here.'

Oswiu had never seen his wife so determined.

'I didn't realise that I'd married such a feisty girl,' he said with a grin, which quickly changed to a grimace when he was ill-advised enough to try and move.

Finan sent his infirmarian and his assistant straight away when he heard but Eanflæd was correct. His penance was to build a new monastery and endow it with enough land to support those who would live there. He chose Whitby as the site and agreed with Finan that it should be a foundation for both men and women. They would live in small huts, as was the Celtic tradition, with separate compounds for the two communities, but they would worship together in the church.

Finan had just started to replace the original timber church on Lindisfarne with one built of stone and Oswiu agreed that the new church at Whitby should also be constructed out of stone.

It took three months for Oswiu's leg to mend; three months when he fretted at remaining inactive. He worried about what Penda was up to and he was concerned that the Witan of Deira would elect someone else as king.

Penda had been weakened by his abortive siege of Bebbanburg and, in any case, was busy completing his subjugation of East Anglia, but Oswiu was right to worry about Deira. When he heard that the Witan had met and elected a new king he was furious. He was even angrier when he found out that they had chosen Œthelwald instead of him. The two might have developed a reasonable working relationship recently but Oswiu still didn't completely trust his nephew. Furthermore, his dream of creating a united Northumbria seemed as far away as ever. He called his clerks together and dictated a letter to go to each member of the Deiran Witan.

~~~

Œthelwald was, unsurprisingly, delighted by his election as King of Deira. He had pretended to support Oswiu for the past few years but, in reality, he had used his position as confidante to get to know the nobles of Deira and to enlist their support. As the son of Oswald, the king before

Oswine, and the grandson of Acha of the original royal house of Deira, he was an obvious choice.

However, his euphoria was short lived. In January 652 a messenger made his way through the snow and arrived at Eoforwīc with a letter from Oswiu.

My dearest nephew,

I know that you will delighted to hear that I am fully recovered and able to discharge my duties as King of Northumbria and Bretwalda of the North properly once more. I rejoiced to hear of your election as Sub-king of Deira and I look forward to your arrival at Bebbanburg so that you can swear your oath of loyalty to me as your overlord and king.

Should this be inconvenient please do not concern yourself. It's time I visited Eoforwīc again and it will give me the opportunity to conduct some long overdue business with the Witan of Deira.

If for some reason I don't hear from you before the start of Lent, I will journey south and join you for Easter, if I may. Of course I mean Easter as observed by our Northumbrian Church and not that celebrated by the Romans.

I look forward to hearing from you,
Your affectionate uncle,
Oswiu.

Œthelwald read the missive with mounting rage. It was Oswiu's unsubtle way of telling him that he would only accept him as King of Deira if he became his vassal. The Easter visit was a thinly veiled threat to invade if he didn't do as he was told. He had no idea what his uncle wanted with the Witan but he was willing to gamble that he wanted to further weaken Deira's position as an independent kingdom somehow.

Once he'd had a night to sleep on it he came to the conclusion that he had little option but to submit gracefully – or at least appear to do so. That would give him time to make secret contact with Penda and plot to get rid of Oswiu.

CHAPTER TWELVE – WAR AND PEACE

652/3 AD

Talorgan was finding that ruling the Picts was anything but straightforward. He knew that Talorc was causing mischief but he couldn't prove anything. Although the former high king had been deprived of his mighty fortress of Stirling, he still ruled the rest of Hyddir and his cousin was King of Pobla. Both Cait in the north and Uuyannid on the north coast of the Firth of Forth had accepted him as high king but that was as far as their support went. However, Ardewr and Penntir were fully behind him.

The problem had unexpectedly come from Dalriada. The death of Fergus of the Isles, one of the sub-kings of Dalriada, had sparked a row over the succession. His clan, known as the Cenél nGabráin, dominated Kintyre, Knapdale, Arran, Jura and Gigha. They supported Máel Dúin mac Conall, the son of a previous King of Dalriada, as his replacement, whereas the present king, Domangart, and the people of Islay and the rest of the isles chose Ferchar Fota, the chieftain of the Cenél Loairn.

Talorc had used the unrest in Dalriada to his own advantage and had paid Máel to launch raids against the south west coast of Cait. This had infuriated its king, Bran, and he was threatening to invade Dalriada if Talorgan didn't do something about it. Talorgan had contacted Domangart but he was too preoccupied with preventing a full scale civil war from breaking out to be overly concerned about a few small raids. So Talorgan did the only think he could think of. He wrote to Oswiu to ask him to come north as Bretwalda and sort out the growing chaos.

'This couldn't have come at a worse time,' Oswiu told his wife. 'Penda is growing in strength again now he has subdued East Anglia. I was sure that he would attack Wessex next as Cenwalh gave sanctuary to Anna but, if I go north, he might well be tempted to take advantage of my absence to invade Northumbria.'

'What will you do?'

'Take a chance and go to Stirling I suppose. I can't afford to have instability on my northern borders whilst I still have Penda thirsting for my blood in the south. If he attacks then you and Ceadda will have to hold Bebbanburg for me. He couldn't take it last time and he won't this.'

'But he'll despoil not only Bernicia but also Deira on his way here.'

Oswiu shrugged. 'It'll be up to Œthelwald and the eorls to stop him. Let's see what my nephew is made of.'

It was early summer by the time that Oswiu reached Stirling. Oswiu didn't delay. He summoned Domangart, Máel, Ferchar and Talorc to meet him and Talorgan there within the week. All but Máel obeyed the summons and so Oswiu dealt with Talorc first.

'You can deny it all you like, but everyone here knows that you paid Máel to launch raids along the western coast of Cait.'

'You have no proof of that and I take exception to your insinuations, Oswiu.'

'You can take what stance you damned well like, Talorc, I don't care. I don't have to prove anything. If you weren't here under the protection of my nephew's safe conduct I'd have you taken out and executed. As you are, I'll give you one final warning. If you play any more silly games I'll hunt you down and take your head from your shoulders myself. I'll also kill every member of your immediate family, including your cousin, to make sure there is no more dissent within my nephew's kingdom. Do we understand one another?'

Talorc gave him a murderous glare but said nothing.

Oswiu's fist thumping the table hard made everyone jump.

'I said do we understand one another?' he said quietly.

Talorc nodded and looked at the ground.

'I'm sorry; I must be going deaf in my old age. I didn't hear you.'

'Yes, I agree, damn you.'

'Just to make sure you keep your word, you'll hand your eldest son, Uurad, over to me as a hostage. You'll stay here as my guest until the boy is delivered to me.'

'But he's a child; he's only seven years old.'

'Good, you obviously care for him. It should ensure your future good behaviour. I wouldn't want to hang such a young boy.'

~~~

Oswiu turned his attention next to Máel. He'd based himself at the almost impregnable Dùn Averty perched on a rock at the end of the Mull of Kintyre. It was a mistake. Oswiu bottled him up there whilst Domangart and the Cenél Loairn pillaged the mainland and the isles

171

where the Cenél nGabráin lived. The men were sold into slavery and the women were married to men loyal to Domangart. It was at the feast held to celebrate the crowning of Ferchar as Sub-king of Islay and the Isles that the messenger from Œthelwald arrived.

Oswiu, it began without the usual flowery preamble, nor did it accord Oswiu the courtesy of being address as Cyning.

Penda has invaded Deira. I met him outside my capital of Eoforwīc but I regret to say that, after a hard fought battle, we were forced to withdraw and took refuge inside the town. Penda, to my surprise, didn't lay siege to me and moved on, presumably to attack Bebbanburg once more.

By the time this reaches you I would expect him to have reached there and, perhaps even have taken it. I'm told that, without your leadership, your eorls couldn't agree on a strategy and failed to mount much of a challenge to Penda's advance.

He is accompanied by his son Peada and his Middle Angles as well as by the East Saxons and some Welshmen under their king, Cadafael ap Cynfeddw.

Your nephew,
Œthelwald,
King of Deira

Oswiu's heart sank. Because of the losses the Mercians had sustained during their last campaign against Bernicia, Penda had evidently needed to recruit the East Saxons and, more worryingly, the Welsh to help him. This was beginning to look like a re-run of the last time that Penda had invaded with Cadwallon of Gwynedd twenty years ago.

'I'm sorry, nephew, I'm going to have to return to Bernicia as soon as possible. Penda has invaded again.'

'I'll send a contingent of my Picts with you.'

'Thank you. I'll call out the fyrds in Rheged, Goddodin and northern Bernicia on the way south. With my warband that should give me enough men to match Penda's army.'

'I'll send a contingent as well, Oswiu,' Domangart told him. 'I've still got to winkle Máel out of Dùn Averty but I can afford to send a fleet of birlinns to relieve Bebbanburg.'

'Thank you both for your support. I'll contact Guret of Strathclyde and ask him if he can spare a few ships to join yours.'

Penda was finding Bebbanburg as hard a nut to crack as he had two years ago. When he heard reports from his scouts of an army four thousand strong approaching down the coast from the north he prepared for battle. He had five thousand and so outnumbered Oswiu; however, two thousand of those were unarmoured Welsh and another two thousand were poorly armed and trained members of the fyrd.

When a fleet of twenty ships appeared north of Bebbanburg he began to rethink his strategy. His own ships, which had been blockading the fortress from the sea, beat a hasty retreat and an hour later the new arrivals started to ferry supplies in to the beleaguered garrison. The Mercian king gnashed his teeth but there was nothing he could do about it.

'We're going to have to retreat,' Peada told him bluntly.

'Have you forgotten the last time?' his brother Wulfhere spat at him angrily. 'I say we stay and fight. With Oswiu dead Bebbanburg will surrender and his kingdom will be ours.'

'You see yourself as King of Northumbria do you boy?' Penda said scathingly.

Wulfhere blushed. That was exactly what he'd been thinking.

'Well, I've got news for you. I'm not prepared to risk everything on one throw of the dice. No, I've got another solution to our problem.'

Two days later Penda and Oswiu met on relatively neutral ground – inside the stone church that Finan had recently completed on Lindisfarne.

'This conflict is bleeding both of us dry.'

'If you'd have stayed out of Northumbria there would have been no conflict,' Oswiu replied bluntly.

'In that event Edwin would probably still be on the throne and you and your brother Oswald would still be in exile. Let's deal with the present and forget about what might have been.'

'Very well. I want to make sure that you never invade my lands again. In return I won't interfere south of the Humber and the Mersey.'

'You'll let me have Lindsey?'

'Provided you retain Hengist as king and he is willing to become your vassal, yes.'

'Hmmm. We will need to find a way to cement our treaty. Oaths are not enough.'

'Not from a pagan, no.'

Penda shot Oswiu a look of hatred but bit back the retort he was about to utter. He was anxious to conclude matters in Northumbria so that he could return south and deal with Wessex. Later on, in a year or two when he was stronger, he would return and settle matters with Oswiu. He would have to gamble that he wouldn't kill Æthelred in retribution.

'I suggest that we arrange a marriage or two between our houses to bolster our new found friendship,' Oswiu continued.

This was something that Penda hadn't considered. He was silent for a while before he replied.

'Who were you thinking of?'

'Your heir, Peada is unmarried. I have a daughter, Alchflaed, who is eleven. I suggest they marry here, in this church. She is too young to bed as yet, but I'm sure that your son can curb his carnal lust for a year or two.'

'Very well, but I'll have to ask him.'

Owiu knew very well that Peada would do what his father told him or Wulfhere would replace him as King of the Middle Angles.

'You also have an unmarried daughter, Cyneburgh. I'd like her to marry my son, Elhfrith, whose fourteen and just starting his training to be a warrior. He's a little young but I'm sure he'd welcome bedding her.'

'She's twelve. I'm not against the match but not until next year. Peada is a man who can control his passions but a boy in the throes of puberty is a different matter.'

How little the father knew his son.

'Very well,' Oswiu conceded. 'But she is to enter the hall of my wife until she is ready to marry.'

Penda nodded. 'I'll go and tell my son the good news. However, I expect you to return Æthelred to me now we have concluded this new arrangement.'

'Very well. Provided you return my chests of silver to me.'

Penda had already spent some of the silver but he nodded. Hopefully Oswiu wouldn't notice that they'd lost weight.

~~~

'No, my men came here for plunder and we won't go home without it.'

Penda was learning that Cadafael was a stubborn, pig-headed man.

'Are you prepared to fight me and Oswiu then?'

'Why would you side with the Northumbrians? They're your enemies; always have been.'

'Not any longer. We are at peace, at least for now.'

Cadafael snorted. 'It won't last. Do you really think that Oswiu has forgiven you for killing his precious brother?'

'No, I'm not a fool, but, like me, he's a pragmatist. Over the past few years we've weakened each other and that makes us vulnerable to our other enemies and, at the moment, I have a lot more of those than he has.'

'Including me if you don't let me have my way over this.'

'Do you think I'm so weak that I'll change my mind because of your threats?'

Cadafael didn't reply. He turned on his heels and stalked away. The next morning he and his men were gone. Oswiu sent Dunstan and the mounted members of his warband to shadow the Welshmen and to kill any who left the main body to plunder or forage. Inevitably some isolated farms and settlements were pillaged and burned as the men of Gwynedd marched south through Bernicia and Rheged but Dunstan's attacks hastened the withdrawal, especially as the inability to do much foraging kept the Welshmen hungry. Then they found their way south blocked by the fyrd of Rheged on the south bank of the River Ribble.

By this time Cadafael's men had been reduced to sixteen hundred and, although the host facing them across the river numbered no more than a thousand, they had the advantage of holding the only two fords. Then the true nature of his predicament struck Cadafael as another thousand men joined his enemy. The newcomers puzzled the King of Gwynedd at first because, although they were Britons like the men of Rheged, their banner was the same as that which his predecessor, Cadwallon, had fought under. Then he realised who the leader of the new host was - Cadwaladr, Cadwallon's son. In his absence he must has enlisted the support of some of his chieftains who had remained behind.

Cadafael wasn't about to risk a battle when the odds were so unfavourable. That night, leaving his campfires burning, he led his men quietly away to the east. Just as dawn was breaking they reached another ford and, under cover of the early morning mist, he crossed the river and turned back to the west.

The men of Rheged had also crossed the river. They launched a night-time attack on the camp but found it deserted. They'd been tricked. However, they were content to leave the pursuit of Cadafael in the hands of Cadwaladr and, as most lived to the north of the Ribble, they returned home, leaving Dunstan to carry shadowing the Welshmen's retreat.

Cadwaladr realised that Cadafael was now almost certainly on his side of the river and was probably heading towards him along the south bank to teach him and his supporters a lesson. He therefore found a good defensive position on top of a small conical hill and dug ramparts and a ditch behind which he would fight.

As the day drew to a close Cadafael's army arrived at the base of the hill and made camp. A couple of hours into the night one of his chieftains came to see Cadwaladr.

'My sentries report that there seems to be something going on. Men are sneaking down the hill and then coming back up again.'

'It sounds as if someone is trying to do a deal with Cadafael.'

'I fear so. You are about to be betrayed, Cadwaladr.'

'Thank you, Owain. Your loyalty won't be forgotten. The next man to leave our camp is to be seized and brought to me.'

Owain nodded and half an hour later a struggling man was dragged before him.

'Hywel,' he said in surprise. 'Why is one of my chieftains sneaking off to treat with Cadafael?'

'Because your cause is doomed. I'm only being sensible and trying to save my men.'

'You own neck more like.'

'So? There are several others who think like I do.'

'I see. Owain, would you please ask all the chieftains to come and see me?'

When they had all gathered outside his tent his gaze swept over them and he made a mental note of those who were looking apprehensive and talking urgently amongst themselves. They were all armed and the two groups seemed more or less equally balanced.

'Thank you all for coming. I'm sorry to drag you from your beds but it has come to my attention that a few of you have been in contact with Cadafael. I've never made a secret of the fact that I haven't forgiven him for seizing the throne after my father was killed. He's not of my family and he had no right to rule. I had thought that all of you supported my claim, but tonight several have sought to treat with him secretly, no doubt with the intent of betraying me on the morrow.'

He stopped as many of the fifteen chieftains started to bombard him with questions. Others talked quietly amongst themselves and more than one hand edged towards the hilt of their swords. Cadwaladr held up his hands for quiet and when most of the hubbub had died down, he continued.

176

'Your men can remain here and submit to Cadafael. The rest of us will depart tonight, but just to make sure we can slip away quietly, you will be coming with us.'

He nodded to Oswain and several of his own men and those from Oswain's tribe quickly moved to disarm and secure those chieftains about which Cadwaladr had his doubts. A few minutes later six hundred of his supporters accompanied by the unarmed chieftains made their way quietly down the side of the hill opposite Cadafael's camp. Each of the traitors had a dagger pressed into their sides to ensure they didn't give the alarm.

Unsurprisingly the sentries challenged the large body of men but Cadwaladr merely replied that he was going to make a surprise attack on his enemy's camp. Most of the men left behind didn't know what their chieftains had been up to or, if they did, they were leaderless and uncertain what to do.

By the time that Cadafael found out that the bird had flown Cadwaladr and his men had crossed the Ribble via another ford to the west and were heading south as fast as they could go. He paused when he was certain he wasn't being pursued for just long enough to hang the treacherous chieftains as a warning to others, and then pressed on heading for the mountain fastness that surrounded Yr Wyddfa.

~~~

The day of Peada's wedding to Alchflaed dawned blustery but fine. The stone walls of the church on Lindisfarne had been finished and the rafters were in place but the thatched roof was less than a quarter completed, so it as just as well it wasn't raining.

When Peada entered the church accompanied by his supporters they behaved in a raucous and unseemly manner until Oswiu grabbed the man his daughter was to marry and pulled him to one side.

'Have you already forgotten the teachings of Abbot Finan? Does your baptism yesterday mean nothing to you, boy? This is the House of God and you will behave respectfully within it or you will have me to answer to.'

For a moment he thought that Peada was going the challenge him and he tensed but the young man saw sense and apologised. He went back to his nobles and, after some hushed whispering decorum once more prevailed.

Oswiu returned to stand beside Eanflæd as their daughter entered. She was small, even for eleven, and was dwarfed by her female attendants. Her mother looked at her and then at the boastful, strutting braggart who she was to marry and she shuddered. She understood why her husband had chosen to marry her off to Penda's son – it was the fate of nobly born women to serve their family's political interests – but she had an uneasy feeling that Peada would ignore Oswiu's strictures about waiting until Alchflaed menstruated before bedding her as his wife.

She looked over at Penda who was standing on the other side of the betrothed couple next to his other sons, Wulfhere and Æthelred. Both the men had satisfied grins on their faces, though Æthelred looked at his eldest brother with contempt. Evidently the time that the boy had spent with her had born fruit. He had readily accepted Christianity and had become more devout than her own children. The attitude of the other two worried her and deep down she knew that the peace that Oswiu had worked so tirelessly for wouldn't last. What then would become of her daughter?

The fact that the Mercian King's daughter was to wed Elhfrith, Oswiu's son by his first wife, the following year might mean that the truce might last a little while , especially as the girl, Cyneburgh, had already been sent into her safekeeping and was therefore something of hostage, just as her brother Æthelred had been and as Alchflaed would be. Perhaps, she thought, she was worrying unnecessarily but, when she glanced at Penda again and saw that Wulfhere was again sniggering at something his father had said, her unease returned.

That night Peada left his new bride alone; not that he would have been capable of much after the copious amounts of ale he'd consumed. The bridal bed remained unoccupied until they returned to Peada's capital of Towcester. Once there, where he felt safe, he decided once he was drunk enough that it was time to do what he'd been lusting after ever since he first saw the girl and that was to make Alchflaed his wife in fact as well as in name. That night he raped her, not once but four times.

In the morning he rose feeling well pleased with himself and he ordered the slaves to display the blood soaked furs from his bed on the outside walls of his hall as evidence of his virility. It didn't take long for the tale to reach Oswiu's ears. He was furious but he ignored his wife's demands that he invade and kill Peada. He needed peace with Mercia more than ever now as Anna of East Anglia had died and his successor, Æthelhere, had made peace with Penda and acknowledged him as his overlord in return for being allowed to regain the kingdom. The death of

Hengist of Lindsey and the peaceful absorption of the former petty kingdom into Penda's domain removed yet another of Oswiu's allies south of the Humber.

Even Oswiu admitted that the war clouds were gathering once more but was determined to do nothing to provoke Penda if he could avoid it. He even forbore to mention the broken seals on the chests of silver which had been returned and the fact that the contents had evidently been pilfered.

CHAPTER THIRTEEN – PRELUDE TO CONFLICT

654 – 655 AD

Catinus watched the young man ride into the fortress at Bebbanburg. He was on sentry duty outside the entrance to the king's hall and he was bored. He admired the stranger's horse and his clothing. It was drab, not like the bright colours nobles wore, but he could tell even at this distance, that they were made from the finest wool and the boots on his feet were made from good quality leather. He led a packhorse laden with a chainmail byrnie, helmet, shield and spear, together with a small chest and a sack which presumably contained his spare clothes. Everything looked new.

As the young man dismounted he noted that his shoulder length fair hair was quite short above his forehead, as he was growing out a tonsure. The new arrival was something of an enigma and Catinus was intrigued.

'Where can I find Ceadda?' the man asked a passing boy, who pointed towards the hall which Catinus was guarding.

'Thank you. Is there someone who can look after my horses?'

The boy nodded and took the leading reins from him.

'I'll put them in the stables, unload your gear and give them a rub down if you like.'

The boy looked at him expectantly.

'You're not a stable boy, are you?'

'No, but I'm willing to go and get them off their lazy arses for a small reward,' the boy said with a grin.

'Here, catch.'

He flipped a small silver coin at the lad, which he caught and tucked away in a small pouch at his waist. He was delighted; coins, especially silver ones, were rare and consequently valuable.

'Can I help you?' Catinus asked as the new arrival walked up to the hall.

'I was told by my father, the Eorl of Dùn Barra, to ask for Ceadda the Hereræswa.'

Catinus now knew who the young man was. He was Cuthbert, the son of Kenric, one of the eorls of the Goddodin and a close friend of the king's. The last he'd heard of Cuthbert he had completed his noviciate at Melrose and had taken his vows as a monk.

'Ceadda's not here, I'm afraid. He's at Eoforwīc advising King Œthelwald on improving the Deiran warband and fyrd.'

His tone indicated that he didn't think much of the Deiran army's capability.

'Oh, who should I see then? I'm to join the king's warband as a warrior.'

'Forgive me for saying so, but most start their training as boys once their voices have broken and are warriors by the time they are sixteen or so. I take it that you haven't been trained?'

'Yes, you are quite right. I'm twenty and have been a monk for the past six years. However, I've decided that I need to experience warfare to complete my education. As to being trained to fight, my father had me trained as a warrior as a young boy.'

'I think you had better report to Redwald, the captain of the gesith in that case.'

Just at that moment Oswiu came out of his hall with Redwald and two other men who were busy congratulating him on the birth of his third child by Eanflæd – a daughter who they had called Ælfflaed.

'Ah, Cuthbert. I'm glad to see that you've arrived safely. Your father wrote to me to explain. Welcome to my gesith. I hope you find what you are looking for with us. This is my captain, Redwald, he'll tell you what to do. You must excuse me, I need to celebrate the birth of my new daughter.'

Redwald nodded at Cuthbert by way of greeting after the king had left them.

'New daughter?'

'Yes, Queen Eanflæd has given birth to a baby girl, Ælfflæd; not that it's any of your business. Where's your baggage?'

'A boy took it to the stables.'

'Go and get it and find yourself somewhere to bed down. Catinus here can tell you what you need to know.'

The two young men nodded at one another a little warily, little knowing what good friends they would turn out to be.

~~~

Alchflaed cowered in her bed when she heard the door to her room open. She knew that it would be Peada on one of his brief but frequent visits. Her slaves and attendants scuttled out of the room as soon as he entered. Ignoring them, he strode over to the bed and leered down at her.

'Looking forward to making love to me again are you, my lovely wife?'

'Please, not tonight. I'm not feeling well.'

It was the truth she was bruised and sore from his attentions over the past month and she was so unhappy that she had given up eating and was now seriously ill. He had torn her inside and, because it never got a chance to heal, his ministrations now caused her intense pain. However, her pitiful pleading only seemed to make him even more randy.

When he left, having beaten her as well as raped her, she was in the deepest despair and wondered how she could commit suicide. She wasn't allowed a knife, except to eat with and that was removed as soon as she'd finished, and she wasn't strong enough to smother or strangle him, even when he was drunk.

She was jealous of Peada's sister who was about to marry her half-brother, Elhfrith. He was now fifteen and was far from being a virgin, but he was nothing like Peada. He was quiet and unassuming but that didn't mean he had a weak character. He preferred to gain his ends by tact and diplomacy but, if he was let down or betrayed he could act quickly and decisively. For the nine years until Elhfrith had gone away to Lindisfarne to be educated with the novice monks they had been playmates and had grown very close. She knew that he would be a caring and loving husband, so unlike her own.

Then one day her chance came. She had developed a fever and Peada was scared about the reaction of both his father and of Oswiu if he allowed her to die, especially if his brutal treatment of her came to light, so he sent for an old woman who was said to be a good healer.

She lived up to her reputation, feeding the girl an infusion of herbs three times a day which brought her temperature down and a broth which restored her strength. She tut tutted over the bruises all over Alchflaed's body and applied a salve to help them heal. She also used a bone needle and catgut to repair the tears that the repeated rapes had caused.

Thankfully Penda had called his son to his side for the wedding of his daughter to Elhfrith so her battered body had time to heal. Once again the ceremony took place in the monastery church on Lindisfarne. It was a repeat performance with Bishop Finan baptising Cyneburgh the day before the wedding; the only differences being the now completed roof and the weather. Unlike the sunny day when Peada had married Alchflaed, the day was miserable. Black clouds scudded across the sky driven by high winds and squally showers beat against the canvas covered windows of the church.

As Alchflaed had predicted, Elhfrith made gentle love to his wife that night and the two found each other attractive; something that would turn to love in time. Peada's lip curled in distain when he saw the happy couple laughing and making eyes at one another at the wedding feast and his thoughts turned to his own wife waiting at Tamworth. He licked his lips when he thought of her. She should have recovered sufficiently by the time that he returned; enough for him to satiate his lust at any rate.

Of course Oswiu had been surprised that his daughter hadn't accompanied her husband but accepted that she hadn't been able to travel because of a slight fever. He offered to arrange for a healer to tend to her, which had alarmed the King of the Middle Angles more than somewhat, but he seemed satisfied when Peada explained that he had a healer of his own. He added that he was certain that Alchflaed would have made a full recovery by the time he returned.

That much was true but the healer had done one last act of kindness for Peada's twelve year old queen before she left.

~~~

Catinus and Cuthbert were amongst the six members of the gesith who accompanied King Oswiu on a boar hunt. The two were armed with boar spears which had a large cross bar below the spear point. Enraged boars had been known to work their way towards their attacker even though the spear point was lodged deep within their guts. A few even managed to kill the spearman before it too died of its wounds. The cross bar was to prevent that happening. The disadvantage was that, if you misjudged your thrust, it was impossible to work the spear deeper in search of its heart or other vital organs.

The other four members of the king's escort were armed with hunting bows. These were short and designed to be used on horseback; however they lacked power and range. Oswiu was a skilful user of the boar spear and to date none of his gesith had had to intervene to save his life.

What Oswiu didn't know was that, on this occasion, he was the prey, not the hunter.

The scent of the boar that the hounds were following had been laid by a group of mercenaries hired to kill the King of Northumbria. The royal party followed the huntsmen and the dogs into a clearing and there the trail seemed to grow cold. Whilst the dogs hunted for the scent Oswiu, his friends and the six members of his gesith milled about, confused by the apparent disappearance of the boar.

Oswiu was in the midst of the hunting party when the attack came. None of them wore any armour so when the shower of arrows hit them from both sides of the clearing six of the riders and four of their horses were hit; one of the former was Redwald. The gesith captain gurgled as an arrow went straight through his neck and emerged the other side. He fell from his horse and, if the arrow wound hadn't meant his eventual demise, the blow to the head by the hoof of his panicked horse certainly did so. Gamanulf and Baugulf placed an arrow in their bows but they could see no target and seconds later they too lay dead.

Ansgar placed his pony between Oswiu and his attackers. He may have saved his master but he was hit instead. Oswiu wept when he saw his body servant struck down and he went to dismount. Had it not been for Catinus' quick thinking he too would have been killed. He grabbed the reins of Oswiu's horse and, telling him to lie down along its neck, he led him at a canter back the way they'd come. Only the king, Catinus, Cuthbert and two others made it out of the clearing safely.

'Catinus, I'm grateful to you for your quick thinking. Now ride as fast as you can back to Yeavering and fetch the rest of the gesith. Bring them back here; we'll follow these murdering scum when they leave the ambush site and we'll make sure you can follow our trail by leaving scraps of cloth along the way. Go!'

Two hours later he returned with the remaining twenty four members of Oswiu's gesith. When they rode into the clearing where the ambush had taken place there was a hiss of anger as the men saw their slaughtered compatriots, including their captain. Then Catinus noticed something - Ansgar had moved slightly. Telling the others to search for the marker left to indicate the start of the route taken by the ambushers, he leaped from his horse and knelt by the boy.

The arrow that had knocked him from his pony had glanced off his ribs and, although he had bled quite a lot, the injury itself was no more than a bad flesh wound. However, he had struck his head on a rock when he fell and that was what had knocked him out so that he appeared to be dead. Catinus reckoned that it had saved the boy's life as the attackers had looted the bodies and cut the throats of those who were only wounded.

He called two of the gesith over and told them to bind Ansgar's wound and make a litter so that he could be carried between their two horses back to Yeavering. No one seemed to question his authority. He was not the oldest by quite some way and he was a Briton who had been born a Mercian; nevertheless he had been sent to fetch them by the king and they respected both his skill as a warrior and his sound common sense. For now he was their leader.

Once Ansgar was safely on his way, the rest followed Catinus along the trail marked out by Oswiu. He had no idea how far ahead of them the king and his small party were but he assumed that the ambushers, whoever they were, would want to put as much distance between the killing ground and themselves as possible before nightfall. He expected them to be on foot but, even so, they could probably cover five miles or so in each hour. Even if they had spent as much as a quarter of an hour checking and looting the dead, they would still be at least ten miles ahead of them. At a canter they could move three times as quickly as a man on foot so in an hour they should have caught them and their trackers up.

He therefore slowed to a trot when he estimated that they had been moving for half an hour. A good half an hour after that they caught up with the king. Catinus dismounted and the king came back to brief him.

'They're about a mile ahead of us and seem to be looking for somewhere to camp. My intention is to surround them and attack them at dawn. There appears to be about twenty of them so our numbers are slightly in our favour, as is our superior training.'

'Cyning, you might like to know that Ansgar survived, although he's wounded and has taken a severe blow to the head. He's lost a lot of blood so his survival is still in the balance.'

'I'm pleased he's not dead and I'll pray that he pulls through. He's been an excellent body servant and I would be loath to lose him, especially as he put himself in the way of an arrow meant for me.'

The Northumbrians settled down for the night tired and hungry. They had never expected to be away for the whole day and had brought few provisions with them. As they settled down for the night, wrapped in the thick woollen cloaks waxed with lanolin that served as their bedding, it began to rain. Although it made his men more uncomfortable, the same would be true of the enemy and, with any luck, it would make their sentries less alert.

Oswiu could have disposed of the sentries first but decided against it. He sent Catinus and half of his men around to the far side of the camp to wait until they heard a single blast on a hunting horn. When the grey clouds in the sky lightened he signalled to one of his men and his horn blared forth.

Immediately the encircling Northumbrians ran forward and overwhelmed the sentries. Seconds later they entered the clearing where they could just make out the men as they awoke from sleep and looked around for their weapons. Only ill-disciplined warriors would sleep without having their weapons to hand. Few got the chance to grab them before they were killed. Those that did were quickly cut down. Within minutes most were dead and the remaining five surrendered.

One had a deep cut to his leg which was bleeding copiously, despite the wadded cloth tied around it. Oswiu had a quiet word with Catinus, who then approached the wounded man.

'I'm sorry you won't be able to keep up with us and it is only a matter of time anyway. I'll save you the agony of a slow death.'

With that he slashed his seax across the man's neck and he collapsed with a sigh that sounded almost like relief.

Two of the other captives nodded at Catinus in understanding but the two younger ones howled their dismay. They looked to be about fourteen and fifteen and so it was them that Oswiu chose to question first. He nodded towards the youngest and Catinus and Cuthbert pulled him away from the others.

'Why did you attack us? Are you mercenaries? Who paid you?'

The boy looked at him blankly; it was plain that he didn't understand English so Catinus tried Brythonic, the language of the native Britons. He didn't understand that either.

'He doesn't speak anything but Oostfreesk,' the elder boy called out in accented English.

'Ah, so you are Friesians,' Oswiu said with a grim smile.

He knew that the collection of islands and settlements along the Germanic coast from Saxony to Frankia was a separate kingdom ruled by a king who lived in the city of Utrecht. The Friesians were mainly engaged as merchants and seafarers who traded far and wide. However, every noble and freeman was obliged to train as a warrior and some hired themselves out as mercenaries.

Oswiu signalled for his men to bring the other youth over,

'Who hired you to try and kill me?'

'I don't know; we only joined our lord's warband a month ago after we'd finished our training.'

'Weren't you told anything?'

'Only that we had been hired to kill some foreign king.'

'Meaning me. Didn't you hear any gossip amongst the older men?'

'Well.' The Friesian hesitated.

'If you tell me all you know I'll let you go instead of selling you as slaves.'

The elder of the two young warriors turned to his friend and a short conversation in a language that sounded similar to English, but was unintelligible, followed.

'He agrees. We'll tell you what we overheard but we don't want to go back to East Freisia. We'd have real difficulty in explaining how we survived whilst our lord and all the others had disappeared. Could we not serve you instead?'

'Perhaps. Not in my gesith - my bodyguards have to prove their loyalty and be chosen by me specifically – but perhaps in one of my warbands.'

Oswiu was thinking in terms of the ones recruited in his vassal kingdoms like Rheged or Goddodin. The elder boy nodded.

'What are your names, by the way?'

'I'm Clovis and my friend is called Egon.'

'Very well, tell me what you managed to piece together.'

Suddenly one of the other captives yelled at him in a language Oswiu didn't understand.

'What did he say?' Oswiu demanded.

'He...' the boy stopped at looked at the ground. 'He said he'd cut off both our balls if we told you anything.'

Oswiu turned on his heels and strode over to the captive who'd uttered the threat. He lifted his tunic and ripped away the man's trews before doing exactly what the man had threatened to do to the boys. The Friesian's face contorted in agony and he fell to his knees. Oswiu watched for a minute and then drew his seax across the man's throat, mercifully ending his torment.

Oswiu wiped his blade on the dead man's tunic and walked back to the two boys, his over-tunic and the inside of his cloak now covered in blood. After that he didn't have any trouble in making the elder of the two talk.

No names had been mentioned but Egon had apparently overheard one of the men close to their lord asking what the king who was paying them had against his uncle. Oswiu only had two nephews: Talorgan of the Picts and Œthelwald of Deira. It didn't make sense for Talorgan to plot against him. Œthelwald on the other hand had always been jealous of Oswiu and he knew the man was ambitious. Perhaps he thought that, with Oswiu out of the way, he could become King of Northumbria.

What a Friesian boy may or might not have overheard wasn't enough for him to charge Œthelwald with treason. However, he would be on his guard now and he'd take steps to court the loyalty of some of his nephew's eorls, particularly those of Elmet and Eoforwīc, who were the most influential.

~~~

'Who do you think put Œthelwald up to it?' Eanflæd asked her husband once they were alone in their chamber off the king's hall at Yeavering.

It had become Oswiu's practice to over-winter at Bebbanburg but to base himself at Yeavering in the summer when he wasn't away visiting Rheged, the Caledonian kingdoms, Goddodin, the more far flung of his Bernician eorldoms and Deira.

'You don't think my nephew planned this of his own accord?'

'No, he may be duplicitous and ambitious, but he wouldn't have dared to try something like this without encouragement and help.'

'The pouch of silver that each of them were carrying gave nothing away. There were a few Roman coins amongst the scraps, and even a few of the new ones that the money lenders in Lundenwic are now producing, but they could have come from anyone.'

'Doesn't Penda now control Lundenwic,' asked Eanflæd.

'Yes, now that Mercia has effectively absorbed the Kingdom of the Middle Saxons, but that's hardly proof. Perhaps it's time I visited my nephew?'

'Won't that be dangerous if he's trying to kill you?'

'He's not that brave,' Oswiu laughed. 'Secretly hiring mercenaries to ambush me is more his style.'

Three days later Oswiu left Yeavering and headed south through the Cheviot Hills. Catinus found himself promoted to captain of the king's somewhat depleted gesith. He was elated by how far he had risen from his humble beginnings a dozen years ago tending sheep in the hills of Mercia, but he'd liked Redwald and he was genuinely sorry that he'd been killed.

Because of the four deaths amongst his bodyguards Oswiu decided to take some of his warband along to make up the numbers. However, they were used to travelling and fighting on foot and few were comfortable riding a horse. To his surprise both of the Friesian boys were good riders and so, somewhat reluctantly, he decided to include them. It would be interesting to see what his nephew's reaction was.

Oswiu had decided to visit Ledes en route. It was the ancient capital of the former Brythonic Kingdom of Elmet and was now the base for Arthuis, its Eorl. Unlike the rest of Deira, it had been a stronghold of the Britons until it had been conquered by the Angles sixty years previously. Arthuis was the son of an Anglian father and a British mother. He hadn't forgotten his heritage and, although the ancient royal line of Elmet had been expunged after the conquest by Edwin of Northumbria, he accepted that Elmet was too small to regain its independence in an England that was increasingly moving from a collection of petty kingdoms to a small number of much larger countries, notably Wessex, Northumbria and Mercia.

Arthuis was a widower who had two sons and three daughters. The girls were all married and his eldest son commanded the eorl's gesith, but the youngest, Galen, had just completed his training as a warrior and was eager to escape his father's rather suffocating company.

It was obvious that Galen was his father's favourite son, which did nothing to endear him to his brother. A career as a member of the eorl's gesith was therefore not an option. An idea began to form in Oswiu's mind but he said nothing for the moment.

When he related the story of the Friesian ambush he watched Arthuis closely but, unless the man was a consummate actor, he obviously knew nothing about it.

'I have two youths with me who were part of the Friesian warband,' he added. 'Clovis, Egon come here. Tell the eorl what you overheard.'

Clovis spoke to Egon in Oostfreesk and then translated the boy's reply.

'He overheard some of the older men in our warband asking each other why a man would pay them to kill his uncle.'

'I don't think they were talking about Talorgan and I only have one other nephew,' Oswiu commented, watching Arthuis closely.

The eorl seemed stunned by the implication of what had just been said and Oswiu relaxed. He nodded at the two Friesian boys, who withdrew.

'I need to know where your loyalty lies, Arthuis.'

189

'You shouldn't have to ask, Cyning,' he replied a little stiffly. 'Œthelwald was appointed by the Witan as king but, as you well know, many have privately acknowledged you as the King of Northumbria. That means I'm loyal to him, but only if he doesn't come into conflict with you. Of course, I pray that never happens but, if it does and I was forced to choose, I would support you.'

'Thank you Arthuis. I only hope that all of the eorls of Deira hold the same views.'

'Some do, some don't. I've heard rumours that your nephew has been busy trying to persuade the Witan to clarify the situation by declaring him free of your control.'

'By persuade I assume that money is involved?'

Arthuis nodded. 'I'm not sure where the gold and silver came from, but I have my suspicions.'

'Penda.'

Arthuis looked Oswiu in the eye but said nothing.

'I see.'

The conversation moved into more convivial areas but later in the evening Catinus managed to have a quiet word with Oswiu. Both had imbibed but neither were drunk.

'Cyning, Galen has approached me to ask if there is a place for him amongst your gesith.'

'Not just my warband; it seems he aims high.'

Catinus shrugged. The gesith were the king's companions as well as his bodyguards and was made up in the main of the sons of nobles, like Cuthbert. Catinus was an exception and there had been others who had won their place on merit.

'It would suit my purpose, I suppose,' Oswiu continued. 'With Galen at my side he would effectively be a hostage against his father's good behaviour, especially as his father seems to dote on him. Does Arthuis know of his request?'

'I get the impression that the lad wanted to know your reaction before raising the matter with his father.'

'Well, as you know full well, we have a few vacancies at the moment. It might be sensible to tie one or two Deiran eorls to my side by giving their sons a place. Tell Galen to talk to his father; if he's agreeable then I would welcome him.'

As Catinus went to leave Oswiu grabbed his sleeve.

'You have earned your place in my gesith but I fear that there has been some discontent since I made you temporary captain. Some of my eorls and thegns have made it clear that they disapprove of a man of low birth in such a cherished position. Even a place in my gesith is normally reserved for nobles and their sons. I fear that I shall have to replace you by a noble when we return to Bernicia, but you deserve better than to be treated so shabbily. I therefore intend to make you the Custos of Babbenburg to replace poor Romand. It's a more responsible position in many ways, but it is a less sensitive one. Some still won't like it, but you are an excellent soldier and you have a wise head on your shoulders, so they will have to accept it.'

'Thank you, Cyning. I don't know what to say.'

'Then say nothing. You've more than earned it.'

When the king's party left Ledes the next day Galen went with them. Catinus had already left on his way north to take charge of the fortress that stood high on the coast; a fortress than even Penda had failed to take. Being custos was a great responsibility and he was nervous. Equally he was determined not to let Oswiu down.

~~~

Now that she was recovered Alchflaed dreaded Paeda's return to her bed but he left her alone for some time. It was only later that she discovered that he had a new mistress. But eventually the poor girl managed to escape his less than tender attentions by killing herself. Her sad death seemed make little impression on Peada and the following night he staggered into the queen's room. He beat her quite badly during his repeated assaults on her body and afterwards, as was his custom, he yelled for a slave to bring him a flagon of ale.

The boy who appeared with it had been enamoured of Alchflaed for some time and he hated what Paeda did to her. He was therefore more than willing to do what she had asked of him. Of course, she didn't tell him that the powder she had given him was a slow acting poison. As far as he knew it was merely a sleeping draught so that her husband would leave her alone for the rest of the night.

Paeda drank the ale and then, mercifully passed out. When he awoke the next morning, unusually still in his wife's bed, he felt unwell but he put that down to his excessive drinking the night before. Once more he called for some ale and once again the same slave brought it to him.

Usually he recovered quickly from his hangovers but this time he felt increasingly ill as the morning wore on and he had to be helped to his own

191

chamber. There his solicitous wife took it upon herself to nurse him, helped by the same slave who had brought him the ale. As time wore on Paeda was unable to leave his bed and was only able to eat broth. However, in time he couldn't even keep that down. When blood appeared in the vomit the wise woman was summoned but all she did was to give Alchflaed more of the white powder.

When the summons came for Peada to join his father with his warband he was a pale, shrunken version of his former self. He sent his men under the command of one of his eorls, explaining that he was too ill to come himself.

That was the first that his father had heard of his son's ailment and he immediately grew concerned. Peada was never ill.

'Father, you can't just abandon your plans because my brother has some minor malady,' Wulfhere told him. 'The East Anglians have mobilised to support us and you've bought off Wessex and the rest of the Saxon kingdoms.'

Penda looked at his son suspiciously.

'It would suit you if Peada died wouldn't it? Then you'd inherit. Well, think again. Peada is twice the man you are.'

The sneer affected Wulfhere deeply. He knew that he would make a better king than Peada ever would. His elder brother had poor judgement and relied on his father's advice far too much. As King of Middle Anglia he was little more than their father's puppet in his opinion. Wulfhere was a clever young man and saw war as just one option to get what he wanted.

To avoid telling his father exactly what he thought of both him and his brother he bowed and left the room. He knew exactly what torment Peada was putting his child wife through and he suspected that she was slowly poisoning him as the only avenue of escape open to her. He wished her well.

~~~

Catinus rode up to the south gates of Bebbanburg and the two sentries, knowing him well, greeted him and let him pass without challenging him. With the court away the two senior persons present were the reeve who ran the household and the commander of the garrison, who was responsible for its defence. Both were elderly and somewhat conscious of their dignity. They were therefore affronted to be sent for by a member of the king's gesith. If he had a message for them from the king it would have been proper for him to have asked for a meeting with them. They were therefore in a belligerent mood when first one and then the other entered the king's hall. Catinus' first words did little to mollify them.

'Thank you for coming so promptly.' The smile that accompanied his words was not returned. 'As you may have heard, both Redwald and Romand were killed three weeks ago by Friesian mercenaries in a cowardly ambush.'

The gasps of surprise told Catinus that he had evidently beaten the tidings back to the fortress.

'Is the king alright...?' 'What happened ...?'

Both men spoke at once until Catinus held up a hand.

'Thankfully the king is unharmed and the mercenaries are dead or captured.'

'Who would pay men to try to kill Oswiu?'

'The king has his suspicions but it would be wrong of me to speculate.'

'Who will replace Romand as custos?' the commander of the garrison asked.

It was evident to Catinus from his tone that the man had hopes of advancement himself, despite his advancing years.

He pulled out two parchments rolled into leather cylinders and handed one to each man.

'I see,' the reeve said looking up from the letter. 'The king obviously has great faith in you to appoint one so young.'

He didn't add and a Mercian Briton to boot. He didn't need to; the tone with which he said it conveyed the sentiment without words.

'Yes he has. Before he appointed me as custos I was the acting captain of his gesith.'

That shut both men up and they nodded.

'Will you want my men paraded so that you can address them?' the garrison commander asked.

'Yes, before rumours start to fly. Shall we say in ten minutes?'

'Ten minutes?'

The man was obviously startled. Catinus had a nasty suspicion that, had he given him long enough, he'd have tried to sow dissention amongst his men.

'No time like the present.'

'Very well, lord, as you command.'

'Yes I do.'

He turned to the reeve. Breda was a cleric, a monk who had been sub-prior of Lindisfarne before Bishop Aidan had sent him to serve the king. His skills lay in the fields of provisioning and the efficient running of a household. Everyone, except the soldiers, were responsible to him from the brewer to the blacksmith, from the cooks to the stable boys. He ran a complex organisation and Catinus was well aware of it. Unlike the commander, who Catinus intended to replace as soon as possible, he needed this man on his side.

'Tomorrow I'd like you to start to show me around. I'm familiar with the defence of the fortress, of course, but I've only a vague idea how about how everything else works.'

Breda looked at him slightly suspiciously. Not one of the previous custos had ever shown the slightest interest in his side of the house.

'Don't worry,' Catinus said with a slight laugh, 'I don't intend to interfere with what you do, unless I can help solve a problem, of course, but I do want to understand what those problems are.'

Breda looked relieved, and he realised that he was pleased by the new custos' curiosity about what he did.

Catinus walked out of the hall onto the grass sward in front of it. Bebbanburg was built on the top of cliffs but they weren't flat. The ground sloped away on all sides from where the hall and the watchtower were built. The garrison was gathered on the incline below him, in front of the warrior's hall.

'Many of you know me as a member of the king's gesith; for those that don't my name is Catinus. I'm sure that rumours have now spread about the ambush in which the former custos, Romand, was tragically killed. The good news is that the king is safe and the ambushers, a group of Friesian mercenaries, have been dealt with.'

He paused at this point to let his eyes sweep over the assembled warriors. He engaged as many as possible in eye to eye contact. With a start he noticed that their commander wasn't present. His lips tightened; he'd deal with him later.

'King Oswiu has been pleased to appoint me as your new custos.'

He waited for the hubbub that this statement created to die down.

'Those that know me will confirm that I treat everyone fairly, but I am not fond of fools or foolish talk. If you have concerns don't discuss them behind closed doors but bring them to me and I'll deal with them honestly and impartially. I know that garrison duty can be wearisome and it tends to blunt your fighting ability. I have therefore decided to institute a programme of weapon training and to run competitions to see who is the best archer, swordsman and rider.

'Yes, I did say rider. I want as many of you as possible to learn how to ride so that we can mount patrols, both along the coast and inland. This fortress has been under attack twice in recent years and we must assume that it could be again. I therefore want to know if any strangers are spying on us. Now, where is your commander?'

He'd again scanned the sea of faces looking at him and was confident that the man wasn't amongst them.

'I see. Well, it is perhaps time that he enjoyed a well-earned retirement. I will need to choose a replacement, however. I want you to select four of your number who you think would make a good leader. I will then talk to them and put them through a series of tests. One will be made your commander and the other three will become watch captains.'

From the excited buzz of conversation he knew that this novel method of choosing their leader had gone down well with them. Any who felt that the sacking of their previous commander was unfair quickly forgot about him in the excitement. He hadn't been unpopular but he kept himself apart from the men and that didn't earn him much loyalty either.

The idea of watch captains was a new one too. It meant that each third of the garrison who were on duty at any one time had someone in charge of them. Catinus' intention had been to give the new commander some support, but they would also improve the effectiveness of the sentries as well. No more would they be able to find a sheltered spot and go to sleep.

'Now disperse; those of you on watch return to your posts. The rest of you, get your armour cleaned and weapons sharpened. You never know when you might need them. We'll meet again tomorrow morning for the election.'

Pleased with the way his introduction had gone down Catinus went off to the hut reserved for the custos and found two slaves there – a boy and his elder sister. The place was tidy but it was obvious that they weren't expecting their master back any time soon. Catinus sent the boy, Leofric, off to collect his gear from the stables and told the girl, who said her name was Sunngifu, to change the straw in his palliase and give the place a sweep.

When Leofric returned he told him to unpack a spare set of clothes and he walked out of the sea gate and down to the sandy beach where he stripped off and ran into the cold, grey sea. Feeling refreshed he ran back up the beach and let Leofric dry him with cloth before getting dressed. The boy told him that he was a Mercian who had been captured with his sister during a raid across the border. The last custos had bought them at a slave auction a few weeks before he was killed so being slaves was very new to both of them.

Catinus sympathised with the boy and his sister, but they were there to serve him and he had to maintain his distance or lose their respect for him as their new master. He therefore merely nodded and told him he would allow them some leeway but they had better be quick learners. He decided to ask Breda to find a slave who could explain their duties to them. He'd never had a slave before so he only had a vague idea of what they should do.

Once he was dressed, Catinus made his way to the blacksmiths. He was just finishing for the day but his eyes lit up when the new custos told him he wanted to order a new byrnie, helmet and sword. His old armour was battered and the mail had broken links. His sword was badly nicked and wouldn't hold a sharp edge. Oswiu had given him a small bag of silver when he had made him custos and Catinus had spent most of it by the time he left the forge. The rest would have to go towards purchasing new clothes more in keeping with his new status, and he supposed Sunngifu would need some to buy food at the weekly market. At least he wouldn't need to worry about meat. There was a dovecote and the local fishermen could be relied upon to keep the garrison supplied with a proportion of their catch in lieu of paying taxes. Furthermore, he would lead a hunt in a few days' time to see if they could add boar and venison to the larder.

When he returned to his hut he found the girl busy preparing an evening meal. He had thought of eating in the warrior's hall but the delicious smell emanating from the cooking pot soon changed his mind. Suddenly something made him think of Conomultus. As king's chaplain his younger brother hadn't gone on the hunt, so he was still at Yeavering. He didn't get on with the queen's chaplain and he'd probably welcome a chance to get away from him for a bit. He'd send a messenger to him tomorrow inviting him to return to Bebbanburg to await the king's return from Deira there.

~~~

Oswiu was still on his way to Eoforwīc when a messenger from King Cenwalh of Wessex caught up with him. He had sought him at Yeavering

196

and been directed towards Ledes. He'd arrived the day after Oswiu had left and had managed to reach him a few miles short of the Deiran capital.

He read the message with growing disbelief, then re-read it before handing it to Ceadda.

To Oswiu, King of Northumbria and Lord of the North, it began.

'You will probably find the tidings in this letter as unbelievable as I did when I first heard it. When Penda tied himself to your house by marriage, not once but twice over, I thought that he genuinely sought peace. I was mistaken.

It seems that this was merely a delaying tactic to give him enough time to build up and train his army and to either buy off or purchase the support of others, namely the East Anglians and the East Saxons. Some reports also mention a contingent from Gwynedd. Most worryingly of all, I am told that your own nephew has been bought by Penda with the promise that he'll make Œthelwald King of Northumbria as his vassal in return for his support.

My sources lead me to believe that Penda has only delayed his attack on you because Peada is ill and he has gone to visit him. Penda thinks he has bought me off with gold but I have no desire to see him as Bretwalda of all England. Therefore name the time and place and I will bring my war host to join you. Hopefully we can then wipe the pagan scourge that is Penda of Mercia from the face of this land.

In the name of Christ, our Lord,

Cenwalh.

CHAPTER FOURTEEN – THE BATTLE OF THE WINWAED

November 655 AD

Penda looked down at the grey and wasted face of his eldest son and pursed his lips. He was no fool and he knew the signs of slow poisoning when he saw it. The froth on his lips and the sunken eyes weren't due to any illness he'd come across. Besides Peada didn't have a fever.

His two others sons, Wulfhere and the ten year old Æthelred, stood by his side as he confronted the healer who was supposedly helping Alchflaed to look after Peada.

'Why are you poisoning my son?'

'I'm not...' the woman started to bluster.

'Don't take me for an idiot! Where is the powder you've been giving him to supposedly make him better?'

The old woman reluctantly produced a small leather pouch containing the white powder. Penda picked up the goblet of water from a nearby table and tipped the contents of the pouch into it. He stirred it with his knife and wiped the blade on the woman's clothes.

'Now drink this for you to prove how efficacious it is.' When she hesitated he added, 'or you can be burned as a witch if you prefer.'

She grimaced and drank the contents of the goblet. Five minutes later she was foaming at the mouth and writhing on the floor. This didn't last long before her convulsions changed to weak twitching. Finally all movement ceased and she was undoubtedly dead, but Penda cut her throat just to make sure.

All the while Alchflaed watched frozen in terror. She was convinced that she was next but Penda seemed to think that she was innocent of involvement; presumably assuming that she was an unwitting dupe. After all, she was only twelve and, as far as Penda knew, his son hadn't even touched her as yet. One glance at the scars and fading bruises on the body under her shift would have convinced him otherwise.

'Take care of him, Alchflaed,' he said with a nasty grin. 'I expect to see him back on his feet again by the time I've defeated your father. If not, with Oswiu dead so is your usefulness to me. However, cure him and I'll let you continue to be my son's wife, so don't let me down.'

The threat was clear. She was caught between two unacceptable alternatives: let Peada die and be killed herself or restore him to health and continue to be subjected to his abuse. She decided that she'd rather be dead. But what really worried her was Penda's intention of killing her father. She had to warn him and decided to take a risk, not knowing that he was already well aware of Penda's perfidy.

~~~

Oswiu arrived at Eoforwīc only to find that Œthelwald was no longer there. However, there was a messenger sent by his daughter waiting for him. The boy was a servant of Peada's but it wasn't long before Oswiu came to the conclusion that the lad was in love with Alchflaed. It had to be the reason he'd readily agreed to steal a horse and ride in search of her father when she'd asked him.

The boy had tried Eoforwīc first and struck lucky. Oswiu appreciated the risk the lad had run and so didn't tell him he was already aware of Penda's treachery. He could hardly send the boy back to Cair Lerion, so he enrolled him in his own household as a servant for his chaplain. Conomultus protested that he didn't need a servant, but he agreed to take him when the boy said that he would like to be trained as a priest. Oswiu smiled inwardly at that. At least he had the common sense to realise that his infatuation with his young queen couldn't lead anywhere.

Œthelwald had apparently left for the south of Deira three days previously and from there he planned to head for Ledes, where Oswiu had just come from. He presumed his nephew was gathering his forces. Certainly the Eorl of Eoforwīc and his warband weren't at the Deiran capital. The city was only guarded by old men and boys still in training.

'This doesn't look good,' Ceadda said when they were alone.

'No, we're caught here whilst it seems my enemies gather to the south-west of us.'

'What will you do?'

'Fortunately there are birlinns and a few merchant ships moored down at the wharf. Send some men to seize them, we'll sail back up to Bebbanburg and muster as many men as we can. Then we march to meet Penda. This time I intend to finish things. Within the month one of us will be dead and the other victorious.'

Oswiu sailed on the fastest birlinn and paid the captain a fat purse for making the voyage in a day and a half. The rest trailed in his wake. They had left the horses behind but there were plenty of others at Bebbanburg and at the breeding farm he kept a few miles away under Dunstan's management.

As soon as he arrived he sent for Catinus. When he entered he nodded at the new captain of the king's gesith, Godric, and at Ceadda, who were the only other men in the room.

'Good. How many horses do you have available Catinus?'

'Over two score, Cyning. I've started to teach....' He started to explain his plan for mounted patrols but Oswiu held up his hand for silence.

'Talk to Godric and decide who your best riders are. They are to carry a message from me to my eorls in Bernicia, Rheged and Goddodin. They are to bring their warbands and meet me at Ripon in two weeks' time. They can call out the fyrd but I haven't got time to wait for them. They can follow on later. Catinus you will bring the garrison from here. The local fyrd can man the fortress in your absence. How many men will that give us, Ceadda?'

The Hereræswa thought for a moment.

'With the gesith, your warband and the garrison, a hundred and fifty from here; about the same number from the eorls of Bernicia; perhaps another three hundred from Goddodin and Rheged. Say six hundred.'

'Penda will have at least three thousand, Cyning; many more if Deira and Gwynedd join him,' Ceadda said, worried by the alarming disparity in numbers. 'We should wait for the fyrd.'

'I'm banking on the Deiran eorls stopping my perfidious nephew from joining the battle. As for Cadafael, I have another plan to prevent him from supporting Penda. I shall send the ships at Caer Luel to attack all along the coast of Gwynedd. With any luck, Cadafael will rush back to deal with the threat. By the time he gets there the ships will be back at Caer Luel and he'll have missed all the fun.'

~~~

When Oswiu arrived below the ridge overlooking the River Winwaed he rode forward with just Ceadda and Godric. Across the other side of the river he could make out five separate encampments. From the banners displayed, the large one in the centre was Penda's Mercians with the Middle Angles on one side and the East Saxons on the other. Very near it

200

was another group with a banner that Oswiu recognised as that of Æthelhere of East Anglia. A little distance away from the rest he saw the banner of Deira and his face flushed puce with rage.

There were a few clues that Œthelwald had been there a little time whilst the others had only arrived recently, the main one being the fact that Œthelwald's men had sited themselves upstream so they had the clean water. Their camp also exhibited more of the detritus that warriors created: discarded animal bones, broken equipment, churned up mud and the like.

He was pleased to see that there was no sign of the Welsh as yet. Hopefully, the men of Rheged would have started their raids on Gwynedd by now and that word would reach Cadafael before he joined Penda.

He'd been grateful for the offer from the King of Wessex to join him but, in the end, he decided that speed was more important than numbers and Wessex was a long way away.

That night a band of picked archers, led by Catinus, crept across the river at a ford five miles to the east and made their way cautiously along the bank towards the camp of the East Anglians. In the middle of the night, when all was quiet, the archers lit fire arrows and sent them arcing into the sky to fall around and onto the roof of the large hut occupied by their king. The thatch was slow to catch, but when it did the roof quickly became a raging inferno and flaming embers dropped down onto the men sleeping below.

When the men inside ran outside to escape the flaming debris and the smoke they were silhouetted against the flames behind them and made perfect targets for Catinus' archers. By now the whole camp was in uproar and the majority of the men who had been asleep in the open were on their feet arming themselves. Those who stood between the archers and the flaming hut joined those targeted by the bowmen. By the time that someone had taken charge and had realised where the arrows were coming from Catinus had ordered his men to withdraw.

The angry East Anglians rushed towards where the arrows emanated from and tried to close with the archers but Catinus had trained his men to execute a fighting withdrawal. One half would rush back to a clearing in the scrub and trees and form up on the far side. The other half would leapfrog them and do the same thing at the next open space. When their pursuers entered the clearing the leading warriors walked into a hail of arrows. It didn't matter that the archers were now firing by the light of a feeble moon, filtered through the clouds overhead. They aimed towards

201

the shadows and the sound. They were bound to hit a few East Anglians and that made the rest wary.

After a while they became loath to venture into the next area of open ground and eventually Catinus' men managed to break contact with them a mile before they reached the ford. It wasn't until after the battle that Oswiu found out that the night-time raid on the East Anglian camp had resulted in the death of their king, Æthelhere, and over fifty of his men. Another thirty or so had been wounded.

The nobles with the army had elected the late king's brother, Æthelwold, to succeed him. The new king, being a devout Christian, had no love for the pagan Penda. After so many casualties he had little trouble in persuading his demoralised army to desert Penda and return home. When they saw them leaving the East Saxons took fright, thinking the whole army was breaking up, and they too deserted Penda.

When Oswiu marched down the incline to the north of the River Winwaed the next morning he was pleased to see the area that had been occupied by the East Anglians and the East Saxons was deserted. Only five hundred and fifty men followed him whereas Penda still had nearly three thousand. However, all of the Northumbrians were trained and well equipped warriors. Penda's army included the fyrds from Mercia and Middle Anglia and they made up two thirds of his army so, in terms of trained warriors, the Northumbrians were merely outnumbered by two to one. Such odds would still have daunted most men but Oswiu had a surprise or two up his sleeve.

For some reason Penda had left it until the morning to start to cross the river. The Winwaed was only a tributary and not wide, but it was more than waist deep and fast flowing after the recent rain. He was therefore constrained to use three fords: one in front of his camp, the one that Catinus had used to attack the East Anglian camp about five miles to the east, and another eight miles to the west.

He put Wulfhere in charge of the Middle Anglians, much to the annoyance of Peada's hereræswa who resented the imposition of a stranger, however royal, to command his men. They set off for the eastern ford. Half of the Mercian fyrd was sent hot foot to cross the river via the ford to the west. This left Penda with a thousand men to force the crossing in the face of Oswiu's opposition. Half of these were trained warriors and the rest members of the fyrd. The former led the way.

Penda sent for Œthelwald and his men but no-one emerged from their camp. He was perturbed but he didn't have time to worry about them; he had enough men in any case.

202

When he received the summons Œthelwald had called his eorls together intending to set off to find out what part Penda wanted him to play in the coming battle but, as soon as they were gathered, they started to argue amongst themselves. Arthius led the opposition against the coalition with Penda with many of the other eorls supporting him. His views had changed dramatically during the time he'd been eorl and he now saw Oswiu as the man most likely to give Elmet peace and prosperity.

Those who were in favour of accepting Œthelwald's alliance with the Mercians were in the minority and had little to offer by way of argument save that it was the king's will. Arthius countered that by pointing out that Œthelwald was Oswiu's nephew and the son of Oswald, who Penda had dismembered. He should therefore support his uncle, and certainly not his enemy. This only enraged Œthelwald, who had to be physically restrained by the other eorls from attacking Arthius.

Œthelwald angrily shook himself free of the men who had held him back and ordered his gesith to arrest the Eorl of Elmet. However, the other eorls stood between them and Arthius saying they wouldn't permit it. The gesith were beginning to have doubts about their king and, in any case, were unwilling to attack the eorls, so they backed down.

The outcome was a stalemate. Œthelwald knew he couldn't commit himself to the fight without his full strength behind him and finally decided that his best course of action was to wait and see who prevailed, then join the winning side. His men therefore packed up their camp and withdrew to a nearby hilltop to watch the battle unfurl beneath them.

As Oswiu's army advanced men ran ahead of the main body carrying hurdles made of wicker which were strong enough to stop penetration by most arrows and spears. These were set up fifty yards from where the ford emerged onto the north bank. Once the hurdles were in position the archers took position behind them and prepared to let loose at the Mercians as they attempted to cross the river.

Oswiu noted that Penda never tried to press home an attack. As soon as his men started to take casualties he would order them to withdraw. He was playing cat and mouse with the Northumbrians; keeping them occupied until the men who'd crossed the river to the east and west could outflank Oswiu and trap him in a pincer movement. It was a good plan, but it was obvious and it was exactly what he had expected Penda to do.

Had Penda bothered to estimate the strength of Oswiu's forces opposite him he would find that they totalled three hundred and fifty and not the six hundred he'd been told that Oswiu had at his disposal. Some of the missing men were members of the warband who could ride, a score of Catinus' men who'd recently been taught the basics and a number of Picts mounted on surefooted ponies. They had all crossed the river under cover of darkness and now, under Catinus' leadership, they kept up pinprick attacks on the Middle Anglians as they made their way to the ford. They would suddenly appear, cast spears and javelins into the column of marching men causing a dozen or so casualties, and then disappear just as quickly as they had appeared.

Wulhere got increasingly frustrated by these tactics and sent men chasing after them. They disappeared into the trees and scrub that bordered the track and were never seen again. Peada's men, already disheartened by their king's absence, the East Saxons' defection and the imposition of the irascible Wulfhere as their commander, grew increasingly morose and disillusioned by their mounting losses with, as far as they knew, no casualties amongst the Northumbrian horsemen in return.

By the time they got to the ford morale as at a low ebb. Catinus had crossed ahead of them and, when they saw the mass of horsemen waiting for them on the far bank, Wulfhere's men refused to fight their way across. He called them all the names under the sun, but to no avail. He then tried bribing them with the promise of a chest of silver for the first man to reach the far bank and kill a Northumbrian. The men stood there in sullen silence and even defied their own nobles and the Hereræswa until eventually the threat of banishment for them and their families changed their minds.

In such circumstances it wasn't surprising that the attack wasn't pressed home with any vigour. As groups of men emerged onto the far bank the horsemen charged into them and cut them down before they could form a shield wall. Had they been able to form a bridgehead and hold it with a shield wall the outcome might have been very different, but the Northumbrian attacks started before they could get organised.

Eventually Wulfhere called a halt and glared balefully across the water at the triumphant horsemen. He had never encountered warriors on horseback before. He'd heard of the tactic as it had been used before in Ireland, but he'd no real idea how to counter a cavalry charge. The Northumbrians had suffered some casualties but nothing like the numbers of his men who'd been killed or seriously wounded.

Meanwhile to the west the second group who were meant to outflank Oswiu had also found their ford held against them. This time their enemy had built an earthworks from behind which the archers under Ceadda's command kept up a slow but steady attack on the Mercian fyrd via arrows fired at high trajectory.

The fyrd made one attempt to cross and, because of their vastly superior numbers, they made it to the far bank though they lost dozens of men on the way. However, once they had scrambled up the bank they found themselves hemmed into a small area by the earthen ramparts surmounted by a wicker palisade, which was all the defending warriors had had time to prepare.

The unarmoured men of the fyrd swarmed up the steep slope to try and tear down the sections of wicker which protected the Northumbrians. The archers had retreated behind the fortifications and were now firing blindly at high trajectory at the men still crossing over the ford. As the first of the Mercians reached the top of the earthen mound the defenders stabbed them with spears. The men they killed rolled down the slope, taking those still trying to ascend with them. None managed to tear the wicker sections down and so the Northumbrians suffered relatively few casualties.

Ceadda watched with some satisfaction as the Mercians eventually withdrew leaving behind hundreds of dead and seriously wounded. The Mercians watched helplessly from the far bank as a few of their enemy removed a section of their palisade and slithered down the slope to finish off the wounded by slitting their throats. They looted the dead and then climbed back up the ramparts with the aid of a rope, which was withdrawn before the section of wicker was tied back in place.

Whilst Penda waited impatiently for his two flanking forces to appear he kept up his desultory attempts to attack Oswiu across the central ford. Eventually his impatience got the better of him and he sent men to find out what was happening. When they came back to report that both his detachments had failed to force their crossing points he flew into a rage and ordered an all-out assault on Oswiu's main force.

It was a disaster. His men were demoralised, knowing that Penda should have secured the ford when he'd had the chance. He hadn't because he didn't want to risk being trapped with the river at his back. His whole strategy had depended on the flank attacks and now that they had failed he was getting desperate. Surely with an army six times the size of Oswiu's he could defeat him? It seemed not as his men streamed back across the river after another failed attempt. He now saw the problem. The Northumbrians had selected their ground carefully so that he couldn't bring more than a third of his army to bear in the space between the ford and their shield wall. The rest of his army were forced to wait, either standing in the river or on the south bank.

He couldn't go on losing men at the rate he was doing and so shortly after noon he ordered a withdrawal. Penda intended to find a suitable place to reform his army south of the Winwaed. With his vastly inferior numbers Oswiu would then be at a tremendous disadvantage.

~~~

As soon as the messenger told Wulfhere to withdraw he did so, which allowed the Northumbrian horsemen to cross the river and re-commence harassing his column as he retreated. Eventually the men of Middle Anglia had had enough and they broke, fleeing south as fast as they could go.

With a whoop of delight the horsemen chased after them, cutting them down like a scythe reaping crops. This increased the panic amongst the routed enemy and they ceased to be any form of threat. Wulfhere and his companions were the only group to stay together and Catinus' men gave them a wide berth and went in search of easier prey. Had they managed to kill him the history of England might have been very different.

Catinus eventually managed to regain control of his exuberant men and they headed west to find out what had happened in the centre.

Oswiu watched Penda withdraw and sent men over the ford to secure the south bank, but he didn't immediately follow up the Mercians' retreat. An hour later Ceadda re-joined him and told him that the Mercian fyrd had also retreated to the south. A little while later Catinus and his victorious horsemen also arrived.

Oswiu turned his attention to the army of his nephew, which still sat on a hill half a mile away. He decided to tackle the Deirans first and his men advanced towards them. Seeing this, and knowing now that his men wouldn't fight other Northumbrians, Œthelwald decided to flee. However, he and his gesith were quickly surrounded by Catinus' men and they kept him hemmed in until Oswiu arrived.

'Well nephew. What are you doing skulking here when the real men are fighting for their homeland against the invading Mercians?'

206

'Penda will win,' Œthelwald spat back at him. 'You and your pitiful handful of men haven't got a chance once you engage him in open countryside.'

'Very true, which is why I have no intention of doing so,' Oswiu replied with a smile. 'The question is, what do I do with you?'

He turned to the assembled Deirans.

'Do you still want this feckless coward as your king?'

The roar that came back indicated all too clearly to Œthelwald that he had gambled and lost.

'I release your gesith from their oath of loyalty to you. When you took it you were led to believe that your lord was an honourable man who was king of a region of Northumbria. That is no longer the case and you cannot therefore be held to your oath. How many of you wish to go into exile with this man and how many wish to serve me?'

Only the captain of his gesith and his brother elected to stay with Œthelwald. The rest declared their loyalty to Oswiu. He turned to Catinus.

'Disarm these three and escort them to the nearest port,' he told him so that everyone could hear what he said, then in a much quieter voice he added 'kill them on the way and bury them where no-one will ever find them. Make sure your men don't loot the bodies and make sure they hold their tongues. I want my nephew to vanish without trace.'

He handed Catinus a pouch of silver before turning away and leading his army back down the hill. Arthius took command of the Deirans and followed him. Now Oswiu had a thousand men behind him.

Catinus left with the surviving fifteen horsemen from the garrison of Bebbanburg. He was unhappy about murdering Œthelwald in cold blood; it went against everything he stood for. On the other hand he owed everything to Oswiu. He decided to compromise. When they reached a dense wood he halted and told the three prisoners to dismount. He took a sword and shield from one of his men and handed them to the former King of Deira.

'I'm giving you a chance. I'll fight you hand to hand. If you win you must swear to become a monk and live out your life in a monastery; if I win, you die.'

Œthelwald's eyes lit up. He had resigned himself to being murdered; Oswiu's talk about exile hadn't fooled him. Now it seemed that this idiot was giving him a chance to escape. He grasped the sword eagerly but before the fight could commence the captain of Œthelwald's gesith spoke.

'What about us? Don't we get a chance to give our lives defending our lord?'

Members of any gesith took an oath to save their lord's life at the expense of their own and many were even prepared to go down fighting if their master was killed.

'Very well. You can fight me afterwards.'

'Catinus this is madness. You'll be tired and perhaps wounded after you've killed this scum,' one of his men protested as Œthelwald went red with rage at his insult. 'Let two of us fight beside you and kill all three.'

'No, I won't ask you to risk your lives. This is my decision and my fight.'

In response the man who'd spoken nodded to the others; they drew their seaxes and killed the two gesith where they stood.

'I'm sorry, Catinus. We couldn't let you do that.'

'Very well. What's done is done and it's on your consciences.'

As he was speaking Œthelwald leaped forward and punched him with his shield so that he stumbled backwards and fell. He brought his sword down on the prone man but Catinus rolled out of the way. As Œthelwald straightened up and was turning to strike at Catinus again the latter swung his sword in a scything motion from where he lay. The blade bit into the back of Œthelwald's thighs, hamstringing him. He collapsed and Catinus thrust the point of his sword through his throat from the kneeling position. He got up and removed the head from the body with one tremendous blow, picked up the head and spat in Œthelwald's face before throwing it aside.

'Dig a deep pit and bury them,' he ordered. 'Then dig around a few plants and saplings so you can pull them up with their roots attached. Plant them over the grave so that no-one will ever find it. No-one speaks of this, ever, or you will join him in Hell.'

He went over to a nearby brook that ran through the woods and washed his hands and face before cleaning his sword. Œthelwald had died in a fair fight, at least on his side, but he felt that it would be a long time before he could forgive himself for killing him.

~~~

Oswiu's army caught up with Penda's by the late afternoon. The Northumbrians set up camp on the other side of the valley from the Mercians and proceeded to erect a wall made of willow hurdles. They weren't much of a defence but they were better than nothing. They probably looked more effective than they were in reality. At any event the night passed peacefully.

When Penda awoke shortly after dawn a frost had coated the ground in white. He was puzzled by the lack of activity in the camp opposite until his scouts returned to report that it was deserted. The temporary fortifications had been a ruse. Now he had no idea where the Northumbrian army was.

Two days later the scouts returned to report that Oswiu was now to the south of them across their line of retreat back into Mercia. Almost at the same time scouts returned from the north to report that the Northumbrian fyrd were crossing the River Winwaed in their thousands.

As soon as rumours began circulating that they were trapped, the Mercian fyrd started to slip away. By the time that the two Northumbrian armies had advanced to within sight of Penda's camp he had less than six hundred men left. Any sensible man would have surrendered but Penda was now an old man and he had no intention of spending his declining years as Oswiu's captive.

Leaving his warband to fend for themselves he led one last desperate charge by his gesith and fought like a demon to reach Oswiu. If he could take the Northumbrian king with him he'd die happy. He never got near him. He was cut down by an arrow through the neck before he got within thirty yards of the Northumbrian shield wall.

CHAPTER FIFTEEN – AFTERMATH

WINTER 655 – 656 AD

Sixteen year old Ehlfrith had just completed his training as a warrior when his father sent for him to travel to Eoforwīc to become Sub-king of Deira. This time there was no election or coronation. Oswiu was in a powerful position now and there was no opposition when he decreed the amalgamation of the two witans – that of Bernicia and of Deira into one. Even then they weren't allowed to elect the sub-king. He was an appointee of his father.

Several of the eorls who had sided with his nephew were replaced and the Eorl of Elmet was quietly rewarded with a small chest of gold. Next Oswiu turned his attention to Mercia. For the moment he allowed the bed-ridden Peada to remain as King of the Middle Angles but he declared himself as King of Mercia. He advanced on Towcester, Penda's capital, with his gesith and a large warband and set about replacing many of Mercia's eorls; either exiling them or forcing them to enter a monastery. His one regret was that he'd failed to capture Wulfhere, but he had taken Penda's youngest son, Æthelred, as a hostage. The boy seemed almost pleased to be back in Oswiu's care.

'Do you think you can hold onto Mercia and Middle Anglia, especially when we need to invade Gwynedd in the spring,' Ceadda asked.

'Probably not, at least in the long term. But I need to make sure that Mercia is no longer a threat to Northumbria.'

'What are you going to do about Peada?'

'That rather depends on him. He's allied to me by marriage and so I'm rather hoping that he will accept me as his overlord. If not, I'll replace him.'

Satisfied that Mercia was subdued, at least for the moment, Oswiu set off for Cair Lerion whilst Catinus returned to Bebbanburg. Before he left the king had confided in him that he would be moving his capital to Eoforwīc. He would still visit Bebbanburg and Yeavering, of course, as well as the more northern parts of his realm, but the kingdom's administration would now be located at Eoforwīc which was more central. Effectively this meant that Catinus would be lord of Bebbanburg.

His one regret was that, having been reunited with his brother Conomultus, Oswiu's chaplain, he would now see far less of him.

Oswiu's arrival at Cair Lerion coincided with a torrential downpour and high winds. The sentries were sheltering from the driving rain and so Oswiu rode into the town with his gesith and a sizeable warband before anyone was aware of his presence.

The news of the battle and the death of Penda had reached the town days before but, with Peada's hereræswa dead and their king incapacitated, there was no one except Alchflaed left to take charge. The eorls were skulking in their halls miles away and the reeve and the custos had fled.

She had breathed a tremendous sigh of relief when she heard that Penda had been killed but was still undecided about what to do. The father might be dead but it was the son who had violently abused her, and he was still alive. When her father stalked into the room, shaking the water from his cloak, whilst she was washing her husband's gaunt frame she was dumbstruck. She hadn't known he was coming and his arrival brought conflicting emotions to the surface.

Her father had been almost a stranger whilst she was growing up and he had forced her to marry Peada. She debated whether to tell him of the abuse she'd suffered at his hands; after all Oswiu had specifically tried to protect her by saying that her chastity should be respected until she started to menstruate. But she had been, by definition, a woman for the past three months. She doubted that her father would understand if her husband's so-called love making was on the brutal side. Many men were like that.

Then she caught sight of Conomultus behind Oswiu just as she curtsied to her father. Her heart lightened as the chaplain had been her confessor before she left Bebbanburg and she trusted him. She was even more pleased to see the servant she had sent to warn her father was standing behind Conomultus.

'Well daughter, I see that you are taking care of your sickly husband as a good wife should. What is wrong with him? The rumours say that your nurse was slowly poisoning him.'

'Penda certainly killed her for it, whether or not it was true, father,' she replied, meeting his eyes.

'Hmmm. I need him back on his feet. If he'll swear loyalty to me I'll leave him as King of the Middle Angles.'

'Cannot I rule them as your vassal, as I'm currently doing?'

'You, a woman? And no more than a girl at that. Out of the question. The nobles would never accept you.'

'They seem to be doing so at the moment.'

'That's because you're my daughter and they are afraid of me. No, it might serve in the short term, but not for long.'

Peada had woken during the conversation and now waved a feeble hand for attention.

Oswiu knelt by his bed and asked what he was trying to say.

'Wasn't the wise woman,' he croaked out. 'Poisoned by Alchflaed.' His head dropped back, exhausted by the effort.

'Is this true? Were you in on the plot to poison him?' Oswiu asked incredulously.

'He raped me the first night we arrived here and has beaten and raped me ever since,' she replied with some heat. 'If I was poisoning him it was only to stop his unbearable treatment of me. I'd rather die than endure that one moment longer.'

'Can this be true?'

'It is Cyning,' the boy behind Conomultus spoke up. 'My mother is amongst those who have helped to treat the whip marks on the queen's back and to cleanse and sew her up her private parts after he viciously raped her. This has gone on from the day the queen arrived here.'

'Thank you. It took courage to tell me that.'

Oswiu became very thoughtful and left the room without saying another word.

~~~

Hild reined in her donkey on top of the ridge above the estuary of the River Esk and looked down on the settlement below her. The warehouses and the halls of the merchants together with the hovels of the poor were scattered on either side of the river with a narrow wooden bridge linking the two. It seemed to her to be a more prosperous place than Hartlepool to the north, where she was currently abbess.

As a member of the Deiran royal house – Oswiu's mother had been her great aunt – she had been selected by Bishop Aidan to be abbess of a small monastery at the young age of twenty. Now she was to become abbess of the new foundation at Whitby. Brother Wigmund kicked his donkey up the rest of the slope and pulled it to a halt beside her.

'I don't think that beast likes you very much,' she said with a smile.

'The feeling is mutual, abbess.'

Wigmund was to be the prior of the new monastery and he would be in charge of the monks.

'What do you think of the site?'

Hild gestured across the estuary to the peninsula on the south side on which the first few courses of stone that would support the walls of a large church could be seen. Œthelwald had halted the construction two years ago and Oswiu had been furious when he found out. Now that he was now longer King of Deira, work had started again.

They rode slowly down to the bridge, paid the fee to cross, and fifteen minutes later they arrived at the masons' yard. Building in stone was not a skill that many Angles, Saxons or Jutes possessed, so the master mason and his assistants had come from Frankia, where stone buildings were becoming more common.

'Sister, brother, welcome,' one of the masons said brushing the stone dust from his clothes with his hands as he approached. He had spoken in Latin. Few of the masons from Frankia could speak the language of the Anglo-Saxons, which was beginning to be called English. Latin was the lingua franca of educated Christians and both Hild and Wigmund probably used it more than English.

'Thank you. Are you the master mason, the man they call Clovis of Paris?'

'No, I'm his assistant, Sigmund. Master Clovis is supervising the building of the scaffolding so that we can start work on the higher courses of stonework.'

The two followed Sigmund to where a small man with a muscular torso was directing the construction of a framework of wooden poles with timber floors every five feet or so. The structure extended for twenty feet and Hild assumed that they would raise the walls to the top of the scaffolding and then move it along to build the next section.

'How is the wall braced to stop it falling inwards or outwards?'

'Well, abbess, the walls are built on a much wider wall of stone which is sunk as much as ten feet or more into the ground. Columns are built inside which will eventually support the roof. The outer walls are tied to these columns by stout lengths of timber as the wall gets higher. In Frankia we have to build buttresses to hold the walls in place as well, but the churches there are bigger than this one will be.'

'How do the columns stay in place,' Wigmund asked. 'The round stones appear to be just placed one on top of the other.'

Sigmund smiled. 'There are rods of bronze running up through the columns which secure each stone in place.'

Hild noticed that a few carpenters had started work on another framework a little distance from the wall and asked about it.

'That's the crane that will lift each block of stone up so that it can be placed correctly. In Frankia we cut and dress the stones so that they are a uniform size and have flat faces, but that takes time. King Oswiu wants the church finished next year and so we are using undressed stone of various sizes with mortar filling the inevitable gaps.'

'Where does the stone come from? We didn't see any quarries on our way here.'

Sigmund pointed to the wharfs that lined the river below them.

'It's shipped in by sea, a barge is being unloaded onto carts at the moment. The stone itself is limestone which is being cut from cliffs further up the coast.'

When Clovis had finished supervising the work on the scaffolding and the crane he came bustling over to meet the abbess and the prior, making profuse apologies for not meeting them on arrival. They spent the next two hours discussing the layout of the rest of the monastery and which building should be of stone and which could be timber. Clovis wasn't interested in the latter; local labour would build them.

'I hear that King Oswiu has dedicated his daughter, Ælfflæd, to the Church,' Wigmund said to Hild as they rode away from the site.

'Yes, to fulfil a pledge he made to God before the Battle of the Winwaed.'

'I presume that she will stay with her mother until she is of an age to become a novice?'

'It appears not. She is to be brought up by me at Hartlepool until Whitby is finished.'

Wigmund was astounded. Ælfflæd was scarcely a year old.

'And has Eanflæd agreed to this?'

'Hardly. I hear rumours that they are no longer on speaking terms and she has denied Oswiu her bed. I wouldn't normally have agreed to accept a child who is still on her wet nurse's teat, but I was left with little option.'

Wigmund didn't reply but privately he thought that Oswiu had been extremely foolish. It wouldn't have hurt to let the girl stay with her mother until she was older. She could hardly start her training to be a nun at the moment.

When they left Hild was satisfied that Whitby would have the most impressive church north of Cantwareburg; far more impressive than the small stone church that Finan had built on the Holy Island of Lindisfarne.

~~~

Oswiu decided that Whitby and dedicating his baby daughter to the Church wasn't enough to thank God for his victory. He regretted his wife's reaction to the latter but he was convinced that she'd understand why he'd done it, given time.

His bother Oswald had built a stone church at Eoforwīc to replace the mean timber one constructed on the orders of their uncle, King Edwin; the man who had usurped their father's throne. But he wanted something grander to commemorate the slaying of his nemesis, the pagan Penda, so he decided to found a monastery with an impressive church like the ones on the Continent that he'd heard about.

Early in 656 he sailed north to discuss his ideas with Finan and arrived at Lindisfarne on a clear, calm afternoon in early February. He also had another matter he needed to talk to him about.

'I need to make confession to you, Finan.'

The Bishop of Northumbria looked at him in surprise.

'Why do you need to make confession to me? Father Conomultus is your chaplain.'

Oswiu looked uncomfortable.

'He was there when I committed this sin.'

'I see. Very well. You'd better tell me what's troubling you.'

'I had intended to leave my daughter's husband, Peada, as King of the Middle Angles after I took the crown of Mercia. However, he had treated her most shamefully after I had specifically told him that he was not to take her to the marriage bed until she was no longer a child. Not only did he disobey me, but he did so in the most degrading and foul way.

'She told me that after enduring such treatment for many months she obtained a poison from the healer called in to treat her for her injuries. The woman took pity on her and gave her a powder to administer to Peada which was slowly killing him. Penda found out and executed the healer. Peada was beginning to recover when Penda was slain at the Winwaed. I went to visit him shortly afterwards and found him still very weak.

'Alchflaed told me what had happened and made a full confession to Father Conomultus. He sympathised with her, I think, and made her fast for a month as penance, so my daughter told me. I have thought long and hard about the situation. I need stability in southern England and I knew Mercia would be difficult enough for me to rule over without adding

215

Middle Anglia. I needed Peada to rule it as my vassal. However, I could not forgive the way he had treated my child, and certainly couldn't allow him to continue his abuse of her once he'd recovered. I therefore told her to continue to administer the poison until Peada eventually died. I heard yesterday of his demise.'

'I see. Would it not have been just as effective a solution if Alchflaed had left Peada and entered a monastery?'

'In a way, yes. But it would have left the problem of who would rule Middle Anglia. I no longer trusted Peada, nor could I forgive him.'

'But you expect God to forgive you?'

'I make no claim to be as wise or as altruistic as God is, bishop.'

'No, but you should strive to be.'

'What is done is done.'

'Yes, it is. Who will rule Middle Anglia now?'

'I had hoped that my daughter would marry one of my nobles so I could make him king, but she has had enough of marriage. She wants to enter a monastery and become a nun and I was unable to dissuade her. I will therefore have to subsume it into Mercia and rule it myself.'

'Will you endow a new monastery as penance for your connivance in Peada's death?'

'Yes, I'd already decided to do so to give thanks to God for Northumbria's deliverance from the scourge that was Penda. I have already gifted the land at a place called Ripon as the site. There are a few settlements and isolated farms there at the moment but the land is fertile and there is scope for expansion. I'm sure settlers will flock there once work starts.'

'Excellent. I even know of a monk who might make a suitable abbot. He was a novice here at Lindisfarne but he didn't get on with his fellow novices, including your chaplain. He finished his education at Cantwareburg and at Rome and had gained something of a reputation as a scholar in Frankia, where he now resides. I believe he has good relations with some of the master masons and tradesmen who have built some of the grand cathedrals there. I'm sure he could persuade some of them to come and work at Ripon.'

'I'm surprised that you recommend a Roman monk.'

'Sadly, we Irish monks are humble folk and there are none who can match the Roman clerics when it comes to building in stone. You only have to compare our poor little church here with that at Whitby to see what I mean.'

'What is his name?'

'Wilfrid.'

If Oswiu had known the strife that Wilfrid would cause him and the Northumbrian Church he would never have agreed to his return but, sadly, he thought that Finan's proposal was a good one and he agreed that he should write to Wilfrid.

Meanwhile Oswiu returned to Eoforwīc to plan his campaign against Cadafael of Gwynedd. He was now recognised as Bretwalda of much of England and of Caledonia, but Wales was still the stronghold of the original inhabitants – the Britons – and Gwynedd and Powys, in particular, had been Northumbria's adversaries for too long.

Author's Note

This story is based on the known facts, but written evidence is patchy and there is some confusion in the main sources about events, dates, names and even relationships between family members. The main events are as depicted, even if the detail is invented. The chronology of events has sometimes been altered in order to suit the story but this is, after all, a novel.

ANGLO-SAXON ORGANISATION AND CULTURE

The leaders of the Anglo-Saxons were constantly at war with one another. Borders kept shifting and smaller kingdoms were swallowed up by larger ones. Kings had to pay their warbands and that took money, hence the need to plunder your neighbours.

The population was sparse and scattered. Agricultural methods were primitive and the crop yields were poor. The peasantry were there to feed the kings, his nobles and their warriors.

Kings usually had a small personal bodyguard of his companions – called a gesith – and a warband - that is a permanent army of trained warriors. These were usually no more than a few hundred strong, if that. Nobles and most thegns would also keep a small gesith or warband to protect them, collect taxes and the like. The rest of the army was composed of a militia called the fyrd. It was made up of freemen who provided their own weapon, and armour if they possessed any. Their standard of training and equipment varied.

When the Anglo-Saxons moved from paganism – about which little is known – to Christianity, being a churchman instead of a warrior became an acceptable career for the well-bred. We know that several kings abdicated to become monks. Other kings usually died in battle. Oswiu died in bed of old age but that was a rarity.

The spread of Christianity started with Augustine in the south and recognised the Pope in Rome as their leader. In the north it was Aidan and the Irish or Celtic church who were largely responsible for the religion's growth. Inevitably the two churches came into conflict, resolved in Rome's favour by Oswiu at the Synod of Whitby.

The Anglo-Saxons were a cultured people, as surviving artefacts testify. The standard of illumination in religious tomes, intricate jewellery and well-made ornaments all demonstrate the high standard of their craftsmanship and their culture.

There was a parliament of sorts called the *Witan*, or more properly the Witenagemot, in most kingdoms. It was an assembly of the ruling class whose primary function was to advise the king and elect a replacement when there was a vacancy. It was composed of the most important noblemen and the ecclesiastic hierarchy, but its membership could be expanded to include the thegns when the most important matters were to be discussed.

Thegns owned land of sufficient size to qualify for recognition by the king as such. A freeman could become a thegn by acquiring more land. Their estate was known as a *vill*, which corresponded roughly to the post-Norman manor.

Apart from members of the royal family, nobles also included the *eorls*. They were appointed by the king to administer sub-divisions of the kingdom. Later the word was combined with the Norse jarl (meaning chieftain) to produce the title *earl*. However Anglo-Saxon earls ruled what had been the old major kingdoms of a dis-united England (for example Wessex, Mercia and Northumbria). The function of the earlier eorl gradually became that of the *ealdorman,* who was a royal official and chief magistrate of a shire or group of shires.

ANGLO-SAXON KINGDOMS

In the early seventh century AD Britain was divided into over twenty petty kingdoms. I have listed them here for the sake of completeness, though only a few of them feature significantly in the story. A few others get a passing mention. From north to south:

Land of the Picts – Probably seven separate kingdoms in all in the far north and north-east of present day Scotland at this time. Later they became one kingdom. The names of the individual kingdoms vary depending on the source.

Dalriada – Western Scotland including Argyll and the Isles of the Hebrides. Also included part of Ulster in Ireland where the main tribe – the Scots – originated from.

Goddodin – Lothian and Borders Regions of modern Scotland – then subservient to Bernicia and part of Northumbria.

Bernicia – The north-east of England. Part of Northumbria.

Strathclyde – South west Scotland.

Rheged – Modern Cumbria and Lancashire in the north-west of England. A client kingdom of Northumbria.

Deira – North, East and South Yorkshire.

Elmet – West Yorkshire. Originally a Brythonic kingdom rather than an Anglo-Saxon one.

Lindsey – Lincolnshire and Nottinghamshire

Gwynedd – North Wales

Mercia – Most of the English Midlands

East Anglia – Norfolk, Suffolk and Cambridgeshire

Powys – Mid Wales

Middle Anglia – Bedfordshire, Northamptonshire and Warwickshire

Dyfed – South-west Wales

Kingdom of the East Saxons – Essex

Hwicce – South-east Wales, Herefordshire and Gloucestershire

Kingdom of the Middle Saxons – Home counties to the north of London

Wessex – Southern England between Dumnonia and the Kingdom of the South Saxons

Kent – South-eastern England south of the River Thames

Kingdom of the South Saxons – Sussex and Surrey

Dumnonia – Devon and Cornwall in south-west England

THE LIVES OF OSWALD AND OSWIU

Little is known for certain about the life of Oswald and Oswiu in exile. More is known about their lives once Oswald became King of Northumbria in 634 AD at the age of thirty. Following the victory at Heavenfield, Oswald reunited Northumbria and re-established the pre-eminence of Bernicia in the North, which had declined under Edwin's reign from 616 to 633. Bede says that Oswald held imperium for the eight years of his rule and was the most powerful king in Britain. In the 9th-century Anglo-Saxon Chronicle he is referred to as a Bretwalda. Adomnán describes Oswald as "ordained by God as Emperor of all Britain".

Oswald seems to have been widely recognized as overlord, although the extent of his authority is uncertain. Bede makes the claim that Oswald "brought under his dominion all the nations and provinces of Britain", which, as Bede notes, was divided by language between the Anglo-Saxons, Britons, Scots, and Picts. An Irish source, the Annals of Tigernach, records that the other Anglo-Saxons of England tried to unite against

Oswald early in his reign; this may indicate an attempt to put an end to Oswald's power south of the Humber, which presumably failed. Other evidence would suggest that it was only Mercia who opposed him.

Oswald apparently controlled the Kingdom of Lindsey, given the evidence of a story told by Bede regarding the moving of Oswald's bones to a monastery there; Bede says that the monks rejected the bones initially because Oswald had ruled over them as a foreign king. To the north, it may have been Oswald who conquered the Gododdin. Irish annals record the siege of Edinburgh - thought to have been the royal stronghold of the Gododdin - in 638 and this seems to mark the end of Gododdin as a separate kingdom. That it was Oswald who captured Edinburgh (or Dùn Èideann as it was then called) is supported by the fact that it was part of Oswiu's kingdom in the 650s.

Oswald appears to have been on good terms with the West Saxons: he stood as sponsor to the baptism of their king, Cynegils, and married Cynegils' daughter Cyneburga. Although Oswald is only known to have had one son, Œthelwald, it is uncertain whether this was a son from his marriage to Cynegils' daughter or from an earlier relationship as Œthelwald would have been too young to be chosen as King of Deira in 651 had he been Cyneburga's son. He was most probably the child of an earlier marriage during Oswald's exile, and this is what I have assumed.

Apart from a list of their names, nothing is known about four of Oswald's brothers. Only Oswiu, who became King of Bernicia after Oswald's death, is mentioned in various records of the time. Although Edwin had previously converted to Christianity in 627, it was Oswald, and later Oswiu, who are credited with spreading the religion in Northumbria. However important their contribution, it was Aidan, Bishop and Abbot of Lindisfarne, who tirelessly toured the land converting and baptising as he went.

Bede puts a clear emphasis on Oswald's saintliness as a king. Although he could be classed as a martyr for his subsequent death in battle, Oswald is normally praised for his deeds in life and his martyrdom wasn't the primary reason for his elevation to sainthood. He was renowned for his generosity to the poor, the austerity of his life despite his wealth, and his ceaseless struggle to promote Christianity.

Oswald was killed by the Mercians in 642 AD at the Battle of Maserfield - a place generally identified with Oswestry - and his body was dismembered. Bede mentions the story that Oswald prayed for the souls of his soldiers when he saw that he was about to die. The traditional identification of the battle site with Oswestry, probably in the territory of

Powys at the time, suggests that Penda may have had British allies in this battle, and this is also suggested by surviving Welsh poetry which has been thought to indicate the participation of the men of Powys in the battle. If the traditional identification of the site as Oswestry is correct, Oswald must have been on the offensive in the territory of his enemies. This could conflict with Bede's saintly portrayal of Oswald, since an aggressive war could hardly qualify as a just war, perhaps explaining why Bede is silent on the cause of the campaign. He says only that Oswald died "fighting for his fatherland". Nor does he mention the other offensive campaigns that Oswald is presumed to have engaged in between Heavenfield and Maserfield.

Oswald may have had an ally in Penda's brother Eowa, who was also killed in the battle, according to the Historia Britonnum and Annales Cambriae; while the source only mentions that Eowa was killed, not the side on which he fought, it has been speculated that Eowa was an ally of Oswald's and fighting alongside him in the battle in opposition to Penda.

SAINT OSWALD

Oswald soon came to be regarded as a saint. Bede says that the spot where he died came to be associated with miracles, and people took dirt from the site, which led to a hole being dug as deep as a man's height. Reginald of Durham recounts another miracle, saying that his right arm was taken by a bird (perhaps a raven) to an ash tree, which gave the tree ageless vigour; when the bird dropped the arm onto the ground, a spring emerged from the ground. Both the tree and the spring were, according to Reginald, subsequently associated with healing miracles. The name of the site, Oswestry, or "Oswald's Tree", is generally thought to be derived from Oswald's death there and the legends surrounding it.

Bede mentions that Oswald's brother Oswiu, who succeeded Oswald in Bernicia, retrieved Oswald's remains in the year after his death. There are various reports about the resting place or places of his remains. Some sources identify both Bebbanburg and Lindisfarne as the resting place for at least part of his body and this seems likely to me. He would have been coming home. Some or all of them may have been moved later, of course.

Oswald's head may have been eventually interred in Durham Cathedral together with the remains of Cuthbert of Lindisfarne (a saint with whom Oswald became posthumously associated, though it's unlikely they would have met in life. Cuthbert was only eight when Oswald was killed) where it is generally believed it remains, although there are at least four other claimed heads of Oswald in continental Europe. One of his arms is said to have ended up in Peterborough Abbey later in the Middle Ages. The story is that a small group of monks from Peterborough made their way to Bamburgh, where Oswald's uncorrupted arm was kept, and stole it under the cover of darkness.

OSWIU, KING AND SAINT

His brother Oswiu became King of Bernicia, possibly as Penda's vassal, after the death of Oswald. However, Oswine was made king by the Witan of Deira until deposed by Oswiu seven years later. Oswald's son, Œthelwald, then became king but he was a constant thorn in Oswiu's side. After he betrayed Oswiu and sided with the Mercians at the battle where Penda was killed (although for some reason his men didn't take part in the battle itself) he disappeared, possibly going into exile or, more likely, Oswiu had him quietly disposed of. Oswiu's son, Elhfrith, became sub-king of Deira as a vassal of his father.

The early part of Oswiu's reign was defined by struggles with Oswine and then Œthelwald to assert control over Deira, as well as his contentious relationship with Penda. In 655 Oswiu's forces killed Penda at the Battle of the Winwæd. This established Oswiu as the most powerful ruler in Britain. For three years after the battle Oswiu's control also extended to Mercia, earning him recognition as bretwalda over much of England.

Oswiu was a devoted Christian, promoting the faith among his subjects and establishing a number of monasteries, including Gilling Abbey and Whitby Abbey. He was raised in the Celtic Christian tradition rather than the Roman Catholic faith practiced by the southern Anglo-Saxon kingdoms as well as some members of the Deiran nobility, including Oswiu's queen.

Oswiu is thought to have had children as follows:

1. Out of wedlock by Fin (Fianna in the novels):
   Aldfrith. King of Northumbria 685 – 705.
2. By Rhieinmelth:
   Elhfrith. Sub-king of Deira 655-664.
3. By Eanflaed:
   Osthryth (dau).

Ecgfrith. Sub-king of Deira 664 – 670. King of Northumbria 670 – 685.

Ælfflaed (dau). Abbess of Whitby.

Ælfwine. Sub-king of Deira 670-679.

Oswiu too was recognised as a saint, though some of his actions weren't very saintly. The first half of Oswiu's reign was spent in the shadow of Penda, who dominated much of Britain from 642 until 655. The once and future Kingdom of Northumbria was again composed of two separate countries for part of Oswiu's reign. The northerly kingdom of Bernicia, which extended from the River Tees to the Firth of Forth, was ruled by Oswiu. The kingdom of Deira, lying to the south of it as far as the Humber, was ruled by a series of Oswiu's kinsmen, initially as a separate kingdom, later as a vassal state.

After Oswiu slew Penda in battle he ruled Mercia for three years as well. The Mercians eventually revolted and installed one of Penda's sons as their king, but Oswiu remained as lord paramount or *Bretwalda* over most of England and, through alliance with his nephew, who was King of the Picts, and his successors, most of Scotland as well.

Up to 664 AD the Roman Catholic Church was dominant in southern England and the Irish or Celtic Church held sway in the North and Scotland. Oswiu called the Synod which met at Whitby that year and he decided to adopt Roman practices, including the date of Easter. After that the Roman Church became paramount throughout the country.

NORTHUMBRIA AFTER OSWIU

When Oswiu died of natural causes in 670 AD, Northumbria was again split into two kingdoms with one of his sons ruling Bernicia and its sub-kingdoms and another Deira and its satellites. They were re-united for the last time in 679. Northumbria flourished under the rule of Oswiu's sons and became culturally important. However, its political decline had already started with the loss of the territory Oswiu had gained in what would become Scotland.

When Oswiu's son, Aldfrith of Northumbria, died in 705 he was succeeded by his son Osred, an eight year old boy. When Osred was murdered in 716 Northumbria's decline accelerated. There were ten kings in the space of eighty years who were murdered, deposed or abdicated to become monks.

On June 8th 793 a raiding party of Vikings from Norway attacked Lindisfarne. Monks fled in fear and many were slaughtered. More raids followed until eventually the invaders, mainly Danes, began to settle. There followed a period of Danish supremacy with England divided in two. The Danelaw in the north included much of Northumbria, but by then much of Rheged had disappeared, swallowed up by Strathclyde. However, the area around Bebbanburg was never conquered by the Danes and remained independent under Anglian rule, though the ruler contented himself with the title of earl.

The story of Northumbria during these turbulent times will be covered in subsequent novels in this series.

Northumbria eventually became an earldom as part of a united England. The last Earl of Northumbria was Robert de Mowbray, a Norman, who was removed from his earldom for joining a conspiracy to depose William Rufus, the son of the Conqueror. Much later there were earls and dukes of Northumberland but the county was defined by the rivers Tweed and Tyne and the county of Cumbria in the west – a pale shadow of the Kingdom of Northumbria that used to be.

Other Novels by H A Culley

The Normans Series
The Bastard's Crown
Death in the Forest
England in Anarchy
Caging the Lyon
Seeking Jerusalem

Babylon Series
Babylon – The Concubine's Son
Babylon – Dawn of Empire

Robert the Bruce Trilogy
The Path to the Throne
The Winter King
After Bannockburn

Constantine Trilogy
Constantine – The Battle for Rome
Crispus Ascending
Death of the Innocent

Macedon Trilogy
The Strategos
The Sacred War
Alexander

Kings of Northumbria Series
Whiteblade
Warriors of the North

Individual Novels
Magna Carta

About the Author

H A Culley was born in Wiltshire in 1944 and entered RMA Sandhurst after leaving school. He was an Army officer for twenty four years, during which time he had a variety of unusual jobs. He spent his twenty first birthday in the jungles of Borneo, served with the RAF in the Middle East, commanded an Arab unit in the Gulf for three years and was the military attaché in Beirut during the aftermath of the Lebanese Civil War.

After leaving the Army, he became the bursar of a large independent school for seventeen years before moving into marketing and fundraising in the education sector. He has served on the board of two commercial companies and several national and local charities. He has also been involved in two major historical projects. He recently retired as the finance director and company secretary of IDPE and remains on its board of trustees.

He has three adult children and one granddaughter and lives with his wife and two Bernese Mountain Dogs between Holy Island and Berwick upon Tweed in Northumberland.

44217999R00139